Return to
the Center of the Earth
and Other Tales of
Steam & Shadows

BY THE SAME AUTHOR

Twenty Thousand Years Under the Sea

Return to
the Center of the Earth
and Other Tales of
Steam & Shadows

by
John Peel

A Black Coat Press Book

Acknowledgements:

Stories Copyright © 2020 by John Peel.
Foreword Copyright © 2020 by Jean-Marc Lofficier.
Cover illustration Copyright © 2020 by Mariusz Gandzel.

Visit our website at www.blackcoatpress.com

TABLE OF CONTENTS

Foreword

I am a man of principles. And one of these principles is, "only write forewords to get a free copy of the book." But, in this case, I am also the publisher and I'll get as many copies as I want, so you could say I'm also an idiot.

Were it not for the fact that, free books or not, John amply deserves this, and not just because he is one of my oldest friends.

I first met John through one of those things you used to affix a stamp to and drop in a colorful box located on street corners—a letter.

I wrote to him to solicit his advice when I was working on my article on *Doctor Who* for the French cinema magazine *L'Ecran Fantastique*, said article which, thanks to Terrance Dicks, later morphed into *The Doctor Who Programme Guide*. (That is a story I've told many times before.)

John was incredibly nice and helpful, something which, over the years, has turned into something of a personal trademark for the Peels. Just a year or so ago, I was looking for an obscure article penned by Talbot Mundy for a 1926 issue of *Adventure*, and who did I turn to in order to get a copy, but John and his adorable wife Nan, who traveled all the way into New York City and went to the central library to find and make a copy of that bit of literary trivia. "Nice and helpful" barely begins to describe the Peels.

After John moved to the East Coast and married Nan ("Mrs. Peel"), we would often chat by phone, and exchange books, magazines, etc. I must have read his *Doctor Who* books, both fiction and non-fiction, on the Daleks and the Time Lords a dozen times. I loved his stories in TARDIS and his short comics tales in *Doctor Who Magazine*. My involvement with the good Doctor has always been more peripheral than it sometimes looks, but after Terrance Dicks, John is certainly the one figure whose work I have constantly enjoyed and admired over the years.

When Randy and I started Black Coat Press in 2003, we had no idea how large it would grow; that is something the credit of which should go primarily to Brian Stableford. Our modest goal, initially, was to translate and publish a few French pulp heroes in order to introduce them to English-speaking readers: Doctor Omega, of course, this amazing proto-*Doctor Who* (except for the time travel and the "bigger inside than outside" bit) invented in 1906 by Arnould Galopin, but also Doc Ardan, The Nyctalope, Sâr Dubnotal, Harry Dickson, The Black Coats, Judex, Felifax, Fantômas, and many more.

A quick way to do this, I thought, would be through a series of anthologies in which modern-day writers would generate their own take on these characters, placing them in (hopefully) clever crossovers with other characters more familiar to our public, such as Sherlock Holmes, Tarzan, The Shadow, etc.

At the time, this type of pulp-themed anthologies did not exist. We were not the first, because my friend, the late and regretted Byron Preiss, had tried his hands at this, but failed. There was no mass market for what is admittedly a niche project. But that was before digital printing and the internet, so I felt the time had come to try this, on a more limited basis, without fears of failure.

So when I launched my "prospectus" for *Tales of the Shadowmen #1* in 2004, I had five writers particularly in my sights: Terrance Dicks, Brian Stableford, Bob Sheckley, Chris Roberson... and John Peel.

And this turned out to be the beginning of a wonderful literary adventure, now sixteen years in the running.

In his play *L'Aiglon*, Edmond Rostand praises the foot soldiers of Napoleon's Grand Army, describing them as "*the little ones, the obscure, the rankless... who walked exhausted, wounded, filthy, sick, with no hope of titles or rewards,*" and yet, they were the ones who erected his Empire. Often, authors of popular literature, even the great ones—look at Paul Féval!—are treated with similar neglect. And that includes truly skilled writers like John.

Most authors, understandably, tend to have their own style and topics they like to revisit; even in *Tales of the Shadowmen*, the majority of our contributors are inclined to be more comfortable with one genre, even one set of characters which they reuse time and again. There is nothing wrong with that, of course. But John is not one of them.

A supremely clever craftsman and a wondrous storyteller, John smoothly transits from gothic to fantasy, detective fiction to SF, the past to the future, and anything in between like a capricious bee looking for pollen. In this collection, and the next one, you will see him bring his own personal touch to literary universes as varied as those of Jules Verne, Edgar Rice Burroughs, Gaston Leroux, Alexandre Dumas, William Hope Hodgson, Lester Dent, Arthur Conan Doyle, and many more...

And to top it all, he makes it look so easy! John is to popular fiction what Fred Astaire is to dancing. Stories flow so smoothly and naturally under his pen, their protagonists are so faithful and convincing, that one accepts them as natural extensions of the original works they're pastiching without the least amount of disbelief.

If you haven't read the stories collected in this volume, I envy you, because you are about to embark on an adventure journey unlike no other through the ever-wondrous worlds of classic popular literature, and encounter a stellar cast that easily dwarfs that of any Hollywood super-production ever contemplated.

En route, mes amis! The game is afoot!

Jean-Marc Lofficier

The first science fiction I can remember reading was Kings of Space *by Captain W.E. Johns (more on him later), and after that came the brilliant* Explorers On The Moon *(Tintin!), but the first real science fiction—the one that grabbed hold of my imagination and really made me love the entire field—was Jules Verne's* A Journey To The Center Of The Earth. *That led me to his other famous (and some obscure) works and I am, to this day, still discovering books of his I've never read before. I have never lost my love for his incredibly vivid and startling imagination, and of those amazing characters he created—such as Captain Nemo, Robur the Conqueror, Michael Strogoff and Professor Lindenbrock. As you read this collection you will discover my attempts to recreate these characters and provide them with further adventures. From Verne, of course, I went on to read H.G. Wells, John Wyndham and, inevitably, that other grand master of exciting worlds—Edgar Rice Burroughs. Tarzan came first, obviously—much as I enjoy a good Tarzan film, though, nobody could ever bring the jungle king to life as vividly and as grippingly as those original tales. And then I discovered the other worlds Burroughs had created—John Carter of Mars, Carson of Venus and then (through* Tarzan At The Earth's Core*) Pellucidar. The next step, for me, was inevitable, really... melding Verne and Burroughs into a single adventure...*

Return to the Center of the Earth

Germany, then Iceland, 1872

I. A Promise Broken

All men when they marry make promises to their wives that they fully intend at the time to keep. Yet, through no fault of their own, sometimes they are compelled to break one or more of those promises. To some men, of course, the abrogation of their word is a small matter and barely concerns them. To others, who truly love their wives and their own honesty, it is a momentous event that haunts their waking moments and disturbs even their sleep. I—whether through good fortune or evil—am of the latter. I had been married to my beloved Gretchen for a mere few years when I was forced to break the one promise she truly wished me to keep.

It was not a promise most men would have ever have had to consider making, but it was the only desire of her heart. Loving her as I did, I had little hesitation in making it. I vowed to her that I would not go away from her again adventuring—more specifically, that I would never again venture beneath the crust of our world. Gretchen extracted this promise from me because I had once engaged in such a journey.

This journey beneath the surface of our planet had been intended by my uncle, Professor Lidenbrock, as an attempt to penetrate to the center of our planet. We had not actually succeeded in this aim, but we had managed to venture to great depths, far below those that any human being had ever expected to accomplish, and we had returned to the surface again through the agency of an erupting volcano. We had then discovered that news of our quest had circumnavigated the globe with greater speed than we had managed to penetrate it, and we were famous by the time we arrived back home in Hamburg. The source of that news had proven to be my uncle's faithful, loose-tongued maid, Martha.

The journey—and my subsequent account of our explorations—had served to make us famous. This had barely impacted my uncle, who had immediately set to work examining and cataloguing the specimens we had managed to bring with us on our return to civilization. He was used to shutting out the world from his life and considerations, so he simply ignored whatever he did not wish to acknowledge and got on with his research.

For me, however, the results were more immediate and satisfying. I was given a teaching post at the University, and my salary allowed me to wed my beloved Gretchen—but not until after, as I have mentioned, she compelled me to promise not to go adventuring again. If truth be told, it was not a promise I had any qualms in making. I am by nature a rather quiet and private person, and my wife and my teaching position fulfilled all of my worldly desires. I should indeed have been more than happy if I could be certain that my footsteps from that point on would be limited to the world above the ground.

This was not, however, to be.

The relative calm did last for a few years. Gretchen and I welcomed a small daughter to share our happiness. Both my wife and Martha doted on the youngster—and I myself was far from innocent in that respect. To my uncle, a baby was merely another distraction to be shut out from his awareness as best as possible. Should my daughter cry, or laugh or burble in his presence he would simply snort and pass by as quickly as possible. Gretchen insisted that she could detect a twinkle in his eye as he did so, but I cannot myself confirm her gentle belief. Despite these distractions, my uncle was happy enough in his work.

I was aiding him in the analysis of one of his igneous specimens one day when there came a nervous rap at his laboratory door. I glanced at the door in puzzlement, but my uncle ignored the sound. He had issued strict orders that he was never to be disturbed whilst working in his laboratory under any circumstances. Martha, taken aback, had asked:

"But what if the house were on fire?"

"What of it?" he rejoined. "Let it burn!"

No amount of pleading had made him agree to change his order under any circumstance. So I was astonished to hear the rapping at the door. My uncle pretended not to hear anything—and, at least at the first, he may not have heard anything. When he concentrates on his work, he can close out the world at large.

Even he could not ignore the second knock. This was no longer nervous and diffident but strong, forceful and virile. "The Devil take it!" my uncle roared. "Go away!"

Instead of wisely obeying this imperious command, the person knocking threw open the door and strode into the room, Martha hovering nervously behind him. I glanced up, wondering who would be foolish enough to disobey Professor Lidenbrock in his own house and saw that the intruder was a soldier—a Captain, to be precise. He wore his full military regalia and if he were on parade before the Kaiser himself. There was not a speck of dust on his clothing, not a place on the metallic trim that didn't gleam, and his leather boots were polished to such a degree that they almost glittered even in the feeble light from the oil lamps.

None of this, of course, affected my uncle in any way. "Are you deaf?" he howled. "I told you to leave. Kindly do so—immediately!"

The Captain ignored his command. His heels clicked together formally and he stared at my irate relative without any visible emotion. "Professor Lidenbrock?" he asked, though he clearly already knew the answer. "I am Captain Manfred Gottfried von Mendeldorf und von Horst. I would ask that you accompany me, please."

"And I would ask that you go to the Devil!" my uncle snapped. "Without me."

"I am afraid that I must insist," the Captain said, not at all bothered by his reception. "Your presence has been requested by An Important Personage." I swear, you could hear the stress he placed on this quasi-title.

"Then have that Important Personage accompany you to the infernal regions," my uncle replied. He tried to turn back to his work, but the Captain took several steps across the room and gripped the Professor by the elbow. "What are you doing?" uncle demanded, though the answer was obvious. Without any apparent strain on his part, Von Horst was drawing the man of learning toward the door. "Let go of me at once!" the Professor cried. "I shall report you to your superior!"

"You may do so immediately," the soldier answered, unconcerned. "He awaits you in your dining room."

14

"My dining room?" This took my uncle by surprise. "Who on Earth would call on me uninvited?" I followed along as he was dragged through the house to discover the answer to his annoyed question.

"I couldn't help it, sir," Martha said, wringing her hands together as she trotted beside me. "They insisted on seeing the Herr Professor immediately. "There was nothing I could do about it."

"I am sure you did your best," I replied, knowing that would indeed have been true. But what could a maid avail against such brutes as this one?

There was a second soldier outside the door to the dining room and—I was later to learn—a small company of them stationed about our pleasant little domicile on Konigstrasse. The reason for such an escort became obvious when we entered the dining room—my uncle still being dragged, and Martha and myself of our own volition. Gretchen was there already, seated calmly and conversing with the man who had so imperiously summoned my uncle without due regard for the possible consequences.

Though I had never seen him before, I recognized him immediately. Accurate sketches of his face were in the pages of every newspaper in the country almost daily. The spreading moustache, the balding hair, the thick build, the elegant clothing—it was Chancellor Otto von Bismarck himself, and here, in our small house!

His eyes went at once to my uncle, and he stood, offering his hand. "Herr Professor Lidenbrock," he said. "I am most pleased to greet you."

"I'd be most pleased if you'd leave, now," my uncle snapped. "I have urgent work to finish." He glared at the Captain, who had finally released his arm. "And take your trained monkey with you!"

"Keep a civil tongue in your head!" the Captain snapped. "Do you not know who you are addressing?"

"Of course I know who I'm addressing," the Professor snapped. "Do you take me for an imbecile? It is Minister President von Bismarck."

"*Chancellor* von Bismarck," his eminence corrected. "As of last year."

"I cannot keep up with the vagaries of politics," my uncle replied. "It's all the same to me. Either way, would the *Chancellor* kindly leave me to my work?"

"My dear Professor," the Chancellor said apologetically, "I fully understand your desire to continue with such important work as you must perform —"

"Good," replied my uncle. "Then leave me to it."

"I am afraid that this I cannot do," Bismarck added in a kindly tone. "It is a matter of grave importance in this political world of ours that you hear me out."

"Politics?" the man of science snapped. "What have I to do with politics? I am a man of learning. I have important work to do. I am no mere politician." It did not seem to have occurred to him that he was insulting the most powerful man in Germany. Once started, however, my uncle resembled a volcanic eruption—one must endure the sound and fury and wait until it abates, and hope that no one is harmed in the meanwhile.

But Bismarck was used to dealing with angry politicians and temperamental monarchs; an annoyed scientist barely gave him pause. "Professor Lidenbrock, I would not be here bothering you if this were not a matter vital to the interests of your country."

"My country? Bah! I am a man of science, and therefore a citizen of the world."

"But, surely, not merely of the *surface* of this world?" Bismarck asked gently.

"What do you mean?" My uncle's interest had been captured, finally, and I could see that the volcano was starting to pass into a dormant phase.

"I mean that I know of your wonderful explorations, my dear Professor," the statesman continued. "Your journey to the center of our world has brought great glory upon Germany—and yourself."

"My journey had nothing to do with glory, either for myself or for this country," my uncle denied. "Which, incidentally, did not even exist when I began my journey."

"But it exists now, and you are a part of it." Bismarck smiled. "And, I believe, a very *important* part of it. I ask you to undertake a mission for the sake of this country—*your* country, now."

"A mission?" Uncle waved an airy hand. "I am not a donkey, to be sent on a journey at the whim of some master."

"It would involve returning to the world beneath our feet," Bismarck pressed on. "A world that only you and your nephew have ever experienced—so far."

"In that you are quite mistaken," my uncle replied. "We also had with us our invaluable guide—Hans Bjelke, an Icelandic citizen and not a *German*. And we followed the trail blazed by my esteemed colleague Arne Saknussemm, another Icelander."

"But it was *your* will and your determination that drove the expedition," the Chancellor insisted. "And it was thus a *German* expedition—that is the important thing."

"It does not matter," my uncle insisted. "Had someone else undertaken the journey, the results as far as science is concerned would have been the same."

"As far as science is concerned, perhaps," agreed Bismarck. "But it would not have been the same for *you*, would it? When you realized that the trip was possible, you rushed to ensure that it was *you* who made it. Being the first to set foot in such *terra incognito* mattered to you—and, I suspect, it still does."

Again, my uncle waved a dismissive hand." I have made the journey; I see no reason to repeat the experiment. Let others follow where Lidenbrock has led."

"But no other person could lead a return to the center of our world other than you with any true hope of success," Bismarck replied. "And this time you would be supplied with more resources—anything you might wish. You would have *my* backing for this undertaking, and that is not without importance in this country of ours."

"But I have already told you that I have no interest in returning where I have already been," the man of science explained, as if dealing with a dunce. "My work is now concentrated on studying what I have already discovered. I can see no point in further exploration."

"Can you not?" Bismarck shrugged his shoulders. "May I ask if you have heard of the Gun Club?"

"Why on Earth should I have heard of it?" my uncle demanded. "They are neither geologists nor mineralogists, else I should have heard of it."

For the first time since we had entered the room, my dear Gretchen stirred and spoke. "Uncle, you cannot possibly be so involved in your work that you have never heard of the Gun Club. They are those American adventurers who so recently sent three men on a journey to and around the Moon."

"Those charlatans?" my uncle cried. "Those fools? Those wasters of opportunities?"

I, too, had been silent to this point—I confess, I was rather awed by the presence of the great Chancellor—but at this terrible accusation, I could no longer be still. "Uncle! How can you say such terrible things about such brave men?"

"Because they were fools," he snapped back. "They went all that way to the Moon, and what did they bring back? Nothing! Not a rock, not a sample, not even a speck of dust! There are so many questions about our satellite that they could have helped answer with just a handful of rocks. But what did they bring back?"

"Themselves, alive," Gretchen said in her kind and gentle manner. "That is no mean achievement."

"It is an achievements accomplished by any couple who take the waters of a spa," my uncle said, dismissing their wonderful explorations. "There is no point in going and returning unless one brings back knowledge!"

"They did not land upon the Moon," I reminded my uncle. "How could they have brought back samples?"

"My point precisely," he said. "They were dunderheaded dolts who planned their explorations imperfectly. Why should I then know anything about them?"

"Because they have announced a further undertaking," Bismarck said. "They, like most of the world, have heard of your greater achievements and have announced that they will repeat your journey."

A cloud passed across the face of the volcano. "They do not possess the key," my uncle said, no longer untouched by the subject.

"They possess guns and other weapons," Bismarck answered. "They feel that they can effect a journey through brute force."

"Explosives?" The Professor was appalled. "The savages! The secrets of our planet are not to be ripped out by blasting powder! They require a gentle hand, a delicate hand, a trained hand…"

"*Your* hand?" suggested the Chancellor.

"Mine or one like it," uncle agreed. He no longer sounded as certain that this did not involve him. "But I don't understand—what do they expect to learn by such violent methods?"

"They expect to *learn* nothing," Bismarck said. "They expect to gain a country. It is their aim to take with them the American flag and plant it within our world and claim all of the lands they discover for their country. They are selling shares and have many rich investors who would gain a great deal from such an enterprise."

"They mean to *exploit* the lands beneath us?" The man of science could not understand the man of business. "This cannot be. It must not be allowed!"

"Precisely!" Having hooked his fish, the politician proceeded to play him in anticipation of landing a large catch. "What must be done is for *you* to lead a fresh expedition to reach those lands below us before they can accomplish this foul enterprise of theirs. It must be the *German* flag that is planted within our world. We cannot allow Americans—and businessmen at that!—to beat us to this important work. If they reach and claim this world first, they will mine it and tear it apart. It is the way of the Yankee trader to exploit rather than to explore. We Germans are well-known as men of science and philosophy—it is *we* who should take command of the exploration of this subterranean world. And *you* must be in command of our party."

My uncle hesitated, clearly no longer as sure of his course of actions as before. "But I have so much work to do here," he finally said, weakly. "I cannot simply run off on an expedition."

"You must," Bismarck urged him. "It is either that or to cede the race to the Yankee traders. If you do not act, they will win. They will take their gun cotton and their weapons and they will blow holes through scientific research to seize their victory—and in so doing they will destroy much valuable information."

"There is much truth in what you say," my uncle agreed. "Very well: I accept that it is my fate to do battle with the forces of ignorance and greed. I *will* return to the center of our globe." Abruptly, he turned to me and clapped a hand upon my shoulder. "And you, my dear Axel, must accompany me."

I had not expected him to agree so readily to the Chancellor's proposal, so that had taken me by surprise. But it was with considerable shock that I received his latest statement. "Me? Uncle!" I protested. "I cannot go with you!" Memories of my previous trip crowded my mind—all of the dangers and terrors that we had faced. True, we had surmounted them—but in many cases this was due in part to luck and in a greater part to our wonderful, taciturn guide, Hans. Who could say whether either would accompany us again on any future endeavor?

"Cannot?" The Professor shook his head firmly. "Don't be absurd—you must be beside me again if I am to undertake this quest."

To face terrible thirst, or to be lost in the utter darkness underground, or to face such hardships or monsters as we had met with on the first trip... I am not a brave man; I confess it. I liked my quiet, peaceful life. I enjoyed the task of teaching up young minds, and of having Martha's wonderful meals, hot and plentiful before me. To exist on preserved foods, eaten cold, under adverse conditions... No, that was not the life for me. Besides, accompanying my uncle would mean that I would have to abandon my beloved Gretchen and our young daughter, and the thought of not seeing their sweet faces for several months was unbearable.

"You may recall, uncle," I informed him firmly, "that when I wed Gretchen, I gave her my solemn oath that I would never again venture beneath the surface of our world. You would not have me be an oath-breaker to my wife, now, would you?"

I could see the indecision written upon his face. The man of science was ready to pooh-pooh such matters, but the uncle and former guardian of Gretchen clearly favored me keeping my word. The two sides of his personality were at war with each other, but I allowed myself to be optimistic that the outcome would be the one I so desired.

But, as before, my darling, treacherous Gretchen did the unexpected. She rose to her feet and took my hands in her own delicate ones. "My dearest Axel," she said, calmly and lovingly. "I am overjoyed that you value the keeping of your word to me so strongly. It has been a great comfort to me these past few years, knowing that you are safe from danger and remain with those who love you." I was touched by her words, and even more resolved not to leave her on such a foolhardy quest. And then she sprang the trap! "But this is a matter that affects the futures both of Science and of our new country, Germany. How could I be so selfish as to insist that you place your word to me over your duties and responsibilities to them?" I began in shock to protest, but she placed her finger over my lips to silence me. "I freely release you from your vow, so you are now quite at liberty to do your duty to Science and Germany. Onwards!—to the center of the Earth!"

II. Our Voyage Begins

My stunned silence was taken, somehow, as overwhelmed gratitude and nothing more was spoken of the possibility of my not accompanying the expedition. I imagine that I did acquiesce to whatever was said following Gretchen's speech, but it was because I was in a state of shock and not one of agreement. By the time my senses had returned, matters had progressed too far for me to be able to back out. Whenever I attempted to broach the subject again in the following days my uncle invariably misunderstood me. He would clap me on my shoulder and say something along the lines of: "Don't fret yourself, Axel! You have not shamed yourself, and will not. We all know that you are a man of your word, but, more so, a man who faces his destiny with courage and conviction!"

Would that I had felt so much confidence in myself!

In his customary manner, the Chancellor of Germany had planned well, and had anticipated all but one problem in his scheme. That one problem, of course, was my uncle. To be fair to the great man, few people have ever anticipated my uncle's mind, and even fewer have ever gotten the better of him. His rank notwithstanding, Herr Bismarck fared no better than the fishmonger at the end of our street.

"No, no and again no!" my uncle cried in response to the Chancellor's suggestion that we find a good, patriotic German volcano as our means of entry to the world below our feet. "In the first place, there are no German volcanoes!"

"But, surely, in our great sphere of influence..." the Chancellor protested.

"And in the second," uncle continued, implacably, "we know that the route down certainly lies within Snaeffels. We do *not* know that any other such route lies within any other volcano. And in the *third* place," he continued, not allowing the great statesman a word, "we know that Snaeffels is dormant. It would be a very foolish act to chance a less somnolent entry point."

"But the volcano is in *Iceland*," Bismarck protested.

"I know that." My uncle folded his arms. "And it is to Iceland we must go."

Bismarck threw up his arms. "Very well, Iceland it is," he agreed. "We have a ship ready and waiting to transport you and the members of your party to the site in question. Any provisions you may need and such equipment you deem necessary should be listed and given to Captain Von Horst." He indicated the military man who had marched my uncle into the room, and who had been silent up to this point. At the mention of his name, he clicked his heels together sharply and gave a smart salute—whether to the Chancellor or my uncle, it was impossible to tell.

"That is simple," my uncle said. "We shall take along almost precisely the equipment we took last time, along with provisions for three men."

"Three?" The statesman shook his head. "You misunderstand the matter, my dear professor—the Captain and his men will be accompanying you on your journey."

"The devil you say!" Lidenbrock exploded. "I cannot be expected to be nursemaid to a group of clumsy soldiers."

"My men and I are *not* clumsy," the Captain protested. "We are highly trained professionals. It is our assignment to nursemaid *you*!"

My uncle glared at him. "In the matter of exploring the world below, there are only *three* experts," he said firmly. "Myself, my nephew and our companion Hans. That is the extent of our party, and on this matter I stand firm."

"You would take along an Icelander and leave behind a good German?" Von Horst cried.

"I know and trust this Icelander with my life," the professor replied. "I cannot say the same about you. I shall not budge on this issue." He crossed his arms again and glared at Bismarck, daring him to issue any fresh orders.

The politician was not so foolish; he was starting to get the measure of my uncle and saw that the only path to getting his way was to make my uncle think that it was the footpath he had himself chosen. "Quite right," Bismarck said, jovially. "You do not know the Captain or his men. I understand that. But you *will* know him by the time you reach Iceland, so there's an end to that problem. As to the Icelander..." He caught the warning flash of fire in my uncle's eyes. "Well, there's no saying whether he will be free to accompany you, is there? It may be that the good huntsman is busy. I understand he collects the feathers of the Eider duck for a living—it may be that he's off plucking feathers." He held up a hand to stave off a protest. "We shall, of course, in deference to your wishes, attempt to secure his services once again. But we must also be prepared in case that worthy is not available. That is only sensible, is it not?"

How could even my uncle argue with such logic?

"The men I have selected for this mission," Von Horst added, "are all experts in matters Alpine. I and they have extensive climbing experience—it barely matters that we climb *down* instead of *up*, does it?"

"If you think that, there is little I can teach you," my uncle replied, caustically. "No good will come of this," he snapped at Bismarck, and then sighed. "Very well, I shall agree to a compromise. The Captain and his men may accompany us for a week. If, after that time, I decide that they are an encumbrance and not an asset, they must agree to return and allow the three of us to proceed alone on our mission."

Von Horst was about to protest, but the Chancellor held up a hand to silence him. "Very well," he agreed, easily. "That sounds quite reasonable."

"But what is to stop him from simply declaring us a problem and rejecting us out of hand?" Von Horst growled.

"The good professor's reputation for honesty," Bismarck answered. "I have every faith that he is a man who is as good as his word—if he promises to judge fairly, then I believe that he will do so."

This considerably mollified my uncle, and planning could proceed without further altercations. My uncle was happy with getting his way, and the Chancellor was equally convinced that he was getting *his* way. Naturally, I was not considered by either man in their further discussions. Both men assumed I would concur with any decisions they made. And, indeed, what choice did I have? My darling Gretchen had assured them I would accompany the quest. I could not make her a liar, nor, to be honest, could I bring myself to disappoint her. She looked at me with such pride and affection in her eyes, and she had no clue that she had betrayed me. She believed me to be a brave man, and so I was forced to act the part, even with a heavy heart.

While the great men talked, I took the opportunity to examine our new traveling companion. Captain Von Horst was clearly career military, and probably from several generations of such men. He stood bolt-upright, as if instead of a spine he had a carbine, unable to deviate from the vertical. His movements were precise and considered, and he was extremely well groomed. I have had very little acquaintance with military men, thankfully, but he appeared to be a fine example of the breed. He interjected comments from time to time into the discussions, and they were always clear and to the point. Yet in all of this, I did not really know what kind of a man he was, not how he would react when faced with the realities of life underground. I full knew that it is one thing to *think* of traveling beneath the surface of our world, and quite another matter when actually *doing* it. In short, I thought the man had potential, but until we had been on our journey for that probationary week, I should not be able to tell whether he would be a good companion or not.

Eventually the talks wound down, and the politician rose to take his leave. He kissed my wife's hand and shook mine. As he grasped that of my uncle, he smiled.

"I have great confidence in you, Professor Lidenbrock," he announced. "The Captain will return in the morning, and then you shall be on your way."

"The morning?" I exclaimed. I had not been following the conversation closely, being preoccupied with my own thoughts. "But surely it cannot be?"

"Whyever not?" my uncle asked, puzzled. "The Captain has already arranged for many of the supplies and equipment we need, and he goes now to secure the rest. Our ship awaits, and we know the road ahead of us. And the members of that infernal Gun Club are well underway in their own preparations to race us on this path. No, indeed, tomorrow it shall be."

"But... but it is not midsummer," I stammered. "That is the time to descend the crater."

"Only when we did not know the right way to take," my uncle said, dismissively. "Now we already know the start of our journey there is no need to wait the change of seasons. Tomorrow it should be." He turned to Gretchen. "You and Martha must help us to pack our few personal items this evening, my dear."

My wife nodded, and then favored me with a radiant smile. "Is this not exciting, Axel?" she asked.

That was not the word I should have chosen.

As for the rest of that evening, I cannot say with any certainty what happened. I must have eaten, obviously, and I know I slept, for I was tormented by terrible dreams. These were partly rehashed memories of my previous trip and partially fears for what might happen on the impending trip. I recall monster teeth that turned into stalactites, both versions of which closed about my body, crushing the life from it. Somehow, though, I did not waken until the morning, and felt surprisingly ready to face the ordeal ahead of me.

My uncle was up and about, eager for the adventure to commence. Martha had laid on a hearty breakfast—"You'll be eating onboard ship next, and they don't have good, fresh eggs or newly-baked bread," she pointed out. "And, after that, only the good Lord knows what kind of food you'll have to endure under the ground." Thoughts of the dried rations we would be taking turned the taste of her good sausages and eggs ashen in my mouth. How would I endure months without good food?

Easier than I would the months without Gretchen, of course. I shall not tell you with what affections the two of us parted, nor of the numerous kisses bestowed upon our daughter. My uncle bore it as long as he could, but then demanded impatiently that our goodbyes cease so we might actually get started on our journey. After a final flurry of kisses, I left my dear Gretchen and daughter and settled into the coach that the Captain had sent to collect us. Our luggage was stowed, and we were off.

Iceland, our initial destination, is a colony of Denmark, and on our previous trip we had started by visiting the latter country and obtaining letters of introduction from colleagues of my uncle. This time, however, that would be unnecessary, as everything had been arranged by Chancellor Bismarck and his right-hand Captain. Hamburg is situated on the River Elbe and is one of the largest ports in Europe. The coach took us directly to the docks where our vessel awaited us. It was a smallish ship named the *Bremen*, but very modern and, as her proud Captain informed us, very fast. Certainly it was very efficient, for we were barely aboard before that worthy and proud gentleman gave orders for us to cast off. By the time my uncle and I were led to the cabin that we were to share, I could feel that we were already under way. I felt quite exhausted from all the activity going on about us and would have gladly taken the chance to rest—hopefully without further night-mares—but that would not be possible with my uncle about. As soon as we had placed our bags in the cabin, he seized my hand and virtually dragged me to the deck.

The buildings and people we lived amongst were already slipping behind us as the *Bremen* sliced its way toward the North Sea. The captain's pride in his ship's speed was not misplaced, it seemed. My old life was being shed as a snake slips its old skin. I was, however, far from eager to grasp my new. No such worries or regrets seized my uncle, of course. Like a prize stallion, he was champing at the bit and eager to be unleashed upon the world beneath us.

Captain Von Horst was drilling his men on the deck. There were six of them and I must confess that they looked very smart. They moved in unison, their faces blank of emotion, following whatever order their commander barked.

The Professor was less impressed. "That sort of thing won't do you much good under the ground," he remarked.

The Captain glared at him. "Efficiency and order are never wasted," he retorted. "My men act as one."

"Then they may also die as one," my uncle replied, off-handed.

"They will not die," the soldier responded. "They are an extension of my will and they are the most efficient of their kind in the German Army. You will find, Herr Professor, that they will be invaluable on our mission."

"Perhaps so," my uncle agreed, vaguely. "Meanwhile, before we leave German waters, I should like the chance to look over our supplies, so that if anything has been omitted, we may collect it on our way."

The Captain looked offended at the thought. "Nothing necessary has been left out."

"You may indeed be right," the Professor said. "But as leader of this expedition, it is my responsibility to be certain."

"Very well." Stiffly, the military man led the pair of us below decks. Behind us, his sergeant took over the drilling of the troops. They were not to be allowed to relax and simply enjoy the voyage, it appeared.

A portion of the main hold had been set aside for the supplies we would be taking along on our expedition. They had all been laid neatly out beside the packs that would contain them. There were, I could see, ten packs in all—one each for the soldiers, the Captain, my uncle, myself, and the final one for Hans. Each had a sign beside it, designating its bearer.

There were the concentrated food supplies I so disliked from the previous trip, but which would serve to keep us alive. There were water containers for each man, as well as small items of clothing such as socks that might need replacing. There was climbing gear and lengths of rope, spread between

28

the packs the soldiers would carry. For them, also, was a supply of ammunition. The scientific supplies—compasses, barometers and so forth—were split between the packs of myself and my uncle. I noted with some satisfaction that there was even a supply of paper and drafting materials beside my pack. I was evidently to be the chronicler of whatever happened, as well as recorder of any lands we claimed. To aid in that there were several German flags to be planted. We and Hans were also assigned a revolver and a rifle each, along with a smaller supply of ammunition for the weapons.

Finally, there were six Ruhmkorf coils, along with the necessary supplies. These portable, strong lights had proven to be absolutely invaluable on our previous journey, and I was certain that they would do so again. Without the clear light they cast, we would hardly be able to move six feet below the ground.

"This appears to be quite adequate," my uncle finally said, after having examined every item carefully.

"More than adequate," the soldier replied. "As long as we are able to find water again on our journey, we have everything here we should need on our journey." Even my uncle was not able to dispute that, though I have no doubt he racked his brain for an excuse to do so.

And so we settled in for our sea voyage. It had taken us two weeks to reach Iceland on the previous attempt, but our Captain was certain that the *Bremen* could make the trip in seven days. "This ship is the most up-to-date in the world," he said, proudly. "A masterpiece of German engineering."

"But we traverse the north Atlantic," my uncle pointed out. "This is not German weather, the seas are liable to be rough and there is always the possibility of icebergs in this season."

"Nevertheless," the good Captain vowed, "seven days!"

The soldiers drilled, my uncle studied the books he had brought along with him, and I worried. What was happening to my Gretchen and our daughter? Were they well? Did they miss me? And I worried about ourselves. What fresh dangers were in store for us below the crust of our world? How many of the dangers we had previously faced would we encounter again? Would we be able to endure this time? And what of Hans? Would his services be available to us again? Would he even be foolish enough to agree to go with us on another expedition? There were so many uncertainties and possibilities, and my mind kept playing them all out, again and again, fruitlessly, as the *Bremen* plowed on.

To my surprise and somewhat to my uncle's chagrin, on the seventh day we did indeed sight land. The lookout gave a cry and gestured. Using field glasses, my uncle confirmed the accuracy of the call.

"It would appear that our good Captain was correct in his faith in his ship," I could not resist observing.

"He was fortunate in the weather," was the scientific man's opinion. This was certainly true, to an extent—despite the lateness of the season we had encountered neither storms nor icebergs, which had helped. But a good deal of the credit must be laid, indeed, to the workmanship of those who had constructed and those who had sailed the *Bremen*. And now, dead ahead of us, lay the first rocky shores of Iceland.

The first and simplest part of our journey was now complete. The more difficult portion was about to commence.

III. A Dangerous Reunion

Iceland is a curious place. It was created from volcanic rock and there are many volcanoes still active on the island. The rock, once weathered, provides good soil for growing crops. When it is not weathered, it gives a landscape that is largely barren and gloomy, broken in places only by water bursting from the ground in what the natives call *geysers*— which are of volcanic origin and frequently hot enough to scald. There are few trees, mostly planted by the hand of man and not nature, so houses are mostly built of the ever-present stone and often fade into the surrounding landscape.

The inhabitants are descendants of ancient Viking explorers, and the island still belongs to Denmark, whose language is spoken here. Unlike their ancestors, the modern Icelanders are peaceful farmers, for the most part, though ancient passions and claims of blood-debt sometimes erupt like the geysers, hot and very active.

Our one-time guide, Hans Bjelke, followed a different profession: he was a hunter, though not with a gun or other weapon. Iceland's main export is the feather of the Eider duck, which makes exceptional filling for pillows and mattresses for the rest of the world. Hans' chosen work was the gathering of such feathers. As the ducks nest in out-of-the-way areas, this is not quite as placid a task as it may sound. Hans had to clamber among the rocks and on sheer cliff faces to reach his prey. As a result, he had become as adept at climbing these inhospitable outcrops as any mountain goat. This had made him invaluable to us as a guide on our last expedition, and my uncle was grimly determined to once again secure his services. This was one decision that I heartily concurred with—there is no man alive I trust as much as that quiet, unhurried man.

In the shadow of the extinct volcano Snaeffels itself, the *Bremen* anchored. I confess to a shudder or two as I looked up at the twin peaks of that once-mighty mountain, knowing it to be the doorway into the underworld that we should shortly hazard. It seemed, though, that I was the only one stricken with any such feelings. My uncle was eager to be off, and the Captain and his men were quite prepared to follow. But first, there was the question of Hans. Could we find him, and would he again accompany us? The Captain was of the opinion that we really didn't need him; my uncle of the opinion that we could not do without him. I, of course, agreed with my uncle—that to proceed without Hans would be foolhardy and possibly deadly. However, I found myself wishing that the guide would be unavailable or else unwilling, and that we should then be forced to abandon our quest.

It was determined, in conference with the *Bremen*'s Captain that my uncle, myself and Captain Von Horst should proceed to search out Hans and that the soldiers and sailors would unload our gear and prepare it ready for our commencement. I am not affected by seasickness or other maladies, but I confess that it felt good to have the solid ground beneath my feet again when we reached Icelandic soil. Of course, the ground was not as solid as it felt—in a matter of days we should be venturing below the land on which we now stood.

The peninsula upon which Snaeffels stood was not close to any of the few small settlements in the area, so it took a little searching to locate a local. If this lonely man was surprised to see a troop of visitors to this quiet land, he gave little outward sign. Both my uncle and the Captain spoke sufficient Danish to be able to converse with this farmer, and he was able to answer their questions, at least in part. My uncle gave him a few coins for his help, and rubbed his hands in some satisfaction.

"Our old friend Hans is somewhere not too distant," he informed me. "It seems that he has become romantically attached to the daughter of a farmer." I was surprised to hear that Hans was prey to such a violent emotion as love, but pleased for him. "There are, however, complications. It seems that he has a rival for her affections, and this other man is noted for a violent temper."

"Then she is sure to pick Hans," I exclaimed. "Who would want to be wed to such a brute?"

My uncle shook his head. "But the brute, as you call him, is apparently quite a wealthy man, and offers the poor girl a very comfortable life. So she must chose temper and wealth or else calmness and more uncertain prospects with Hans. Still, what this little drama means is that Hans is in the habit of visiting the girl and her family on a fairly frequent basis, and so our best chance of intercepting him would seem to be to call on the farmer and simply wait."

"For how long?" Von Horst asked, impatiently. He turned to me. "Your uncle neglects to inform you that it seems that we are already behind in this race to the center of our world."

"I was about to tell him," the professor said coldly. "But my nephew is a man of emotion, and I felt that he would prefer news of our old friend first."

I glanced from one to the other. "Will *one* of you please tell me the news?"

"The Gun Club arrived here in Iceland a week ago," my uncle replied. "Being Americans, they made their presence known from one end of the island to the other. They have spent coin quite freely and were last seen three days ago heading on this very path toward…" He gestured dramatically at looming Snaeffels. "They have begun their journey ahead of us, it would seem."

"That is not good," I observed.

"It is not," agreed the Captain. "I think spending any time waiting for this local guide of yours is wasteful—we should head directly to the peak and begin our own descent."

"That would not be wise," my uncle informed him. "It hardly matters that they are ahead of us—they are traversing lands unknown to them, and may quite easily chose one or more of the many passages that lead nowhere. A few days here or there is meaningless. We know the correct path to take."

"Another reason why we do not need a guide!" Von Horst exclaimed.

"On the contrary," the professor said, refusing to change his opinion. "Hans is not to accompany us to lead the way— that is *my* task. He is to be with us to offer advice and insight, and to help us when things get rough. And, I assure you, they will get very rough indeed." He grinned widely at this hellish prospect. "Our chances of survival and success will probably depend highly upon this man, a man the Gun Club members do not have. Either we secure his services, or else I go no further."

The Captain could see when he was beaten. "Very well," he agreed. "Let us check that our camp here is being prepared, and then we can go on a search for this treasure of a man." He hurried to retrace our path back to the slight harbor where the *Bremen* was waiting.

"I am glad he has seen the sense in what we desire, Axel," my uncle commented. Sense? I could see no sense at all in any of this! But nobody, least of all Herr Professor Lidenbrock—was interested in *my* opinion.

Von Horst took the time to issue a few orders to his men back at the camp. This seemed unnecessary to me, as the men had the building of our temporary abode quite well in hand, but the Captain was one of those men who seems to feel that nothing will get done correctly unless he give detailed orders. And he complained of *us* wasting time! Eventually, convinced that affairs were well in hand, he joined us again and we made our way to the young lady's farm.

As I have mentioned, Iceland is for the most part a vast, rocky wilderness. Grass grows in abundance, and, with proper farming methods and diligence, other crops can be coaxed to do so. Many farmers keep sheep and goats, which provide them with milk and cheese as well as rare meat dishes. For transportation, most Icelanders rely upon their own legs, but there are quite a few small, shaggy ponies of an even temperament and good work ethic. Since there are few trees, most houses are built of the omnipresent volcanic rock. The domicile we reached proved to be quite typical of the island.

The farmer was a tall, muscular man, now a trifle past his prime. His wife was a sturdy matron, mother to a brood of children I was not quite able to number. Aside from their ebb and flow within the house, many had chores to accomplish and so were in a constant state of motion. There were at least six children, and perhaps as many as ten, apparently equally distributed between the two sexes. The object of Hans' affection proved to be a slender blonde girl some nineteen years of age with a ready smile and a polite manner. It was not difficult to see why she had two ardent admirers, and probably would have had more if she lived in even a small city instead of the backwaters of this island. Her name, I gathered, was Habby.

My uncle conversed with her and her mother—the father went about his work, using his mouth mostly to clench a pipe that he sometimes paused to light—and was able to ascertain that Hans was in the nearby hills and expected to show up as a guest for dinner later that day. We were graciously invited to partake of the meal also, which my uncle gratefully accepted for the three of us. When he passed along this information Von Horst was not happy.

"I prefer to eat with my men," he stated. "It is better for discipline that they see their Captain sharing their rations rather than eating in luxury."

"Hardly luxury," the professor said amiably, gesturing at our surroundings. "These are good folks, yes, but I would hardly term this *luxury*."

"My point is that I should be with them," the Captain snapped. "And I do not like the idea of waiting about for this Hans of yours. If he is in the hills, let us go and seek him out. The sooner we know if he will accompany us or not, the better."

My uncle glanced about at the turmoil around us. The father of the family might be taciturn, but the same could not be said of most of his offspring. My uncle disliked noise and confusion, so I was hardly surprised when he agreed with the Captain. He explained to our hosts that he and I would be back with Hans later, and that the Captain would not. We took our leave of the family then, though several of the children, curious and pleased with their unexpected and strange visitors, flocked about us like starlings as we left the farm house and started on our way. Thankfully for my uncle's temper, none of them strayed too far from the house and in a matter of minutes we were alone with our thoughts.

I was anticipating meeting our old friend again and hoping he would agree to accompany us once more. But having seen Habby, I doubted it—what man would want to abandon her to his rival simply to go on a possibly doomed adventure? Habby made me think of Gretchen again, and how much I missed her. If I could have my choice, I would never have left her; I should certainly not blame Hans if he turned us down. Thinking thoughts alternately gloomy and nostalgic, I hardly noticed the path we were taking into the hills. My uncle was leading the way with his usual conviction and I simply followed along silently. The Captain brought up the rear of our small group as silent as I.

I was jolted back to the present when my uncle gave a loud hail. I glanced up and saw a familiar figure a short distance above us in the rocks. It was our good Hans, making his way down the mountainous slopes toward us. I was so pleased to see him again that I was pulled from my reverie and my legs, unbidden, started forward quite swiftly. I found myself running to greet him.

Then, above the pathway to my right, I heard a loud cracking sound. I paused and looked upward. With a shock, I saw that a portion of the rock face several hundred feet above us had broken free of the hillside. Huge boulders crashed down the slope, and stones clattered through the air. Dust and noise abounded, and the entire mass began descending toward us. My uncle and the Captain, below us, we not in the pathway of this mass of volcanic material, but Hans and I were directly in its path. I heard faint cries from below, but my attention was almost entirely seized by the crashing, tumbling army of stone. For a moment I was paralyzed with indecision.

Hans had no such problems. He leaped forward, as agile and sure-footed as any goat, and he grabbed a hold of me, pushing me before him. I went willingly with his motions, but there was no chance we should be able to evade the lethal avalanche descending upon us.

Then I saw the escape was not Hans' plan. Instead, he propelled us underneath a slight overhang above the pathway, barely more than a bump in the rocky surface. He pushed me against the wall, and gestured for me to hold myself in as tightly as I could. I obeyed his unspoken command, and he, in turn, stood close beside me in a similar manner.

The rocks and boulders crashed down toward us and I was convinced that we would perish. An image of my dear

36

Gretchen filled my mind as I thought I should never see her again, and then I gasped and choked as the dust accompanying the avalanche reached us, filling my nose and mouth. As the noisy rockfall crashed about us, I coughed and choked. I was struck several times, but thankfully only by smaller stones. The volcanic rock was sharp, though, and left streaks of blood on my skin. The overhang, slight as it was, proved to be sufficient, as it turned aside the larger boulders. Only the lesser stone and dust reached us. In moments, the terrible avalanche was over, and we could bend and move as we coughed to clear our throats and mouths.

After a few moments, I heard my uncle and the Captain crying out our names as they approached us. They had to tread carefully, as the pathway was strewn with rocks and scree. Hans and I started down toward them just as carefully. In a matter of moments, we were together, and my uncle grasped both of my arms.

"My boy, are you well?" he asked, anxiously.

"Merely minor cuts and scrapes," I assured him. "Hans, as ever, looked out for me."

"Ah! My good Hans!" my uncle cried, clasping the hand of our old friend. He spoke to him heartily in Danish, quite volubly. Hans, as was his manner, waited until my uncle had finished and then answered with a few calm words. "He says he is fine, and somewhat surprised to see us," my uncle reported. The pair of them spoke for a few minutes while I managed to return myself to some semblance of order.

"It seems quite a coincidence that there should be a landslide just as we meet up with Hans," I observed.

"Coincidence?" The Professor shook his head. "My boy, neither Hans nor I believe it to be a coincidence."

"I concur," Von Horst said. "The timing is highly suspicious, is it not?"

"Indeed." My uncle smiled. "Hans feels it is the work of his rival for the young lady's hand. He is noted for his temper and his dislike of obstacles to his plans."

"I'm not so sure," I said slowly. "It seems to me that it would be an awful coincidence that his rival decided to strike at precisely the time we come here to solicit Hans' aid."

To my surprise, the Captain announced: "I agree with Axel—it *would* be too much of a coincidence. I suspect that it is much more likely that the Gun Club has left an agent behind to ensure we cannot follow them."

"Would they go to such lengths as to try and kill us?" my uncle asked. "It seems a trifle extreme, even for Americans."

"They may not have intended to kill anyone," Von Horst replied. "They may only have intended injury to members of our party to slow us down. No, I feel that Axel's suspicions may well be correct."

The Professor dismissed the matter. "Well, it is of no consequence now—neither Axel nor Hans were injured, and our expedition can proceed."

"*If* Hans agrees to join us," I pointed out. "He has yet to be broached on the subject. He may not wish to leave his sweetheart to the mercies of his rival, especially if the man *was* the one attempting to kill Hans."

My uncle nodded and engaged in an earnest conversation with our guide. Hans, as ever, was calm and spoke little, and in the end my uncle beamed. "He has agreed to accompany us, on the same terms as before," he announced.

"And Habby?" I asked, curiously.

My uncle chuckled. "Hans has a definitely individualized approach to romance," he said. "He is of the opinion that the decision must be hers and hers alone. He aims to tell her of his plans and inform her that he wishes to marry her on his return. If, while he has gone, his rival's suit wins out, then he believes that clearly the young lady was not the woman he took her for, and he would be well rid of her. He did add that he does not expect this to happen."

I turned to Hans and shook his hand gratefully. If we were to undertake this madcap quest, I felt we had a much better chance of returning now that he had agreed to accompany us. Hans seemed to understand my mood and he nodded solemnly. I then realized that no obstacle now stood in our way.

We were on our way back to the center of the Earth...

IV. Our Party Is Complete

We returned with Hans to the farmhouse of his young la-dy. The chaos there had died down slightly with the approach of supper. As Habby's mother dished out the meal—consisting of a thick fish stew that was surprisingly tasty—Hans took Habby outside to speak with her. They were gone so long that they almost missed the meal entirely, but when they did reap-pear both of them looked very happy. It seemed that our guide's proposal had met a sympathetic response.

The decision had to be passed along to her parents, and met with their considerable approval. The father disappeared off and then emerged from an inner room with a bottle that appeared to have been stored for a while. He insisted on drinks all around to seal the engagement, and I managed to sip what-ever the concoction was without gagging too much. Habby's younger brothers and sisters weren't allowed any of the alco-holic toast, but they seemed to have many comments of their own directed at the happy pair which—from the way my uncle raised his eyebrows—I assume were of light-hearted jokes in somewhat poor taste, much like that of any family anywhere.

It was arranged with my uncle that Hans would settle his affairs and join us at our camp in the morning. I assumed that he would also take a long and perhaps tender farewell of his bride-to-be and wanted as few witnesses to this as possible. Captain Von Horst was impatient with all of these matters, but he was wise enough to know that he could not hurry my uncle along. When we eventually left, shortly before sunset, he could barely conceal his impatience.

"There is still much to do," he snapped. He glanced back at the farmhouse. "Can we rely on your man to be with us at the appointed hour?"

"If Hans says he will do something," my uncle replied, "then no power on Earth can stop him from keeping his word. He will be with us at daybreak and we may be on our way." This answer mollified the soldier somewhat, but he still kept up a swift pace back to our camp.

Here we had two surprises to greet our arrival. One of the soldiers hurried up to the Captain, saluted briskly and informed him that one of the men had suffered an accident. It appeared he had been out on the volcanic rock and lost his footing. He had slipped and fallen, seriously injuring his leg. The Captain rushed to examine the man, and emerged from his tent a few minutes later looking angry and concerned.

"A foolish accident," he said. "The man disobeyed my orders and went off alone. He hasn't broken his leg, but it is severely sprained and he is quite unable to move it now after hobbling back to camp on it. We shall be one man short on our expedition tomorrow."

My uncle shrugged. "That hardly concerns me," he replied. "I have said all along that there are too many of us as it is. One less seems like a good move to me." Then, having clearly realized how callous he must sound, he added: "Nevertheless, I trust your soldier will recover."

The second surprise was even less likely than the first, and considerably more puzzling.

It seemed we had a visitor. An *American* visitor, waiting in our tent to speak with us.

"An American?" Von Horst asked, astonished. "Here? What could he want with us?"

My uncle snorted. "Let us go and ask him," he suggested.

We moved to the tent he and I were to share. Oil lamps had been lit since night had fallen, and as we entered, we saw our visitor in the light of one such lamp. He rose to his feet to greet us, and I was impressed by my first sight of him. He stood more than six feet tall, and was thick-bodied and muscular. He was dressed in a nautical jacket and cap, and there was a sailor's sack on the ground beside him. His eyes flickered back and forth over the three of us, and then he extended a large hand toward my uncle. "Professor Lidenbrock, I assume?"

"Indeed." My uncle shook his hand. "And you are…?"

"My name is Ned Land," he answered.

"And why is an American visiting us?" the Captain demanded. "Did you have something to do with the attack on our guide?"

"American?" Land was almost roaring. "I am not an *American*, I am *Canadian*."

"It is the same thing," Von Horst insisted.

"No, sir, it is not!" Land growled. He looked as though he might start a fight over the insult. "And I don't know what attack you speak of. I have not fought anyone today—yet."

"American or Canadian," my uncle said, hastily, before the Captain could make matters worse, "the question remains: what are you doing here?"

"I wish to join your expedition," Land said, folding his arms across his chest.

The Captain appeared about ready to explode with rage, but my uncle waved him to silence. "And what do you know of our expedition?"

"Why, that you're off to the center of the Earth," Land said. "I am a harpooner by trade, and my ship is docked at Reykjavik. I heard that you were here, and so I came along to offer my services."

"A harpooner?" The Captain seemed undecided whether to rage or laugh. "We have no need of such a man."

"Begging your pardon, but I suspect that you do." Land smiled grimly. "I read the account of your first expedition, and you spoke of a sea of monsters." His eyes lit up with passion. "I have been a sailor for more than twenty years and have crossed every ocean on the surface of this world. The call of a fresh ocean, one seen by few human beings, that stands ready to challenge and be challenged… How could I resist?" He glanced at me. "You, I take it, are the chronicler of that expedition. You spoke of giant sea beasts that almost killed you that time." He reached into the shadows of the tent and produced a large harpoon. "With me and this, you would have no need to fear a recurrence of the threat."

His simple statements and his air of confidence encouraged me. I found myself taking a liking to this seaman, wherever he was from. I could tell by the stiffness of his pose and the barely controlled anger on his face that the Captain did not agree with me. Still, neither of our opinions mattered, as my uncle had the only real vote on the matter, and it all depended upon what he thought of Ned Land. After a moment's contemplation, he spoke up.

"What you say might be true—and I say *might be* advisedly, since there is no way of knowing the hazards that we face. But the Captain is quite right in one respect—there *has* been an attack on one member of our party already; how do we know that you were not the man responsible?"

"Because I say so, and I do not lie," the sailor answered simply.

"For which statement we are expected to take your word?"

Land glared at the Captain. "I have sailed the seven seas all my adult life," he said slowly. "I have been from Cebu to Valparaiso, from pole to pole. In all the world there is not one man who knows me who would call me a liar. If you wish to be the first, I am willing to debate the matter." His fist clenched the harpoon and raised it slightly.

I could see that the Captain was unlikely to back down, and that blood might well be shed in the next few moments. I had to do something to prevent it, so I said, swiftly: "I am certain that the Captain did not mean to call you a liar, Mr. Land. But if you might happen to have some sort of credentials…"

"Credentials?" Land blinked, and I could see his grip loosening on his weapon. "Well, that's something easily arranged. Here, lad, hold this for me." He promptly tossed the harpoon in my direction—thankfully not point-first!—and didn't even bother to look to see if I had managed to snatch it from the air. Luckily, I managed this without fumbling or dropping the harpoon. Land picked up his sailor's kit bag and rummaged through it for a moment before producing a small bundle carefully wrapped in wax papers. He untied the bundle and passed a letter across to my uncle. "It's from Professor Aronnax—I don't know if you've ever heard of him?"

"Indeed we have," my uncle replied. "I have read his books on the subject of marine biology. There are one or two points he makes that I should like to debate him about, but on the whole he is a solid and reliable researcher."

I stared at the Professor, wondering if that was all he knew of the famous man. "And of his adventures with Nemo and the *Nautilus*," I prompted.

"Who? What?" My uncle glanced up a moment from the letter he was reading. "What are you babbling about, my boy?"

"The mysterious submersible that was sinking ships in the world's oceans just a few years ago," I explained. "Professor Aronnax and his companions aided in ending the menace." I looked at Ned Land with fresh respect. "Were you one of them?"

"Aye," he agreed. "I was there—though *menace* is perhaps not the best word to describe Captain Nemo."

"I don't know what you two are talking about," my uncle declared, folding the letter and handing it back to Land. "But Aronnax speaks highly of your skills and loyalty in that missive, and I am inclined to accept his judgment of you, Mr. Land." He held out a hand. "Welcome to our expedition."

"I protest!" Von Horst rather predictably exclaimed.

"I rather thought you might," my uncle said. "But it is my place to decide these matters, and I say he accompanies us. His particular skills could prove invaluable."

"We have supplies for only ten men," the Captain argued.

"And one of your men can no longer accompany us," the Professor replied. "Therefore Mr. Land can take his place."

"I had planned on using a *German* in my man's place."

"I'm sure you were," my uncle answered. "But this is a scientific expedition, and science knows no national boundaries. My decision stands."

The Captain was furious, but he could see that there was little point in arguing further. Instead he turned to the sailor. "How is it that you did not accompany the American expedition, but waited for us?" he asked. "It seems rather suspicious to me."

Land shrugged. "I would have joined the American expedition if it were possible. But my ship did not dock until yesterday, and they had already set off. Then I waited for your party."

"You see?" Von Horst pointed out to my uncle. "The man has no loyalty."

"The man *had* no loyalty," the sailor corrected. "But now I have been accepted as a member of your party, I *do* have loyalty. I assure you I will do my utmost to make this expedition a success."

"Capital!" the man of science exclaimed. "Well, now that is all settled, I suggest we have our evening meal and then settle down for the night—tomorrow is liable to prove a very busy day for us, gentlemen."

I looked from my uncle's calm face to Ned Land's smiling features, and then finally to the Captain. His visage was clouded with anger at being over-ridden in this matter. I had a strong suspicion that my uncle's heavy-handed manner of dealing with the issue might have serious repercussions once we were below the surface of the Earth. It was not merely my natural timidity that made me worry about what the future had in store for us all.

V. Descending

We were all up early—I because I had not slept well because of my worries, the others because of excitement (my uncle), duty (Hans) and discipline (Captain Von Horst and his soldiers). Ned Land rose early simply because of long years of doing so at sea. We had our last well-cooked breakfast thanks to the cook from the ship, and then our journey began. We shouldered our assigned packs, seized our rifles and walking sticks and set off along the coast road that led up the slopes of Snaeffels. The morning was cold but calm and the exercise kept us all warm. Once we descended into the volcano, we would find the temperature more amenable.

Conversation at this point was kept to a minimum and we all entertained our own thoughts. Mine were of Gretchen and our daughter and the possibility that I might never see them again. I should have been a very glum conversationalist if there were any to join in. Thankfully there were not.

That first day saw us climb to the waiting crater. This part of the journey was arduous but unremarkable. We were in the shadow of nearby Scartaris most of the time—the same mountain shadow that had pointed the way for us on our previous trip—and, though the views were spectacular, they were as nothing for those yet to come. It was evening by the time we reached the summit of Snaeffels, and so we prepared a camp for the evening looking down on the volcano's crater. As before, there were three deep shafts that would lead to the heart of the mountain.

Ned Land grinned cheerfully. "A strange sight for a sailor," he decided. "And there won't be an ocean for me to hazard for quite some time now." He pointed to the center shaft. "That is our path, I believe."

"Hardly," my uncle replied, with a slight smile.

Land scowled and glanced at me. "Your published account of your trip —"

"Said that the center descent was the correct one, yes," my uncle interrupted him. "That was *my* suggestion."

"It is not?"

"It is not," the Professor answered. "That learned man Arne Saknussemm went to great lengths to hide the correct entrance—and for good reasons. I persuaded my nephew to do the same. He named the *incorrect* start of our journey.[1] I believe it to be a wise choice."

Land's face was split by another of his huge grins. "Then if the Gun Club is relying on your manuscript to show them the way —"

"Then we need not fear that they have a few days head start on us, because they will have taken the wrong route," my uncle confirmed.

Ned Land laughed uproariously at this, and spent most of the evening chuckling as he thought upon the point. He was undoubtedly the happiest man in our camp that night, and I the glummest. But even the longest and most depressing night comes to an end, and in the morning we began our real journey.

The shaft below us was five thousand six hundred feet deep. Needless to say, we could not descend so far in one attempt. We therefore followed our former method of travel, lowering ourselves by rope some two hundred feet at a time down the left hand shaft. There were numerous small shelves and ledges on the way down the volcanic vent, but none large enough to hold all of our party at once. As a result, we made the descent in three separate groups. The Captain, my uncle, Hans and I led the way. Ned Land followed with two of the soldiers and then the final three military men made up the third party. Each group left at hour intervals so that there would be no chance of our bunching up on the way down.

Fortunately, we all had good heads for heights—or, more accurately, depths—as the climb down was for most of the journey a descent into an abyss without any view of the bottom. Had any of us slipped and fallen it would have been a horrible fate. Though every time I missed a firm grip or foothold I had visions of plunging to my death, I was always able to rectify my error and continue the descent.

---

[1] I leave it to the reader to decide whether there is any greater truth in *this* account of our journey.

We rested several times on that descent as it was extremely exhausting work. We were all in good shape, though, even my uncle who was at least ten years older than any other man in the party. Despite his age, he was as agile and excited as a young goat, stopping from time to time mostly to examine our surroundings. There was not, at this stage, much to see, because we were in a vent that had once contained lava, and the walls were coated with hardened igneous rock. Still, it all interested the man of learning, and he would make the occasional note in his pocket journal.

On we went, further into the depths, passing below the surface of the earth outside before our feet finally touched solid ground. Here there was a horizontal passageway that showed the way we were to go. A few feet inside the tunnel was absolute darkness, as sunlight could not penetrate it. My uncle led the way inside and lit his Ruhmkorf coil, which cast an electric glow over the rocks.

"Let us wait here," he said, cheerfully. It will be some two hours before the last of our party joins us." The Captain seemed impatient to press on, but understood the need and nodded curtly. Hans, phlegmatic as ever, simply sat with his back to the tunnel wall and fell into a swift sleep. I prowled back and forth until the next party reached us.

"An odd journey for a sailor," Ned Land commented, as his feet touched ground. "But I've been aloft often enough in the past for that trip to have seemed familiar enough." He peered into the gloom ahead of us. "But this next stage looks to be something else." He started forward, but my uncle held his arm.

"Do not go out of sight of the rest of us," he advised. "Distances and directions down here can be very confusing and it is far too easy to get lost." He gave me a sympathetic glance at that remark, knowing I had done precisely that on our former trip.

"I have a sailor's instinct for distance and direction," the whaler replied. "But as there is no sea in sight, I'll take your wise advice and promise to stay within view of your lamp. But

I am intrigued, and would like to take a glance around." He grinned at me. "Maybe you'd be kind enough to accompany me, lad?"

I shrugged and acquiesced—looking around was better than sitting and waiting. Together we walked further into the tunnel ahead. Within twenty paces, the light from my uncle's lamp was all we had to see by. I could have lit my own coil, but it seemed better to save it for when it might be more urgently needed. The sailor had been examining the walls of the tunnel, and he called my attention to a short mark in the rock, perhaps six inches long and quite horizontal.

"This is really why I wanted to call you aside, lad," he said, softly, worried that his voice might carry. "It's clearly the mark of something striking the wall—a backpack, I imagine. I saw a few more of these back at the base of the shaft. It looks as if the members of the Gun Club might be ahead of us after all."

He was quite correct in his deduction as to the cause of the marks—they were made by something striking the wall at a height of about five feet from the ground. I could think of no natural cause for such marks. I could, however, dispute his conclusion. "It does not show that anyone is ahead of us," I replied. "Merely that someone has passed this way before, and we certainly know that—this is the route we ourselves took on our previous journey. Down here where there is neither wind nor rain to erode such marks, it is impossible to determine their age. They could simply be the marks we ourselves made on our last descent."

"Well, that's a relief then," he said. "I was worried about upsetting the Captain and the professor by saying anything about these scrapes around them. I'm glad to hear my fears aren't well-founded."

I touched his arm. "I do not say that the Gun Club is *not* ahead of us," I cautioned him. "Merely that these marks prove nothing either way. You will find that many things are very different down here than they might have been on the surface of our world."

In order to make Land's excuse plausible to the others, we looked about for a short while before returning to the main party. My uncle had been verbally sketching out the path ahead of us to the Captain, who was visibly restraining himself from plunging on ahead and letting his men follow behind as they arrived. My uncle, once again, cautioned that our party should not separate; well enough did I know the consequences of such an action. Though impatient to be off, Von Horst forced himself to wait until the last man joined us. At this point, we formed a single line, Hans in the lead, and we began the task of retracing our steps.

For the next several days, nothing of any great interest occurred. We experienced nothing out of the ordinary as we knew this portion of the journey well enough to take no wrong passages. The days were simply filled with walking, climbing, resting and eating our rations. We were frugal with our water supplies, mindful that this precious liquid might not be so simple to find down here.

Ned Land found everything fascinating, out of his native element as he was. He listened willingly to every lecture my uncle gave as we walked about the rocks and fossils we passed. The sailor was an intelligent man, and a quick study. Soon enough he was pointing out the shells of extinct marine life so well preserved in the tunnel walls, and mispronouncing their taxonomic names with great gusto. If the Captain or his men found any interest in the sights, none of them showed any evidence of it. They were men on a mission and devoted their attention and energy to that cause.

At the end of our first week's travel, we had made good progress. Having avoided errors we had made the first time around, we were much deeper and further along on our journey than the previous time, and it was now time for two things. First, as had become our habit on the previous adventure, Hans received his weekly pay for his services. He accepted the coins solemnly and stowed them in his pack.

Secondly, it was time for my uncle's promised decision about the Captain and his men. We were gathered together in a small cluster in a cavern some hundred or so feet long, thirty high and sixty deep. Each of us had managed to find a boulder to act as a seat, and two of the coils were lit to provide a faerie light that glinted off the rocks about us.

"When we began this trip," my uncle said, "I had my reservations, Captain, about the size of our party. However, I find myself in the position of having to admit that my worries have proven to be unfounded. You and your men have caused no delay in our progress, and you appear to have adapted to this strange life of ours down here rather well. If you are in agreement, then, I would propose that you remain members of our group for the rest of our journey."

"Naturally I agree," Von Horst replied. "We are here because of our duty, and that duty to Germany remains unchanged. We shall accompany you every step of the way."

To seal this agreement, the two men shook hands solemnly. Ned Land grinned, and I admit I was glad that we should have the company of the soldiers for the rest of the journey. Though they did not socialize with us at all, they were not a burden, and I was glad for the extra numbers. I could not then—nor indeed can I now—tell you the name of a single one of them, but that was how they wished it.

For myself, I was more than glad that we had Ned Land along. Hans was a good fellow, but he rarely spoke, and when he did it was in Danish, and only my uncle understood him. Land, on the other hand, spoke several languages pretty fluently, so he and I could converse without trouble. As the Captain stayed with his men in our rest times, and with my uncle the remainder of the time, I was sincerely glad for the sailor's company. We had become good friends by this point, and we had exchanged our tales. I filled him in on the events of my previous plunge into the Earth, and he responded by telling me of the adventures he had faced whilst captive of the strange Captain Nemo. When those tales had run out, he'd turned to speaking of his days on the high seas, and of hunting the great whales. Though his tales sometimes sounded a trifle fantastic, his quiet, earnest manner made me believe his every word.

He soon had evidence for one of my own tales. We were descending a sloping passageway when there was a faint murmuring ahead of us. The Captain signaled a halt and turned to my uncle.

"Could we have caught up with the Gun Club?" he asked, softly. He worried about sound being carried down these passageways, as sometimes the acoustics could make sounds from miles away sound as if they were right beside one.

"I don't know," the scientist admitted, just as softly, and just as disturbed. Despite everything, were we in second place after all in our mission?

Hans, however, was quite certain he knew the reason for the faint sound. "Vand," he said, in his normal voice.

"Vand?" my uncle echoed. Then he laughed. "Of course, Hans is quite correct, as usual."

"But what does he say it is?" Ned Land demanded. "You forget that we don't speak Danish."

"Oh, he means *water*."

The sailor frowned. "We have reached the underground sea already?"

"No, no," my uncle said, impatiently. "But I'm surprised that Axel hasn't recognized where we are. Come along." He led the way briskly forward, and we trailed behind. I racked my brain, trying to work out why I should know this passage of so many. It finally came to me as we reached the source of the murmuring sounds.

"The Hans-bach!" I exclaimed, and indeed it was that underground river, named for its discoverer, Hans. On our first trip we had been threatened by an acute shortage of water when Hans saved us by discovering a subterranean river flowing behind the rock wall of our tunnel. He had hacked a hole through to it, and water had gushed forth, saving our lives. And here, years later, we now faced the remains of that flow. It demonstrated how much underground water there must be that this river—now reduced to a gentle stream—had lasted so long.

And, as we quickly discovered, it was still extremely hot.

"There is a great deal of water associated with volcanoes," my uncle lectured. "In Iceland, these super-heated streams sometimes burst forth at the surface into powerful fountains known as *geysers*. They have also been reported in sections of the United States. I suspect there is now one less erupting on the surface of our planet, having been diverted down this passageway." He pointed onward. "And, as before, the faithful Hans-bach will lead our way for a while now."

We paused to refill our canteens, though we had to wait for a while until the water was cool enough to drink, and then continued on our way, descending once again.

Ned Land shook his head. "I had thought, lad, that I had seen almost all there was to be seen associated with water. But a stream miles beneath the Earth that runs hotter than a bath—now *that's* a new one for me." He chuckled. "I can see that this trip of ours in going to be very educational."

VI. The Shores of an Ancient Sea

On my previous journey I was able to provide exact dates and distances for our travels. This time, however, I am quite unable to do that for reasons that will shortly be made perfectly clear. Instead of being able to peruse my notes, I am forced this time around to rely upon my memory. Again, for reasons that will be made abundantly clear, those memories are not as accurate as I might have wished. So I am afraid that vagueness is all that I can offer. It is a poor excuse for a scientist, but cannot be helped.

We followed the path of the Hans-bach downward for the next few days. A trip to the center of our world might sound exciting, but day after day of walking, resting, eating and sleeping is far from enthralling, especially when much of it varied not at all. One tunnel through ancient rocks is much like any other tunnel. One rest-stop on convenient rocks varies not a whit from any other. The meals we ate were cold and monotonous and my sleeps—at the very least—were broken by the longing I felt to see my wife and child again. From time to time there might come some excitement if my uncle discovered a new vein of some igneous rock which he felt compelled to point out to everyone. From time to time Ned Land might laugh or marvel at some oddly-shaped rock. Other than that, the soldiers marched in grim silence and I was lost in my own thoughts, save for the times of conversation with the sailor, or with my uncle over matters scientific. Despite the potential perils and the urgency of our mission, boredom was our greatest foe.

And then we heard the sound of a great thunderclap from ahead of us. Even Hans appeared startled at this unexpected intrusion into our silent world. Save for the low murmur of the flowing Hans-bach, and the sound of our own footsteps, the world below ground is almost uniformly silent. With no native light, there are no plants, and without plants there is no animal life. There is no wind, for the air does not hurtle about, and so there is little enough to cause any noise. Hence our surprise and shock at this great roaring boom.

Captain Von Horst immediately signaled his soldiers. Dropping their packs, they immediately raised their rifles and set off at a trot. Hans fell in behind them, though without losing his pack. Ned Land was hot on his heels, and my uncle and I followed at the rear. We carried our own packs as at the time I had my coil lit and my uncle would not abandon his instruments for any strange noise. Down the passageway we plunged, following those ahead of us, and then into a large cavern. Here we halted, gathered with the others of our party.

The cavern was some fifty feet long, about twenty wide and over a hundred feet high. Stalactites and stalagmites abounded, and there was the faint sound of dripping that showed some subterranean waters were causing both to grow slowly over the millennia. At the far side of the cavern were two possible exits. I recalled that the left-hand one was the passageway we should take, and before that exit was a huge jumble of rocks, partially blocking access.

Hans said something in Danish to my uncle, who nodded and gestured at the pile. "That was not here the last time we passed this way," he said, confirming my own recollection. "It is partially blocking the road we must take."

Von Horst scowled. "The Americans must be ahead of us," he declared. "They must have caused this obstruction in the hopes of slowing us down or stopping us." The thought was alarming. Was the Gun Club willing to stop us at any cost?

"That is one explanation, to be sure," my uncle admitted. "There are, however, others."

"Such as?"

"If you examine these rock shards you will see evidence of recent growth of minerals on pieces. This shows that this debris once made up a stalactite, like so many above us." He gestured at the roof of the cavern. "It is possible that this one simply accumulated too much material and it was unable to stay suspended any longer."

"But we heard an explosion," Von Horst objected.

"No; we heard a noise that could be *interpreted* as an explosion. If the rock had merely fallen and shattered, these passageways could produce echoes and reverberations that would have made it sound similar to an explosion."

Von Horst clearly wasn't convinced. "And it just happened to fall as we approached?" he asked. "And it just happened to partially block the way we must take?"

"Coincidences do occur," my uncle replied calmly. "I do not say that is how it happened, merely that is it how it *may* have happened."

"Besides," Ned Land put in, "from everything I've heard of the Gun Club, they are very used to employing explosives. If they blew up this rock with the aim of blocking our way, I think they'd have managed a better job of it. We can clear the pathway is a few minutes, so it hardly holds us up at all." This seemed a valid point to me and to my uncle, but Von Horst remained skeptical. Still, proving Land's point, we had the pathway sufficiently cleared to allow us to proceed within fifteen minutes.

We were all quiet as we did so. Von Horst was probably listening for any signs that the Americans were ahead of us, but I was wondering whether the fallen stalactite had been a work of coincidence or of human agency. The idea that we might be following a party willing to take drastic action to slow us down or stop us was quite unsettling.

Was it possible that the Americans had realized that my uncle had tried to trick them when he convinced me to put the false entrance to the underworld in my manuscript? Had they taken advantage of their few days' lead on us to plunge ahead of us? Could we have been trailing them all of this time? There was no way to be certain, just as there was no way to discern whether the fall of the stalactite had been the work of Nature or the hand of man. As we all worked to clear our passage, we were all lost in such somber thoughts. After all of our efforts, we might still be in second place. To have gone through all that we had, and to see our efforts come to naught... It was too much to contemplate.

By early afternoon, we were able to continue on our way. Now, however, we were looking all about us not for whatever we could learn of the world about us, but to see if there was any evidence that we were on the Gun Club's trail.

There were marks from time to time on the walls and on the ground before us. The problem was, as I had explained to Ned Land at the start of our quest, that it was impossible to discern whether they were the marks we ourselves had left from our first trip or whether they were evidence of others before us.

We continued in this feeling of despair and uncertainty for several more days. Even Ned Land, normally talkative and cheerful, was uncommonly silent and withdrawn. As ever, only Hans seemed unaffected by our concerns. As long as he received his weekly pay when it came due, he was a happy man. If he was missing his young lady's company, or worried about her actions while he was gone, neither showed on his open, unworried face. He did his job as he always did, and left worries or cares to others more suited to suffering them.

Unlike Hans, I certainly suffered. Atop missing my little family and worrying for my life, I now had the terrible premonition that it might all be for nothing after all.

Finally, however, came the day we had been anticipating for so long. We came down a long tunnel, Hans in the lead, as usual, when the guide called back: "Vind!"

Wind! Even I understood that much Danish. *Wind!* Down here, far below the tumultuous weather on the surface of our planet, there could only be one source of wind. Excited again at last, we rushed forward and exited the tight passageway to stand within an immense cavern, almost unimaginably large. Our coils were no longer needed, as the place possessed a light source of its own. Far in the distance, near the roof of this great cavern, was the glow of an aurora, similar to those found in the polar regions of the surface world. Here, though, the glow was continuous and bathed the entire realm in a mockery of sunlight.

Ned Land whistled, and then grinned. "Now *this* is a sight!" he exclaimed. "Light and a stiff breeze—and I can hear the sound of waves, unless I am much mistaken."

"You are quite correct," my uncle said. "The Central Sea lies before us. Come, let us go and see it!"

The prospect of a break at last in the monotony of stone walls close about us had even the soldiers excited. We rushed together as a troop through the rocks and stalagmites, lit in strange and beautiful colors from the glow of the aurora, toward the waiting sea. The sounds of the waves and the whistling of the wind were wonderful to hear, and then we broke out onto the shore.

Ahead of us, fading into the distance, lay an immense body of water. Waves lapped or crashed upon the shore about our feet. It was impossible to calculate how large it must be, or how much water it held. Land, Von Horst and the soldiers stared at it in awe. It almost felt as though we had somehow been magically returned to the surface of our planet even though we all knew we were deep within the Earth. At our backs were the huge walls of rock that then rose over our heads and helped to contain this world within a world.

"Magnificent!" the Captain said, in an almost breathless tone. "This, *this*, is the start of New Germany." He signally one of his men who removed his pack and extracted from it a small flag bearing the emblem of our unified Germany. Von Horst took it carefully from the man and moved back about a dozen feet from the edge of the ocean before plunging it upright into the ground. "I claim this new land in the name of the Kaiser and the peoples of Germany!" he cried. The five soldiers gave a cry of acclaim. The Captain was almost glowing from patriotic fervor.

I confess that I had quite a different reaction to this statement. It seemed to me that any attempt to annex this inner ocean as part of Germany was both futile and a case of hubris. This world was its own master, without the need for the hand of man. Ned Land was as silent and inscrutable as Hans. My uncle, however, could not restrain his own emotions.

"You are claiming this land?" he asked, derisively. "What? Are you to move settlers down here? Do you envision starting up a factory on the shores of this sea? Or do you wish to sail a battleship or run a ferry here? My dear Captain, I can see no use for patriotism down here."

"You are mocking our Kaiser?" Von Horst asked, his face flushed.

"Not I!" my uncle assured him. "I rather think it is *you* who mock him by attempting to claim a land he cannot use. What will you do with this vast realm now that you have it?"

"But you agreed to lead an expedition here in order to claim it," the soldier protested.

"No," the man of science answered. "I could see that you were determined to come here on this mission of yours, and I knew you would not succeed without my help. But my aim was never to claim this land, but in the hopes of demonstrating the futility of your desire." He gestured about us. "There is nothing here for you or your superiors. This world exists on its own terms and is ruled by creatures you cannot conquer or understand. It is not a place for politicians to try and claim or squabble over. As we explore further, you will understand what I mean. All we can do here is pass through it and seek to understand as much as possible. It is not our land, and never will be."

"You are a traitor," Von Horst exclaimed, his face livid. "You mock Germany and our Kaiser!" He turned to his men. "Arrest him!"

"Arrest me?" My uncle laughed. "And then what will you do with me? Is there a jail nearby you can throw me into, or a dungeon where I can be chained up? Captain, you are being foolish."

"You will bow to my authority," Von Horst snapped. "If you resist, I can have you shot."

"Oh, that would be most sensible," the professor mocked. "Can you even retrace your steps to the surface of this world?" He held up his notebook. "The only route back is within this book—and it is written in a code of my own devising. If you have me shot, you may as well then shoot yourself and stave off a lingering death."

The captain was starting to feel less secure in his authority. He gestured at Hans. "He is your guide—I am sure he will know the way back."

"That may be so," my uncle replied, unworriedly crossing his arms. "But he speaks only Danish—and I am the only other member of this party who shares that tongue. So the only way you would ever know what he knows is through my assistance. My dear Captain, please stop posturing and use your mind for a change. Things must remain as they are, however you feel about matters." He gestured at the flag. "If it makes you happy to plant that here, then do so—but don't expect it to mean anything."

The Captain was livid, but I could see that he understood how things were. Confronting my uncle was a pointless exercise that would only serve to test his power. My uncle could be infuriating at times, but in this matter he was quite correct—there was little that Von Horst could do to him down here. What my uncle was forgetting was that we would, hopefully, not be down here forever. Once we regained the surface of our world, I had a strong suspicion that any resentments the military man felt now would be multiplied twentyfold, and that he would make my uncle pay dearly for his mockery. I resolved to have words with the Professor when we were alone and caution him against further challenges to Von Horst. I was by no means certain, of course, that my uncle would listen.

"So," the Captain said, finally, barely restraining his temper, "what would you have us do now?"

My uncle gestured at the expanse of the Central Sea. "That is our way forward," he explained. "It is time for us to build rafts to enable us to navigate it." He turned to Ned Land. "Do you think you could take the lead in the construction of a pair of rafts?"

Land grinned widely. I could see that he was eager to be out upon the waters of this unexplored ocean; this was why he had accompanied us. "I can do better than that," he vowed. "With the aid of these stout fellows —" He gestured at the soldiers, Hans and myself "—I am certain I can construct vessels that will serve us well." He inclined his head toward Von Horst. "With your permission, Captain, I should like to borrow your strong lads to collect the timber we shall need for the work."

The Captain looked puzzled. "I see no timber," he said. "Merely rocks."

"Farther down the coast is a veritable forest," I informed him. "Though not one such as we have on the surface of the world. It should supply us with all the materials we will need. It will take a few days to gather the materials and construct our craft, so this would be a good time to set up a base camp near the forest."

"Very well," the Captain agreed. "Let us take a look at the forest and we shall establish a camp there. And my men will aid in chopping down the trees."

I couldn't resist a grin of my own. "It's not trees, Captain—it's mushrooms."

"Mushrooms!"

"Indeed," my uncle said. "But mushrooms the like of which our world above has never seen."

We wound our way along the shoreline of the Central Sea. There was a strong breeze coming off the waters, and Ned Land laughed as he walked beside me. "The journey so far hasn't been one for a sailor," he commented. "But this! This was worth walking all that way to see. An unknown ocean, un-navigated and uncharted. This is what a sailor lives for, my lad."

"Our last trip on these waters was far from entertaining," I observed drily. "We suffered through an electrical storm and the clash of leviathans."

"But that time you didn't have Ned Land with you." He grinned again. "Things will be very different this time, I assure you."

I hoped that he was correct, but in these strange lands it is always best to expect the worst—far too frequently that is what arrives. But I had no idea how terrible things were about to become.

VII. Betrayal!

Walking along that shore, with the sea to our right and the strange electrical glow in the air, one might almost imagine oneself back upon the surface of our planet instead of miles beneath its surface. That is, until one looked up and saw the rocks curving up above our heads on the left until they were lost in the light. The stalactites thinned out and then we caught our first glimpse of the weird mushroom forest. On the surface of our world, often hidden from the rays of the sun, mushrooms achieve a height of but a few inches. Down here in the underworld, illuminated by an electrical glow that clearly possessed strange properties that normal light does not, mushrooms achieved a much greater height.

Ned Land gave a loud, clear whistle that echoed about us strangely. "I've seen sights from Zanzibar to Zebu," he murmured, "but never anything like this!"

Starting with a few scattered individuals of lesser height, the mushrooms spread before us, many of them topping forty feet tall. Large caps crowned stalks the size of trees, though possessing no branches. It was possible to discern different varieties of growths—most were tall and pale, like our earthly counterparts, but some had riots of odd color. Some were tall and thin, reaching toward the looming roof of rock, while others were shorter and fatter, more like the size of a small hut. The soldiers were all stunned by the vista before us, and even I—who had seen it before—found it profound and moving. Where there is water, light and heat, it appeared, life will find a way to exist.

My uncle, ever practical, gestured toward the forest. "The stalks of the gigantic mushrooms are as strong as wood," he commented. "There are many that have fallen in the electrical storms that ravage this world and we should be able to collect sufficient for our needs quite quickly."

Ned Land nodded. "I'll have to test the... well, I suppose calling it *wood* is incorrect, but it's what I'm used to saying... the wood, then, to make certain it's suitable, but I see nothing wrong with your basic plan."

At that moment, there was a strange howl in the distance that made everyone pause.

"What is that?" the Captain demanded.

"One of the inhabitants of this land, I should imagine," my uncle said lightly. "There are creatures within these forest that feast on the mushrooms, naturally—and other creatures that prey upon those beasts. We should have nothing to fear from them as long as we are careful."

"Animals down here?" asked Ned Land.

"Certainly," my uncle replied. "Life down here follows the same natural laws as it does upon the surface of our world. Where there is vegetable life, there is animal life to feed upon it. And where there is animal life, there are predators to snatch up what they can. Besides, you already knew that there are monsters in the waters—why are you then surprised to hear that there is life upon the land?"

"I simply never made the connection," the sailor admitted, a little ashamed. "This land is so austere and strange that I never imagined life upon it—but the sea is wild and beautiful and life there seems natural to me. The prejudices of a sailor!"

The Captain licked his lips. "Animals mean fresh meat," he said. "After so long on dried rations, that sounds delightful. I shall send two of my men off hunting—tonight we shall feast!"

"Perhaps it would be better for Hans to accompany them," my uncle suggested. "He is, after all, a hunter by profession."

"No!" the Captain said, sharply. "My men will go alone. Your guide is strong and will be of more use here helping to haul the wood that we require."

It did not surprise me that he did not want Hans to accompany his men—he had made it abundantly clear that he felt that the two non-German members of our party were somehow inferior creatures and not to be entrusted with any important tasks, and that they were more suited to menial labor. It was an attitude I did not care for, but there seemed to be little to be gained in remonstrating him for it.

Ned Land stepped forward. "Aye, he's a big boy," he agreed. "I'll take him along with me and Axel here and we'll scout about for fallen mushrooms and test their wood." He rummaged in his pack for a moment before straightening up, holding a large, heavy knife. "I have to be certain we can carve the wood." He turned to the professor. "Ask your man to bring his ax and to accompany us, if you would."

My uncle exchanged a few words with Hans, who nodded and pulled his ax from his pack. "I shall remain here with the Captain," my uncle decided. "This would seem to be as good a spot as any for our camp."

I shed my own pack, retaining only my own knife and a rifle. I doubted any of the local fauna would venture close to us, but I was comforted by its presence. Ned gave me one of his cheery grins and led the small party off into the mushroom woods. Two of the soldiers set off in a slightly different direction. In a few moments Ned, Hans and myself were alone in the strange growths. As we walked, Ned was occupied with something in his hand, and then I heard him give a sailor's picturesque curse. "What is the matter?" I asked him.

He held out his hand. In his large palm rested a bullet that he had pried open, spilling dark powder onto the skin. "When the Captain seemed so adamant that our friend Hans should not go hunting, I was seized by a sudden suspicion. I palmed one of the bullets I had been issued when I retrieved my knife."

"So?" I asked, puzzled.

"So," he said, grimly, "this bullet would not fire. It is filled with coarse black pepper, and not powder."

I was confused. "What does this mean?"

"It means that the Captain does not trust me—nor Hans, most likely—with live ammunition." He stared at the rifle I carried. "The question now is whether he trusts you and your uncle with it."

This thought was very disquieting. I opened up the breech of my rifle and extracted the bullet. As he had feared, when Ned Land opened the cartridge, pepper once again spilled out.

"So," he said, slowly, "you and most probably your uncle also have weapons that will not fire. Only the Captain and his men are armed."

"That's not good," I said. "We are unable to defend ourselves. He has placed our lives at risk."

"My lad, you are very naïve," the sailor said. "It is possible that he intends to do more than risk your life. If the three of us and your uncle were not to return from this expedition, who would ever think of blaming the Captain? He, after all, would be the one telling the story of our fate."

"You think he would do that?" I asked, aghast. "But *why*?"

He shrugged. "I do not *know* that this is his plan," he said. "Merely that it *may* be so. I think we should all prepare ourselves in case that is what he has in mind. You must take the opportunity to speak to your uncle alone and warn him of my suspicions. But we shall *all* take care and not let our suspicions slip. If he knew we were aware of his schemes, he might advance his timetable. For the moment I think we are safe because he needs us to construct our vessels. But after that?"

"But he needs my uncle for his map," I protested. "He knows he cannot decipher it without him."

"And what need does he have for the rest of us?" the sailor asked. "He might possibly require you as a hostage to ensure your uncle's compliance, but Hans and I are likely to be deemed superfluous. It all depends upon what his aim is and at the moment we do not know it. But we are aware that he *has* plans, and so we must make some of our own. It is essential, however, that he not know we are onto his schemes."

I glanced at Hans. "And what of him?" I asked. "How much of this does he understand?"

"He will understand all of it shortly," Land replied. "I can converse with Hans well enough with my little Danish. You learn a lot of languages living at sea, my lad."

"Then I will speak with my uncle at the earliest possible moment," I promised. "Who knows? Perhaps he can make some sense of this."

As it turned out, he could—but not the way I had expected. We had gathered quite a supply of fallen mushroom stems that the sailor thought looked promising, and returned with them to camp. While he and Hans set about turning these into usable planks and such, I managed to get my uncle aside and speak to him. When I told him of our discovery, he merely shrugged.

"I know all about that," he said. "And have since the expedition started."

"You *know*?" I cried. "And said nothing?"

"Keep your voice down low, my boy," my uncle admonished me. "I would prefer that the Captain not overhear this conversation. Yes, I knew—and I said nothing. Axel, my boy, you're a good man, but I don't know if you're a good actor. I was afraid that if I told you what I knew, you might blurt it out, honest soul that you are, or eye the Captain and his men in ways that might arouse their suspicion."

"But you knew," I persisted.

"From the first day," he admitted. "I inspected our equipment while we were on the ship, you may recall. The Captain was wise enough to lay out live ammunition then, so that everything looked normal. But when we received our packed bags, I saw that the ammunition in it had been changed. The only reason for this I could think of was that blanks had been substituted. And I realized that if mine had been tampered with, then so had yours and that of Hans and Mr. Land. The only reason for this that came to mind was that the Captain wanted to be certain of having an advantage over us. I do not know why he should want that, but it was clear that he intended to control us in some way at some time."

"But what can we do about it?" I asked, appalled.

"I have already done something," he replied. "The real reason I wished to stay with the Captain and set up camp was because the soldiers had to leave their packs here while they hunted and worked. I was able to seize the opportunity to exchange all of mine and Hans' blank ammunition for live rounds. Now *we* have the advantage, for the Captain believes us powerless and his men to possess the only live ammunition. I am not yet certain how we make use of this, but any advantage must be to the good."

My uncle never ceased to amaze me. I was astonished and proud of his cleverness, but annoyed at being kept in the dark over it all. Still, though my pride was hurt, it was more important to plan for our future. "So what are we to do now?"

"Act as if nothing were wrong," he replied. "We build our two ships and continue our little expedition as planned until we discover what the Captain's intents are." His face clouded. "I fear they may be grave for our companions."

"You think he means them harm?" I asked.

"I think he has already attempted harm. The attack on Hans back in Iceland—I do not believe it was engineered either by the Gun Club or by his romantic rival. I suspect—but cannot prove—that the injured soldier we were forced to leave behind was the person who began the rock fall that was aimed at Hans, and that he himself was injured as he effected it."

"You think he means to kill Hans and Ned Land?"

My uncle held up an admonishing finger. "That is merely one interpretation of the facts," he cautioned me. "It may or may not be the correct one—but we should take the possibility quite seriously. Inform Mr. Land of my suspicions, but admonish him to take precautions but no precipitous actions yet. We must see how things are planned before we act."

My uncle appeared calm and in control of himself, but I did not find it as easy to keep in rein my own temper. That we should be so betrayed! I wished to face down the Captain and confront him with what we knew of his treachery—but my uncle was quite correct. That would avail us nothing. They were still six to our four, and they had twice as much ammunition as we had. Besides which, they were trained fighting men, and we... Well, I had no doubt that in a fight both Hans and Ned Land could more than hold their own. But my uncle and I were mere academics and completely unused to physical combat. It galled me to do nothing, but my uncle's advice had been good.

I hurried back to Ned Land. While I was supposedly helping him to work on the shaping of our vessels, I informed him quietly of the conversation I had just had with my uncle. The sailor thought about this for a few moments before replying.

"It seems to me that your uncle is right—at the moment the Captain has the advantages. But since we know he must be intending to act, we have an advantage there as he must assume we are still completely unaware of his actions. He is an egotist, and such men feel themselves superior to others. He is sure to believe he has us completely fooled. We must all act dumb in order to maintain his false state of belief. In the mean time, I shall endeavor to follow your uncle's example and exchange some of my bad ammunition for one soldier's good supply."

"I shall do the same," I vowed.

Land laughed and clapped my shoulder. "I think not, my friend," he said. "You're a fine fellow, and I'm glad to have you on my side, but your hands lack the required subtlety for the work of thievery. Leave that to me, and I shall slip you some good bullets as the time passes. Now, we have real work to do—shaping our boats!"

The two soldiers returned later, carrying two small, dead creatures my uncle and I readily identified as *eohippus*, a miniature ancestor of today's majestic horses. The men had sighted a small herd of the creatures grazing, and had brought down these two. When my uncle had named and described them, Ned Land expressed his wonder.

"Ancient horses supposedly dead these past few million years?" He shook his head. "This is a strange world we are in, indeed."

"Not at all," my uncle replied. "It is only logical. Some 13 years ago a British scientist, Charles Darwin, published his book *On The Origin Of Species*. In it, he proposed that creatures evolve over time to adapt to changes in their conditions." He spread his arms. "Down here, there *are* no changes in conditions. It is logical, therefore, that since there is no need for animals to evolve, they do not. So plesiosaurs in the seas here remain masters of their ocean and small ancestral horses still roam these strange forests. It is eminently sensible."

I licked my lips as the fresh meat roasted over a fire. "What is eminently sensible to me," I pointed out, "is that we are going to have fresh meat again for the first time in many weeks."

Ned Land laughed. "I think you have the best of this discussion, my lad."

Our "evening" meal—though there was neither night nor day down here, we allowed our pocket watches to rule our days—was a reasonably jovial affair. We were all, soldiers included, glad for this change in our fare. Though the meat was a trifle on the tough side, I could not recall a time when I had eaten better. The only thing marring our enjoyment of the feast was the strong and certain knowledge that we were to soon be betrayed.

VIII. At Sea

The small vessels that Ned Land designed and supervised as we all helped to build them were a great improvement upon our previous attempt. The mushroom stalks proved to be remarkably wood-like in their qualities, enabling us to make planks from them and then to form them into the requited shapes to construct the boats. Naturally, we did not have metal for nails, but the sailor showed us how to use "wooden" pins and wedges to hold the planks together. Over the course of the next several days our two boats took shape. I refer to them as boats, but they were actually little more than elongated canoes, to which Ned Land added out-riggers, such as those he had seen in the South Seas, to make them far more stable.

All of this took time, of course—again, I cannot be sure of exactly how long, but it was certainly more than a week, but less than a month. Von Horst allowed us the use of three of the soldiers each day to aid with the construction, while he and the remaining two went hunting, to keep us supplied with fresh meat. At least, that is what he claimed, though later events make me now disbelieve that assertion. Tensions were quite high—partly because of the confrontation between my uncle and Captain Von Horst, but mostly because of the fact that we knew a betrayal was in the offing. While Ned Land kept us busy constructing the boats, my uncle and Hans managed to swap out more of our ammunition with that of the soldiers who helped us. I never did learn their names, as they had no interest in conversation and simply obeyed Mr. Land's orders as they were given.

The hunting parties proved to be very productive. We ate well, and were able to smoke and preserve a goodly store of meat in case it should be needed on the rest of our trip. On our previous voyage, the Central Sea was as close as we actually managed to approach the center of the Earth; shortly after we crossed it, we were hurtled back to the surface through the agency of an active volcano. We sincerely aimed to avoid the same route this time—we had been more than fortunate not to have been cooked on our last journey—and would seek a route leading us deeper into the Earth.

"It may be that our predecessor Arne Saknussemm managed to get no further than this, either," my uncle said over our supper one evening. "We discovered his initials carved on a rock beside the tunnel that took us back to the surface. There may be nothing more ahead of us than a return to the sunlit world above us. But I cannot accept that as inevitable, and am determined that we should press onward—and, hopefully, downward."

"That is my aim also," Von Horst agreed. "We are ordered to reach the center of the Earth, if at all possible." He glanced out across the waters of the Central Sea. Because our light was caused by electrical phenomenon, unlike on the surface there was no night here. Every hour of the day was as bright as any other. In the distance, churning the waters and lighting the sky, was a vast electrical storm. "Yet are you certain your boats will be able to withstand such weather, Mr. Land?"

The whaler laughed. "No sailor knowingly would engage a storm such as that," he observed. "Such forces of nature could swamp and sink much sturdier vessels than we are constructing. No, I do not propose crossing the ocean at all."

My uncle glanced at him sharply. "But we *must* cross it," he insisted. "If there is a way ahead, it is on the far side of the waters."

"Well now," the sailor said gently, "in the first place, we don't know that for a fact." He gestured about us. "There are many grottos around here, and any number of side passages, any of which might be the road downward for us."

"Far too many for us to explore in several lifetimes," the Professor objected. "And none with any certainty that it doesn't peter out pointlessly. We should look for more evidence that the esteemed Saknussemm has gone before us."

"But he, in turn, must have had a reason to select the passages that he did," Ned Land pointed out. "And there is no telling how many times he had to backtrack to advance. And what if your supposition is correct? That he got no closer to the center of the Earth than this sea here before us?" That thought shut off my uncle's objections for a moment. "In the second place," the sailor continued, "I have seen no evidence that this Icelander built a raft himself—the only indications of previous work at this site are those you and your companions left last time. This leads me to believe that your medieval explorer went on foot around the edge of the sea."

I had to confess that he made a good point there. "It's likely, uncle," I argued. Then, confused, I asked Ned Land: "But in that case, why the need for us to build boats?"

"Because of my third and final point. I suggest that we do not venture out too far at sea, but instead follow the coast and camp each night ashore. This way we shall be able to scout about and see if we can strike further evidence of the path our predecessor took and if he went deeper before returning here. And we shall be able to look for routes that he might not have taken that look likely. And, to cap it all, we shall be able to avoid the monsters of the deeps that almost killed you on your last trip. Such monsters need the depth to swim and feed, so they will not be able to venture close enough to the shore to imperil us."

For once, the Captain actually seemed enthused by Ned Land's ideas. "I agree whole-heartedly," he said. "It is a most sensible plan and gives us the greatest chance of success."

My uncle was still not convinced that we would not be better off striking across the sea, but even he was willing in the end to defer to the judgment of our only nautical member. If was thus decided that when we were able to launch our vessels we should stay close to land and scout the way as we went, camping each night upon the shore. I confess I was much relieved—I had no desire at all for another encounter with the pleisosaurs and ichthyosaurs we had narrowly escaped before. I had seen quite enough of the supposedly-extinct monsters to last me several lifetimes.

And so, with everything agreed upon, we embarked upon the sea-leg portion of our voyage. The Captain insisted on being in the lead vessel with Ned Land and two of the soldiers. I made up the final member of that crew. My uncle and Hans were to follow with the remaining three soldiers in the second boat. I didn't feel comfortable being confined with Von Horst in a small vessel, but there was little choice. I was, at least, glad of Mr. Land's company.

As he had promised us, the outrigger construction proved to be remarkably stable and a completely different experience from the raft we had previously employed. Each of the boats had a mast, to which we had rigged whatever canvas we had as sails, but the main motive power was our muscles driving oars. We were all, even my uncle, in good physical shape thanks to our continual exercise, and we soon learned to stroke in unison to power the boats faster. The rhythm we built up was quite effective, and sped us through the waters. We stayed in fairly shallow waters about a hundred yards from the shore line as we headed east around the sea.

There was little of any consequence for the first three days. We rowed, rested and allowed the wind to drive us, and scanned the shoreline. We saw animals from time to time that my uncle and I named from our studies, many of which were considered extinct thousands or even millions of years ago. Most were herbivorous, like the small herds of *eohippus* that seemed to infest the area. Twice we heard the sounds of some animal in pain and the cries of some ancient hunter, but we saw nothing. Evidently there were predators, but they did not venture to approach either the water's edge or our evening campsites.

There was an abundance of fish in the sea, and Ned Land rigged fishing lines for both boats. I cannot tell you with what pleasure we dined upon freshly roast fish when we camped for the "night". Neither the sailor nor my uncle was able to name the species we devoured, but most of them were quite delicious.

Gradually, as we sailed and rowed east, the landscape changed. The forests of giant mushrooms thinned out and were replaced by ones of gigantic ferns and trees common to more prehistoric eras of our planet. With this change came different creatures inhabiting the forests. I was able to recognize a family of *Brontotherium*—prehistoric relatives of the rhinoceros, but with twin horns on its huge snout, and a small herd of the immense *Megaloceros*, the fabled Irish elk, seven feet tall and with twelve foot antlers. Smaller creatures abounded, but stayed hidden from direct view. I could hear my uncle expounding upon these marvels in his own boat, and I could scarcely blame him—seeing these creatures finally in the flesh, perambulating and feasting was a dream unrealized by most paleontologists. His excitement was more than understandable, but I was also more than a trifle apprehensive. The final creatures that I saw and recognized were mastodons, those extinct relatives of the elephant, but of huge stature. These I had seen on our last trip to these regions and in the company of a nebulous figure that had terrified me more than any other we had encountered. This had been some twelve feet tall and shaped like a man. My uncle and I had fled from its presence before it could see us and we were never able to ascertain if what we had seen had indeed been some antediluvian species of *homo*. We were more than content to allow that mystery to remain unsolved.

Von Horst, however, seemed excited by the sight of these immense pachyderms and ordered the boats to make land immediately. Despite my protests and those of my uncle, the soldiers obeyed his command and we were forced to alight on the beach barely a mile beyond the great beasts.

"We shall set up our camp here," the soldier commanded. "I shall go with two of my men to explore the region."

"It is not safe," my uncle protested. "These mighty beasts we have been seeing are not used to mankind—there is no predicting their behavior. You may be courting your own deaths."

"That is none of your concern," Von Horst replied. "Do as you are told, and allow me to follow my orders."

"Your orders?" My uncle looked at him sharply. "And what orders might those be?"

"At this moment, no concern of yours," the soldier said. "Ready the camp and start the evening meal. When we return I shall explain further." True to his word, he wouldn't speak to us again before he and two of his men marched into the woods, their rifles at the ready.

Hans looked disturbed and asked my uncle a question. There was a short discussion carried on in Danish that left neither man happy. When it was concluded, Hans set about making a fire and I questioned my uncle about his conversation.

"Hmm?" He seemed very preoccupied. "Oh, my boy, don't bother me about that now. We have other things to concern ourselves over." And he refused to discuss the matter further.

I therefore turned to the only other man I trusted and asked Ned Land what he thought was going on. "The Captain clearly has instructions to do something he does not wish us to know about," he said. "This means he is fairly certain we shall not approve of those orders. Whatever he is up to, I'll wager it doesn't bode well for the four of us." He scowled. "It might be well to keep your rifle close at hand—you can always claim it's because these gigantic beasts are making you nervous. Heaven knows, their presence is affecting me." I rather felt that was because he was itching to hunt them, to be honest. Land was used to chasing monsters of the sea, and these were their closest terrestrial equivalents.

So we were a pretty quiet group as we set up our camp, each lost in his own thoughts. Mine were quite black. Whatever was happening, I felt that a confrontation was now inevitable. Unfortunately, I was quite correct.

The Captain and his soldiers returned as our evening meal—more fish and *eohippus* meat—was ready, and he refused to speak until after our meal was concluded. Then he finally gave in to my uncle's persistent and sharp questions.

"We merely explored the area," he insisted. "It would seem that we are in a region of monsters from the antediluvian past."

"And hence not a safe place for a camp," my uncle snapped. "So why, then, did you insist that we set up for the night here?"

"I have my reasons."

"Perhaps you would care to share them?"

"They are none of your concern," Von Horst replied.

"I am the leader of this expedition; *everything* that affects it in any way is of my concern." My uncle folded his arms stubbornly. "If you expect my further cooperation, then I must be fully informed as to what the objectives of this mission are, and what secret orders you have been given."

The Captain considered for a moment, and then nodded. "Very well. You would discover them soon enough anyway." He waved his hand about us. "I have been instructed to find the creature you referred to as *the Shepherd*."

That comment made me shudder. He was referring to that peculiar hominid my uncle and I had witnessed who appeared to be treating a herd of mastodons as if they were domestic sheep. It had been a strange and terrifying figure, one we had both been glad to flee before it should have observed us.

"And why would you wish to do that?" my uncle asked. "Surely not simply to study the beast?"

"No, of course not." Von Horst dismissed the idea contemptuously. "But where there is one such creature, there are surely more of them. There must be at least a family unit and perhaps even a larger grouping."

"All the more reason to avoid even one of them," I said. "One is frightening enough—more of them would be abhorrent."

"You are a frightened chicken, not a man!" the Captain snapped. "Forever balking at shadows. Only a child is frightened by the unknown."

"And a wise man," Ned Land put in quietly. "Only a fool is not cautious when faced with a situation he has never dealt with before. I should take Herr Axel's concerns with a bit more respect—he has been here before—and you have not."

"Anyway, whatever the state of my nephew's nerves, why do you court death by seeking these shepherds?" The Professor in my uncle was curious. So was I, even though I was the subject of the Captain's insults and ridicule.

"I have been tasked with capturing and returning to Germany one of the youngsters of that species," Von Horst replied.

We were all quite astonished by that reply. Even my uncle could think of nothing to say for quite some time. It made no sense at all to me. Nothing I could think of could explain such bizarre orders. I glanced at the faces of my uncle and the sailor and saw that they were equally as confused as I. Finally, my uncle asked: "And why would you wish to attempt that?"

"Because Chancellor Bismarck himself has ordered it," the Captain said. "Can you not imagine the results of an army of such soldiers? Their appearance alone would terrify all opponents! Twelve foot soldiers fighting for the Motherland—a glorious sight!"

My uncle stared at him aghast. "You cannot be serious!"

"Never more so."

"This is madness," the Professor snapped. "These creatures, whatever they may be, belong *here*, among their own kind, not on the surface of our world! You cannot snatch them from their families and enslave them."

"They would not be slaves—they would be soldiers!" Von Horst said, enthusiastically.

"Soldiers you would have fight for a land and cause that is not their own," Ned Land growled. "They *would* be slaves, in all but name."

"They would be invincible!"

"*If* they can be taken to the surface of the world," I pointed out. "And if they were tractable enough to be trained. Has it not occurred to you that these conscripts of yours might not go along with your plan? That they may have a negative opinion of it?"

"Their opinion does not matter," the Captain said. "I have my orders, and I shall carry them out." He held up his rifle. "*We* have firearms, and they have only clubs. If there is protest, we can deal with it."

My uncle shook his head vehemently. "You are speaking of bringing war to this world," he exclaimed. "I cannot allow it! I *will* not allow it!"

"Then you have reached the limits of your use to me," Von Horst snapped. He nodded to the closest of his soldiers. "Kill him."

Before any of us could move, the soldier raised his rifle and fired point-blank at my uncle.

IX. Flight!

By good fortune, the bullet that should have ended my uncle's life turned out to be one of those he had switched earlier; instead of killing him, the soldier stared at my intact uncle in confusion.

"Now, my friends!" Ned Land roared. He lashed out at the closest of the soldiers, felling the surprised man with a single blow. He then scooped up his own rifle and pack. Hans clearly had been anticipating some such event, for he also jumped one of the startled warriors and sent him crashing to the ground before grabbing his own equipment. I had been unprepared, but seeing their actions I promptly followed suit, lowering my head and charging the closest soldier like a bull. I succeeded in knocking him down and snatched up my own pack and rifle. I followed hot on the heels of the sailor as he rushed into the ferns and trees close to the camp.

We ran as fast as we were able, dodging branches and following some trail created by the local fauna. I did not look back, but after a moment I heard the whine of bullets being fired behind us. Some of these were the blanks, but there were live rounds mixed in with them. Fortunately the forest at this point was quite thick, and none of the soldiers had a clear shot. I did not stop to plan or think, these events having taken me completely by surprise. Instead it was all I could do to keep up with the sailor I followed.

I realized that my uncle had been expecting some kind of confrontation with the Captain, and this must have been what he and Hans had been discussing earlier. I was more than a little hurt that he had not thought to confide his suspicions to me also, so that I might have been better prepared for what was happening. I realized, though, that it was not through any distrust of me but simply because he was too worried to even think of telling me.

On we plunged, getting further from the beach, our transportation and the fury of the Captain. We were, however, getting closer to potential trouble in the forests. There might be any number of the Shepherds about, along with local predators. I was about to call out to Ned Land and suggest we halt and gather our breaths for a while when the sailor himself called out for a halt.

Panting, exhausted and aching, I was glad to comply. I was bowed over, gasping for air, but still able to look around me. We were deep in the forest now, with ancient trees towering over us and swathes of ferns to hide us from pursuit. As I gasped for air, Hans emerged from the depths, still as impassive as ever, and—thankfully!—behind him came my uncle. He looked a trifle battered, but still in one piece. When he had regained his breath, he smiled at us and said: "Splendid. We are all still together."

"No thanks to you," I retorted, still angry over events. "You might have warned me that this was in store."

"Didn't I?" He looked puzzled. "No, I don't think I did, did I? I'm sorry, my boy, but I had a lot to think about and it simply passed from my mind. And I didn't exactly anticipate that the Captain would attempt to kill us. I had expected he would simply try and detain us. It really is very foolish of him—now he has driven us off, how does he expect to retrace his path to the surface?"

Ned Land gave a sharp bark of a laugh. "Do you think you are the only one capable of keeping a journal?" he asked. "One of the soldiers has done the same from the start. I'm sure the Captain believes he can find his way home again easily enough."

"And he aims to take along one of the ape-men from this world as a prototype soldier," I pointed out. "I'm sure none of us want that to happen. Warfare that involved these creatures would be too terrible to contemplate."

"We can hardly prevent him," Mr. Land said. "We surprised him with the substitution of fake bullets for real ones, but I am certain he will be sorting through his supplies right now and weeding out the blanks. We ourselves have some ammunition, but we are not soldiers and could not prevail in a pitched battle."

"No indeed," my uncle agreed. "Nor would I suggest that we risk our lives to attempt it. I think we shall have to rely on the natives of this land to defend themselves. The Captain's plan to steal one of the young of these ape-men might not be as simple as he thinks. He is making a very common mistake—he is assuming that modern man with his technology is of necessity smarter than ancient man. But to have survived all these millennia those ancient men must have been as intelligent as we are, merely lacking the technology. But this is *their* land. They grew up here, they live here, and they know it intimately. The Captain lacks those advantages."

"Perhaps so," I agreed. "Perhaps these locals need no aid from us. But you are forgetting, dear uncle, that *we* are still in trouble. The Captain wished to kill us in case we might interfere with his plans—I doubt he will have changed that aim simply because we fled."

"Axel is correct," Ned Land agreed. "The Captain will undoubtedly make hunting us down and killing us his first priority. We cannot stay here and talk for much longer—we must set off again and attempt to hide our path so that he cannot simply track us down. They are six to our four, and they have more training and experience at warfare. We are at a distinct disadvantage."

"Not entirely," my uncle said, a twinkle in his eye. "We have one weapon that he does not." He tapped his temple. "We have my scientific brain." He glanced at me. "Yours, too, Axel, though it is still forming. In any event, I believe we should be able to out-think him."

"Not unless we first out-run him," Ned Land replied. "Let us get moving once more."

We moved on, attempting to be as cautious as possible while still maintaining as much speed as possible. We did not want to make it easy to track us, but we had to balance that against the need to get away from the soldiers on our trail. From time to time we heard sounds of movement in the trees, but as no soldiers materialized, it was probably simply local wildlife that we had disturbed in our passage. We were fortunate that we did not stumble across the paths of any predators in our flight.

After a short while, though, we heard the distinct sound of a rifle. The great cavern we were within caused some echoes, and it was impossible to determine how far away the shot was. Nor did we know why it was fired. Ned Land speculated that it was a signal from one soldier that he had stumbled upon our path, but there was no way to decide whether this was true or not. We had to assume that they were indeed on our trail and keep on moving.

We were extremely fortunate in having Hans as our guide. He was uncanny in his ability to select the easiest paths for us to traverse, and he moved with barely a sound through the forest. Ned Land was surprisingly quiet for all of his size, but both my uncle and I appeared to stumble upon every stick that could break and every stone that could be dislodged. Probably these sounds didn't carry very far, but at the time I thought a blind man could track us with ease.

I cannot tell how long we fled. In that land where there is no change in the quality or quantity of the light time is very difficult to track. I recall glancing at my pocket watch and seeing that it was 7:15, but whether that was before or after noon, I couldn't say. Nor does it really matter. When there is no change from one hour to the next, one day to the next or even one month to the next, what is time but meaningless measurement? So we fled—whether for hours, days or weeks, I cannot say. I do recall stopping several times to eat and sleep—short, fitful naps rather than long, refreshing rests. We had no real idea where we were heading; we were simply following Hans, who, when asked his opinion simply stated: "*Fremad!*"—"Forward!"

As so we went. We did not dare hunt fresh meat, but we had amassed a good supply of smoked meat from our time beside the sea, so food was not a problem. There were plenty of brooks and streams within the forest so we had ample fresh water. We were suffering mostly mentally, from a fear of being caught, and physically, from the exertion to escape from that fate.

I did notice that, as we fled the sea, we were drawing closer to the walls of the great cavern we were in. After a while, the trees and ferns began to thin out and we could see immense rock walls parallel to our path. What we required was a passageway that might lead us out of this area and into fresh pathways that might take us deeper—or higher. Once we were on rocks, we should leave no clues for our pursuers, and we could duck into any passageway fairly certain that we would not be followed. Of course, we should have no way of knowing whether that tunnel would lead anywhere, as we had surely passed far beyond the travels of the famed Arne Saknussemm by now.

But the fact of the matter is that there was no tunnel to follow. The wall of rock was unbroken in either direction as far as we could see. I could only conclude—and here my uncle agreed with me—that we were in some fault zone, where slippage of the rocks in some ancient earthquake had caused a rift in the solid rock, and one area had fallen lower than the other. Until we reached the full extent of this rift, there would be no chance of finding a passageway we could follow. All that we could do was to press onward.

As so we did, constantly on the move, save for short periods of rest or sleep. It is all very hazy to me now, but at the time it was desperate and as swift as we could make it. We walked, we rested, we ate, we slept—over and over again. We had lost all purpose in our lives but this. To this day, I waken from nightmares of being lost in these prehistoric jungles, with some great evil on our trail.

Finally, though, it ended. One day Hans stopped and gestured for us to do the same. At first I couldn't imagine why he had called the halt as we had been only walking a couple of hours and it was not yet time for a break. But he called to my uncle and gestured ahead. The two of them spoke together urgently in Danish for a time, while Ned Land and I seized the opportunity to sit on a fallen log and rest. I was weary and discouraged, exhausted from the relentless trek, as were we all. But I looked up into my uncle's face when he came across to me and saw him grinning widely.

"There is a way down!" he exclaimed. "Hans has found a tunnel ahead of us."

A way down... Slowly the news permeated to my befuddled brain. I blinked and then started up from the log. "A tunnel?" I questioned.

"A tunnel," my uncle confirmed with another smile. "Come, see for yourself."

The four of us hurried ahead. Apparently Hans had been scouting—I had not even noticed he had been gone—when he had discovered our fresh path. After about ten minutes, the jungle thinned to nothingness. There was a stretch of rock about forty feet long, and there, in the wall of stone, was an entranceway to a tunnel. It stood some fifteen feet high and appeared to plunge downward at about a five degree angle. Light didn't penetrate more than about twenty feet, so there was no telling how deep it might go.

"It may be a dead end," the sailor cautioned, lest we get too excited.

"There is only one way to find out," my uncle replied. "We go on."

"Wait," I said. "There is only this one tunnel—no others."

"We need only one," my uncle said, "provided it is the right one."

"But Von Horst and his men will know we have taken it," I pointed out. "If they are still on our trail, we shall not lose them this way."

"True enough," my uncle agreed. "But what other choice do we have?" He gestured in both directions. "Solid rock as far as we can see. This is our only chance to leave this immense cavern. Once below, there should be further opinions for us to take, but here there is nothing. We must follow this pathway."

"Let us at least look and see if there are indications that this may lead down," I begged. "It may be that Arne Saknussemm still leads our way." No one objected to my suggestion, so we examined the area close to the tunnel entrance for any signs that someone had been here before us. Within moments, Ned Land gave a cry and called us to him.

There, upon the ground, was a knife. It was of good steel, with a bone handle. The edges were sharp and there was dried blood on it. The sailor looked at my uncle. "Could this belong to your explorer?" he asked.

"It could not," the professor said with certainty. "The knife is untarnished and the blood cannot be too old. Storms ravage this area from time to time, so if it were hundreds of years old, it would have washed clean and rusted by now. No, this weapon could not have been here longer than a few months."

"It cannot be from the Captain's men," I said. "We saw all of the equipment laid out in the ship before we began, and I do not recall any knife like this in the inventory."

"Quite right, my boy," my uncle agreed. "So there are only two possibilities left to us. The first is that the Gun Club expedition has passed this way before us and one of its members dropped this weapon."

"And the second possibility?" Ned Land asked.

"That it belongs to some native of these lands."

The sailor scowled. "Those prehistoric Shepherds you saw?"

"No," I answered. "That knife is made for a person with a hand near in size to our own—the Shepherds would need a weapon twice that size at least. Besides, it is made of steel, which requires manufacturing. We have seen no evidence yet of any mining or forging in these jungles."

My uncle beamed at me. "Quite right, Axel, quite right," he agreed. "You're using that brain of yours at last. Yes, if that belongs to some native, then it is a man we would recognize as a man of near our own kind. That it was dropped here suggests that there is probably a destination at the end of this tunnel in that case. Or, if it belonged to a member of the Gun Club, it means we may find allies ahead of us. Either way, it is clear that this is the way we must progress. Onward!"

So decided, we entered the passageway ahead of us. For the first time in many days, we had to fire up one of the Ruhmkorf coils for light. The eternal glow of the aurora was now behind us as we started back downward again. We had hopes once more to look forward to—and fresh fears. If it was the Gun Club ahead of us, would they actually prove to be friends or foes? And if it was some unknown native of these regions, how would they react upon seeing us? Ned Land told us stories of native people of the South Seas, encountering strangers for the first time. Some were warm and welcoming, others suspicious and murderous. There was no way to know how our hypothetical natives might behave, so we worried—or, at least, I did.

Downward we went, the light from our coil casting eerie shadows on the walls. Several times I mistook an oddly-formed shadow for movement and started with shock, but I seemed to be the sole member of our party inflicted with such nervousness. As always, nothing bothered Hans; Ned Land was used to venturing into fresh lands, so he was an old hand at this; as for my uncle—well, he had fresh rocks to examine, and this kept his mind from worrying about the unknown.

At one point my uncle gave a cry and we stopped. My heart was pounding, but it turned out that the professor had simply discovered the fossil of an unknown marine vertebrate in the wall. He was quite excited about it, and insisted on a short halt while he sketched it. I failed to see the reason for his excitement—yes, a fossil at this depth was certainly unusual, but we were close to an underground sea, so it was not particularly unlikely that we should discover a fossil here.

"My dear Axel," my uncle admonished, "this specimen proves that the Central Sea has been here for millions of years, and that it once extended to these depths, covering a much larger area than it does now. Don't you find that exciting?"

"When the Captain may be closing in on us while you scribble?" I asked, annoyed. "No, I do not. There is a time for science and there is a time for sanity."

He snapped his notebook shut. "Very well, then," he said with a sigh. "Let us continue. Axel, there are times when I despair of ever making a proper scientist of you."

"I should be happy if you do not make a corpse of me!" I replied.

And so we descended. The passageway had no side tunnels, so we were not tempted to stray from our course, and no indications that it would peter out. It gave every indication of being a true pathway. We found no other evidence of life within its confines, though. The floor was solid rock and could not carry footprints, and there were no other dropped or discarded items. We were back to our routine of walking, eating and sleeping. It lasted for at least a week without any indication of change until finally Hans—in the lead as always—called for a halt. He gestured to me to turn off the coil, and I did so at his bidding.

Our eyes adjusted to the sudden gloom—and then I realized that it was not entirely dark. In the distance was a faint spark of light. How Hans had managed to detect it, I shall never know, but he had somehow seen it and realized its significance.

We had reached the end of the passageway and ahead of us was a fresh source of light!

Even I forgot my fears momentarily as we were enthused and rushed ahead, almost galloping down the tunnel to its conclusion. None of us was at all prepared for what greeted us as we emerged from the passageway and into fresh air.

Stretching ahead of us as far as the eye could see was a fresh jungle—thicker, greener, more lush than the one we had left beside the Central Sea. We could hear the sounds of birds and beasts, and somewhere close by the tinkling of falling water. The air was warm and humid. And above us shone the Sun!

The Sun! We looked at each other in confusion. We had been descending constantly from the cavern that held the Central Sea! How, then, could we have possibly returned to the surface of our planet? Surely it could not be possible?

It was not.

My uncle gripped my arm. "Axel!" he exclaimed. "Look at the slope of the earth!"

At first I did not understand what he meant. But then it dawned upon me with a sudden shock. There was no horizon. Instead, as I looked at the ground in front of us, I could see that it *rose* in a gentle but consistent slope. Behind us, of course, lay the rock from which we had emerged, but in every other direction the earth rose away from us, fading into the distance. There was certainly nowhere on the surface of our world where any such effect had ever been noted.

"What does it mean?" I asked, confused and bewildered.

"Mean?" My uncle gave a great laugh. "My boy, it means that we have reached the center of the Earth at last! And it is not rock, nor molten lava, but a great spheroid inhabited by a central sun! We have discovered a world within our own world, a world on the *inside* of a gigantic sphere." He gestured upward, toward the strange sun in the sky. "There, my boy—there is the center of the Earth!"

We were witnessing our first views of the world that we should soon discover had a name—*Pellucidar!*

X. First Steps in a New World

Pellucidar! Though the name was unknown to us at that first moment in which we stepped into it, we would soon learn at least a few of its secrets. But our first thoughts were still to put greater distance between ourselves and Captain von Horst and his men. At least out here in this immense fresh world we had a greater chance of losing our pursuers.

And so we set off, Hans in the lead, myself and my uncle together and the good Ned Land bringing up the rear and constantly checking behind us. My uncle was like a schoolboy at Christmas, almost giddy with excitement. He wished to stop constantly to examine specimens of plants and shrubs as we passed them, but this we could not allow. We hurried him past them, and he would cry out a farewell to them, including their Latin names. His disappointment at losing one specimen was abated as soon as he saw the next. I promised him that we would halt as soon as we dared, and he could explore to his heart's content. In the meantime, however, we had to hurry.

I really cannot express just how strange and provocative this world we had stumbled upon was. It was extremely unnerving at first to see the land rising upward all around oneself, instead of staying flat and natural as it does on the surface of our globe. It was as if we were scurrying along the bottom of some immense basin that stretched for thousands of miles, until lost into the distance or the light from that strange central sun. It created a strong feeling of oppression, as if one could expect the walls of this world to suddenly start like an avalanche towards one. It was days before I lost that terrible sensation.

And then there was that sun—though it appeared to cast about the same quantity of light upon us as did Sol upon the surface of the world, it was clearly much smaller than the true Sun, and much, much closer to us. How was it powered? Of what strange form of matter did it consist? I threw these questions at my uncle as we traveled, partly out of curiosity and partly to keep his mind occupied so that he wouldn't stand still and look at another floral distraction.

"Those are good questions, my boy," the Professor replied. "And ones I fear will prove to be very difficult to address, since we scarcely yet know what forces power our external sun. Do the same processes at work in Sol work here inside the Earth? I should doubt it, myself. Any force capable of flinging light and heat across millions of miles of airless space would be far too intense to power a smaller sphere within the heart of a planet and shine through merely hundreds of miles of atmosphere."

"Indeed, uncle," I agreed. "But how, then, could this peculiar arrangement have come about? Science has surely agreed that the Earth is a compact spheroid. We have a rough weight for it—six by 10 to the power 24 kilograms. That allows us to estimate the density of the planet, and allows for nothing like this huge hollow we now find ourselves within."

"Then science is wrong, my boy. It has been wrong in the past and no doubt will be wrong in the future. But science progresses by discarding the false and seizing the new truths we discover. I would say that we can account for the missing mass that should be filling this hollow space by theorizing that the central sun that we see before us is vastly denser than packed earth or even heavier metals."

"Perhaps so," I conceded. "But how is it that we have come to be walking on the *inside* of this hollow Earth, when we began our journey the right-side up on the surface?"

My uncle laughed. "Nothing is more obvious, my boy," he replied cheerfully. "It is by the same process that enables a person in the Antipodes to stand right-side up on the bottom of the world—the change is accomplished gradually, so slight that it isn't even noticeable as one travels. As we descended, we must also have been turning 180 degrees without being aware of it."

This was all a bit much for me; I have not the scientific mind possessed by the wise Professor Lidenbrock. I must have looked a trifle confused and glum, for my uncle laughed again and gestured at the path we were taking.

"Then here's another little conundrum for you, my dear Axel—why do you have no shadow?"

I glanced down and saw that he was not technically quite accurate—I *did* have a shadow, but one cast directly downward, so it was extremely small and tight to my feet. The answer to that was quite obvious, even to me. "Because the sun is directly overhead," I replied.

"And yet we have been traveling for about two hours now, and when we started the sun was *also* directly overhead."

That news made me stop, shade my eyes and stare upward. My uncle, as always, was quite correct: the sun *was* directly overhead, and the sun had also been directly overhead a few hours previously. That puzzled me for a moment, and then I laughed. "Of course! This secondary sun is *always* directly overhead because it lies at the exact center of the Earth! The planet revolves about it."

"Good, my boy, good. Now—deduce from that. What does this fact tell us?"

I considered for a moment and then realized what he was getting at. "If this orb is always overhead, then it can never set."

"Admirable, my dear Axel, admirable. And what follows from that?"

"There can be no night here," I said, slowly. "This is a land of perpetual day, like the polar regions in the summer."

"Far more so," the Professor said gravely. "There, at least, the sun will eventually start to rise and set again. Here in this world it can never do so. Conditions here can never change. This world has known only a single day, and will continue to know only that single day until the source that powers it should die out, and then a single, endless night will descend upon this world. Time as we know it cannot exist here."

"But that cannot be!" I exclaimed. "We can measure the passage of time—we estimated we've been walking two hours already, for example."

"I did not estimate it—I measured it with my watch," my uncle contradicted me. "And our chronometers are the only means we have to measure the passage of time here. There is no morning, noon or evening here, so time is constant. It is always *now*. And another thing follows from this, my boy—there can be no seasons, either."

I grasped the reason for that quickly enough. "Because the seasons are caused by the inclination of the Earth's axis toward the sun," I said. "In the winter, the hemisphere is slightly farther away, and in the summer slightly closer. But here, at the center of the Earth, every region is equidistant from the central sun and can never get closer or farther away."

"Quite so, quite so," the Professor agreed happily.

I gestured about us. We were travelling through a fairly dense forest. "Then how do things grow here?" I asked him. With neither spring, summer, autumn or winter, how do the plants know when to flower, the trees to shed their leaves..."

"Ah, but *do* they, my boy?" he asked excitedly. "Oh, I can see that this is going to be a world that will repay exploring most handsomely! A man might spend a lifetime here just attempting to unravel its mysteries!" He rubbed his hands together in anticipation.

Ned Land must have been listening in to at least a portion of our discussion because he let out a heavy snort. "Maybe for you as a gentleman of science," he said. "But I had rather planned on spending the rest of my lifetime back on the surface of this world, not living like a mole in the heart of it. Can you find us a way out of here again, Professor?"

"Oh yes, I'm certain of that," my uncle said. "As our own descent has proven, there are connecting passages between our own world and this. We know of the one behind us, but there are undoubtedly more of them. And that would explain a few mysteries, I might add."

"Such as?" the sailor prompted.

"Such as the plesiosaurs that inhabit the Central Sea. There are too few for a viable breeding population there, and they could not have survived there for the millions of years since they died out on the surface world. This land in which we now find ourselves must be their breeding grounds. I fancy that in the seas here such creatures and much more must thrive and reproduce. The same would go for the terrestrial animals we have encountered. Sooner or later we shall stumble across herds of such creatures, I'll wager." He looked at the sailor with twinkling eyes. "As for passages back to our world—well then, they must exist because they help to explain some of the mysteries of science. There are tales around the world of strange creatures—one or two at most—that are sighted and that cannot possibly exist. However, if such creatures as live here were to stumble onto a passageway that leads outside of the crust of our world, why, then, that would be perfectly reasonable!"

At that moment Hans halted and gave a sharp motion that indicated we should be silent. We immediately did so, and I wondered what our sharp-eared and —eyed guide had noticed that we had not. We were walking through thick forestland at this point. As we stood there, we could hear bird cries and songs, and then, faintly, rustling sounds. A smile crept onto the face of our guide, and he indicated that we should stop, so we did so.

A moment later a group of deer slowly emerged onto the faint track we had been following, some fifteen feet ahead of us. They appeared as startled to see us as we were to see them—all, that is, save Hans, who had somehow heard their approach. He had his rifle up and fired before the panic-stricken family could dart back into the hidden depths of the forest.

All save one, who had crumpled and fallen, shot expertly through the heart.

"Well done, my friend, well done!" Ned Land enthused. "An end to eating the jerky at last! Fresh meat for our feast tonight."

"Not *tonight*," my uncle corrected the harpooner, "for in this strange world night will never fall, save at the end of its days, as in some Nordic myth, and then it will be endless night."

"Let's not quibble," Ned Land laughed. "Whenever it may be, thanks to our good friend here, we eat well!"

Hans had stepped forward, his knife drawn ready to start the process of preparing the slain deer. Ned Land was lowering the pack he was carrying to go to his aid when there came a fresh player to the stage.

There was a low growl from the trees, and then a blur of motion. As if from nowhere, a large, powerful form now stood on the pathway, its amber eyes turned balefully in our direction. It was a huge cat, standing a good five feet at the shoulder. It was striped like a tiger, and its powerful body rippled with muscles. As it growled again, my attention was drawn to the two scimitar-like teeth that protruded from its upper jaw. This was some saber-toothed cat, the likes of which no man had seen since the end of the last Ice Age. Though it was clearly a powerful hunter, it was obvious that it was also an opportunistic thief should the chance arise.

It wanted the deer Hans had killed. For my part, I was quite willing that it should have its desire. Even armed with modern rifles, I was by no means certain we would be able to take down such a monstrous creature as this. Much as I would enjoy fresh meat, I wasn't sure that it was worth fighting for. Hans, however, didn't even flinch. Armed only with his knife, he crouched over his kill, refusing to back down. The tiger growled another warning, but Hans merely raised the knife slightly.

Ned Land seemed to barely pause for thought, either. He had, strapped to his pack, one of the harpoons he had brought along on the expedition in the hopes of spearing some gigantic sea monster. What faced us now was no aquatic animal, but as far as the sailor was corned, one monster was as good as another. He drew the harpoon and let his pack fall.

Somehow the tiger realized who was the greater threat. It turned its attention from Hans to Ned Land. The sailor faced this creature of the land with as much aplomb as he must have faced the giants of our terrestrial seas. He stood, feet apart and braced, the harpoon steady in his hand. The tiger must have been desperate for food, for it seemed to sense it was in danger. But it, too, did not lack courage, and it refused to back down. Instead, it crouched and sprang.

Ned Land did not—as I had expected him to—throw the harpoon. Instead, he merely moved slightly aside and then thrust his weapon with all of his might into the great cat, burying the hard iron point deeply between the tiger's shoulders. The huge paws caught him a glancing blow, thrusting him aside as the tiger landed on the pathway. It stood there, mouth agape and roaring its defiance. Somehow I managed to gather my wits and raised my rifle for a killing shot, but it proved unnecessary. Ned Land knew his job well, and the roar of the tiger was its last effort. Its great heart must have burst, for there was a sudden outpouring of blood from its mouth, and it collapsed, lifeless, to the ground.

Hans hurried to the sailor and helped him back to his feet. The Icelander's normally impassive face was split by a broad grin, and he clapped our nautical friend heartily on the back, almost sending Ned Land sprawling again. Then our guide looked down at the massive dead beast and shook his head in wonder. He had, of course, never seen a monster such as this in his life before. Nor had any of us, and I would have been heartily glad for some reassurance that we never would again.

The sailor reclaimed his harpoon and started to clean it. Then he stopped, staring over my shoulder. "We are not alone," he said, quietly.

I looked around, and saw what he meant. Silently, a small group of men had slipped from the shade of the trees. There were six in all, tall, muscular and also on the hunt for food, it would seem. Each man carried a long spear tipped with a stone point. They were all very much alike—dressed only in loin-clothes, with rough sandals. Each had a belt that held a stone knife. Their skin was a reddish hue, darker even than the natives of North America, and they had long, dark hair and eyes almost as dark.

Were these primitives also planning on attacking us to steal our deer? We held ourselves at the ready, but made no hostile move. "Let us wait and see what these men have in mind," my uncle said softly, and it seemed a good suggestion to us all. Would they be friendly—or should we be attacked?

XI: Back To The Stone Age

After both sides had stared at one another for quite a full minute, my uncle stepped forward slightly. "Can we assist you gentlemen in some way?" he enquired.

Ned Land snorted. "I'd hardly call them *gentlemen*," he grunted.

"Now, Mr. Land, there's no need to be rude," my uncle said. He looked expectantly at the six warriors. They looked at one another, and then one nudged a second with the butt of his spear. The "elected" individual glared at his companion, but stepped forward and spoke earnestly for several sentences, not a word of which did we understand. He then waited and looked at us.

"Perhaps we should try another language?" the Professor mused.

"Begging your pardon," the sailor said, "but I've heard many a tongue spoken on my various voyages, and not a one of them sounded like *that*. And they don't look like scholars to me who might understand Latin or Greek or some other dead tongue."

"I fear you are correct, Mr. Land," my uncle agreed with a sigh. "But what are we to do?"

"Well, uncle," I said, "they've made no move to attack us, which means that while they may not exactly be friendly, neither are they actively hostile. Why not make an overture of friendship by offering to share our food with them?"

My uncle beamed. "A capital idea, my boy! There are times when I do believe you're actually learning to use that mind of yours." He turned to Ned Land. "You have probably had more experience with less civilized people than any of us. Perhaps you would care to conduct the negotiations?"

"Right you are," the sailor agreed amiably. He looked to the savages and made a point of finishing cleaning his harpoon first, to make the point that we were far from helpless. Then he gestured at the dead deer and the slain tiger. Then he spread his arms toward the six men and then gestured to the rest of us. His meaning was abundantly clear, that he was inviting them to share with us.

The warriors conferred briefly in their strange tongue, and then the one who had been elected leader made a point of laying down his spear and his knife before stepping forward. He held out his hand and when Ned Land did the same, the warrior clasped his arm and grinned widely.

We were friends, it seemed.

I need not tell you how much that relieved us all. These stone-age savages had never seen a gun before, and probably thought that our weapons were merely clubs. The metal-tipped harpoon, too, was something utterly new to them, but at least that they could recognize as a weapon, and Ned Land as a skilled warrior. They were much taken with our burly sailor, and kept looking from him to the slain tiger in admiration. Later, when we were able to converse with them after learning their language, we discovered that very few people had ever managed to kill what they called a *tarag*. Ned Land was held, therefore, in great respect. Back at their village, the women pried loose the two great teeth and handed them to the sailor as a trophy. He was more than happy to receive them, and wore them on a thin cord about his neck from that moment on.

At that moment, however, the warriors simply helped us pack up the two kills, gutting them where they lay and leaving the entrails for the scavengers. They also made two carrying poles and strapped the kills to them. Four of the warriors were elected to carry these, while the remaining two walked with us alongside them as we traveled to their village. My uncle seized the chance to converse with their spokesman as best he could, learning words for things as we walked along.

Our new companion managed to tell us that his name was Halar, of the Sarak people. He made an effort at grasping our names, though he couldn't quite get his tongue around "Axel", which came out more like "Askel", but it was close enough for me to understand him. Despite their savage appearance, the men turned out to be remarkably open and friendly.

"Don't make the mistake, my boy, of thinking of them as ignorant idiots," my uncle warned me. "They may be less technologically advanced than we are, and their grasp of science may be rudimentary to non-existent, but there's nothing wrong with their brains. This is their world, and they are clearly very well suited to it.

Their world, it turned out, was Pellucidar, the first time we had heard this name.

We soon reached their village—I say *soon*, but it was, of course, impossible to tell how long it took us. My uncle's watch had stopped, which was strange, as he always kept it wound. Then Ned Land discovered that *his* watch had also stopped, something it had never done in all his days of voyaging our surface oceans. As a result, we had absolutely no way to measure time, for the sun, of course, was constantly overhead, no matter how many hours or days might have passed. We could only estimate our journey, then, by the fact that we were not tired when we reached the village, and therefore judged that our trip was not a long one.

We were the center of attention from the moment the women noticed us. Our clothing was considered strange and somewhat amusing, and many of them pinched at the cloth and commented amongst themselves about it. For their own part, the women wore almost as little as the men—short skirt-like things and halters for their chests—leaving large areas of their skin uncovered. Whilst this would never have passed muster in polite society, our sailor, at least, approved of it. And, truth be told, the women were as beautiful as the men we met were handsome. Still, they all made me realize just how much I missed my dear Gretchen. And the tribal children made me miss my own daughter.

The children were lively and happy, investigating every-thing. The younger children wore no clothes, and the older ones dressed as the adults. Everyone seemed to be in good health, something we noted with interest. My uncle, in fact, had started our visit with trepidation.

"I've no doubt these people are as friendly as they would seem," he informed me. "But it is not treachery I fear but dis-ease."

"Disease?" I asked him, surprised.

"Yes, my boy. Recall the lessons of history. When the Europeans first voyaged to the Americas, they met peoples who had never known European diseases, and who had germs of their own that *we* had never before encountered. As a result, neither side had immunity to the sicknesses that plagued the other. Whole peoples were wiped out as a result. And he we are, in a world that may possess diseases more deadly than the Bubonic Plague—to which the natives may be utter immune. Or the slightest sneeze from one of us might give these friend-ly fellows a cold from which they may never recover."

"But these look to be the healthiest people I have ever encountered," I objected.

"Which does not mean they are not the carriers of some fatal malady," my uncle warned. "We must take great care to observe one another—yes, and the natives!—for any signs of illness or infection, and if it does occur, we shall have to enforce strict quarantine measures. We can take no chances, my boy. If even one of us gets ill, we dare not even think of returning to our world. We could become plague bearers such as the world has never known!"

I confess, he scared me greatly with these terrible thoughts. To be exiled here, never to see my Gretchen and child again! That terrified me more than the thought of dying of some unknown illness.

As it turned out, of course, my uncle's fears were groundless—the inhabitants of Pellucidar have great immunity to any kind of disease. In fact, in all of the time we were among them, I never even heard a single child sneeze. But it was several weeks—I *think* it was weeks—before we felt sure we would be safe.

But back to the events of that first day. Ned Land was the hero of the hour. I have mentioned that he was given the great teeth of the tiger, and that he wore them proudly. This made him very popular with the laughing ladies, who value strength and skill in hunting more than anything else. My uncle was sure the sailor received several offers of marriage, which he thankfully did not understand or accept. The women then skinned and cooked the deer and tiger. I was rather surprised at the latter, since I have always understood that carnivores for some reason make poor eating. But the members of the Sarak tribe wasted nothing, and the tiger was cooked and devoured by them with every evidence of great enjoyment. I for my part stuck with the venison, which was a trifle burnt but absolutely delicious after so long on our rations.

The tribespeople did not practice agriculture—my uncle hypothesized that they were still at too primitive a level of culture for that—but the women and children had gathered some roots and plants from the forest, which they made into a kind of stew to go with the meat, and so we ate very well. After a hearty meal, almost everyone elected to sleep. There were a few guards posted, for there are a number of animals in Pellucidar that will happily attack and devour people, as well as other dangers of which we were quite unaware at the time.

Another consequence of the perpetual, unwavering daylight in this world is that there is very little variation in weather. It was constantly like a warm summer day, hence the lack of clothing by the Sarak people. Truth be told, I was a trifle uncomfortable in my own clothing, but nothing would induce me to shed any of the layers. Both Ned Land and Hans, however, went shirtless after a short while, though neither went quite so far as to resort to loin cloths. This warmth also meant that bed sheets were unnecessary, as, indeed, were houses as such. The people had only slight shelters to shade them from the sun while they slept.

In truth, they slept much less than we do in our world, though neither I nor my uncle could account for that. Our best guess was that perpetual sunlight may have affected the human need for sleep somehow, but there was no way for us to test that hypothesis, so it remained little more than a conjecture. But we discovered that our own need for sleep much reduced while we were in Pellucidar, though now we are home and safe in our own beds, we have reverted to our earlier need for several hours a night.

I found their lack of housing most peculiar, but my uncle—as always—had a ready explanation for it. "These are a primitive people," he reminded me. "They have few possessions, all of which they can easily transport with them. Because of the weather, they have no real need for shelter, so why should they build houses?"

"But what about... privacy?" I asked.

He laughed, good-naturedly. "They understand privacy differently than you or I," he said. "They do not know greed, either—for no one has more or better than anyone else. Envy? Pfah! Theft, too, is likely unknown."

"You think them faultless, then?"

"My dear boy, they are still human beings, and, as such, I am certain must be prey to sins—just not the ones we fall prey to. Jealousy and anger probably exist here as much as in our world."

This was true enough—the people here had their faults, but various crimes that exist all too frequently in our world could not thrive here. What was there to steal when your neighbor had only the same things you had, and when the identity of the thief would be transparent almost immediately? The only thing one person might have that another wanted was food, but that was held in common anyway. The men hunted and everything that was brought back was shared with the tribe. The women and children gathered roots, fruits and edible plants which, again, were shared.

People being people, no matter where they lived or what sort of culture they possessed, they still managed to have human emotions and thus human conflicts. Men angered one another, and these arguments sometimes ended in fights. They were rare, however, for all able-bodied men were needed to hunt to feed the tribe, so the chief of the tribe was empowered to settle conflicts when they arose, and his word was law.

I sighed. "You make this place sound almost like Paradise reborn," I said to my uncle.

He glanced at me and shook his head. "My boy, one thing I have learned in life is that where there may appear to be a paradise, then there is also a serpent in the garden."

In actual fact, there were two serpents in this garden—one of which we had brought with us...

XII: The First Serpent

As I have already mentioned, our good friend and companion Ned Land proved to be most popular with the unmarried females of the Sarak. His skill as a harpooner made him a reliable provider as a hunter. We had been accepted into the tribe quite easily, and as a result we now had duties to perform. My uncle was excused from hunting on account of his age, but Ned Land, Hans and I accompanied the other men on their expeditions, under the leadership of Halar, who had always been accepted before as the greatest hunter. But Halar had never killed a *tarag*, so he soon found his status challenged by the regard everyone felt for Ned Land.

Any other man might have been jealous, but this was not in Halar's easy-going nature. Instead, he appeared to be glad to have such a skilled hunter to add to his parties. The sailor, of course, had no desire to usurp Halar's position as chief of the hunters, and readily accepted the other man's orders and friendship, so this was not a problem.

There was, however, another problem, and one not so simple to sort out. Among the unmarried females was Alaya, daughter of the chief, Tomak. Alaya was acknowledged as the most beautiful woman of the tribe, and rightly so in my opinion. I thought her almost the equal in looks to my darling Gretchen, though her temperament could hardly match that of my dear wife. She was tall and lithe, extremely pleasant to look at, and, as I have mentioned, the chief's daughter. This made her the most eligible catch in the tribe, and don't think that she was not aware of this fact! As much as anyone in the tribe of Sarak, Alaya was spoiled. The men all vied for her favors, and the women all sought to be her special friend to gain status. And Alaya—Alaya played everyone off against everyone else.

It had apparently been understood that she and Halar would be mated—but that was before our arrival, and the ascent of Ned Land to most successful hunter. For such was indeed the case. The men of Sarak all had their stone weapons, which were surprisingly effective in their skilled hands, but Ned Land had his invaluable metal-tipped harpoon, a far better weapon.

We all had our rifles, too, but we refrained from using them as much as possible. Our ammunition was severely limited and we conserved it against a true need. Besides, the tribe had no concept of what a rifle could do, never having seen a firearm before, so they didn't even recognize them as weapons. As a result, when we went hunting Hans and I used spears and knives of stone that the tribe made and presented to us, while the sailor used his harpoon. One of us would take along a rifle, in case of emergencies, but it chanced that we never really had occasion to use one.

Alaya had seen the shift in status of Halar, and even though Ned Land didn't press his situation, it was evidently very obvious to the women of the tribe, and to none more so than Alaya. She found excuses to be close to the sailor, to hand him some delicacy at the feasts, or to fetch him water when he was thirsty. He, for his part, enjoyed the attentions of the most beautiful of the women of the tribe, and enjoyed spending time and attention on her. I could not wonder if he was not falling in love with the savage maiden, and mentioned this to my uncle.

"I had not noticed," the Professor said, thoughtfully. "But this might complicate matters for us."

"How so?" I asked. "Surely his emotions must remain his business?"

"Yes, yes," my uncle said impatiently. "But how will this affect our little group? I do not imagine that you are in favor of our staying here for the rest of our lives?"

I thought—as I did so often!—of my dear Gretchen and our girl, and shook my head vehemently. "No indeed!"

"Good. Nor do I, or Hans, - who is eager to get back to the girl he was wooing. I had thought to remain here merely a short while to build up our strength, to learn what we can, and to sharpen our language skills. Tomak assures me that there is only one common tongue throughout all of Pellucidar, which I find quite peculiar but helpful. I am building up a map of this area of this subterranean world and hope we can set off soon to explore it. Given that Captain von Horst is undoubtedly close to the place where we entered this world, I do not think it wise to attempt to return to the surface through that passageway. I am hopeful that we may be able to discover an alternate route, and propose that we set off again on our journey quite shortly."

"You think some alternate route exists?" I asked him, eagerly. I had not considered the possibility myself, and had assumed that we would have to retrace our steps to return to the surface.

"I believe there must be others," he answered. "It would be most logical. But finding one may take some doing. It is clear these primitive peoples have no inkling that there is another world, let alone that it is reachable from here. If we are to escape, then we must discover a route by ourselves. Allow me to think on that, and let us assume one will be found." He looked a trifle worried. "Now—will Ned Land accompany us or not, do you think? I must confess that I have grown used to his company and find him exceedingly helpful as a member of our expedition. I would not gladly leave him behind—but if that is the way his heart may carry him, neither would I attempt to compel him to go with us." He clapped me on the shoulder. "My boy, you are quite close to him—perhaps you would be good enough to sound him out and ascertain his intentions?"

I promised my uncle that I would do so—but events precluded me from carrying out that intent, events provoked by Alaya herself.

As I have said, she was rather spoiled and tended to take for granted that what she desired would be immediately given her. It appeared that she currently desired Ned Land, and had laid her plans to take possession of him. But her plans were not progressing as swiftly as she had hoped, for the sailor was proving difficult for her to pin down. She was not the only unattached girl flirting with Ned Land, though she was undoubtedly the prettiest. However, all of the girls seemed to me to be extremely attractive—perhaps their scant attire had something to do with that!—and certainly it seemed as if that might be the case with our harpooner.

Annoyed by her lack of success, Alaya elected to attempt to allay her annoyance in that time honored female way— taking a bath. In our world a lady might simply order her maid to prepare her water for her and then take a leisurely soak to her heart's content, but in this primitive society there were no baths, no heating and no maids. Instead, the accepted method of bathing was to simply undress and plunge into the closest river—away from prying male eyes, of course. This is what Alaya elected to do, taking along a handful of her close friends, probably with the intent of complaining about men in general and Ned Land in particular.

I should at this point explain that we had heard for some time a curious expression amongst the members of the tribe, and one that made little sense to any of us. A mother might warn an unruly infant to behave or "the Mahars will get you." We took it to be the generalized kind of warning that parents always give to keep their children in check and thought nothing more of it. However, the phrase was also used in some of the few laws that these people had. On the whole, their legal system was quite simple and splendid: don't do anything to anyone else you wouldn't wish done to yourself. And in most cases, the punishment for breaking this law was simply that the offense would be repeated upon the offender. As my uncle had noted, there was very little law-breaking for the very reasons he had given.

There were, however, a few injunctions that were more specific. One of these was that women should never travel more than a quarter mile from the village unaccompanied by a warrior—"else the Mahars will get you." Again, we thought little of this, given the dangerous nature of Pellucidar in general. We had already encountered one *tarag*, and were told that these ferocious sabertooths had no fear of man. And there were other animals almost as dangerous, such as the *jalok*. We had not encountered any of those, but they were described to us as something like a large, ferocious wolf that frequently hunted in packs. So the admonition against going unaccompanied by an armed man made perfect sense—to everyone but the spoiled Alaya, who was having nothing to do with any man if she could not get the one she desired.

It seemed that her favorite spot to bathe was almost a mile from the village, where the river twisted and made a pleasant pool, and she decided to go there with her friends. And, of course, she informed no one in the village of her plans, partly so that nobody could try and dissuade her and partly because she was annoyed and didn't wish to talk to anyone other than her silly friends.

Meanwhile, we were in the village having a time of leisure. Our last hunting trip had been a success, and we had brought down a *thag*—a kind of oversized elk—with enough meat on its bones to last everyone for almost a week. If it were possible to measure a week in this land! The men were using their free time to repair their spears and knives, or to make new ones. I was watching one of the skilled craftsmen preparing a new blade the way it had been done during our own Stone Age, fascinated by the swift and assured way he used a stone to flake a flint core. In his own way, this man was just as much a craftsman as any watchmaker or instrument maker in our world. As I have said, the men of Pellucidar are not stupider than the men of our world—they simply have less access to information than we have. When it came to living the lives they did, I doubt if any modern men could do as well, let alone better. The stone axe or knife or spear maker was a skilled craftsman, working with precision and care.

It was while I was watching him work that one of the lazing hunters gave a cry and pointed to the path to the river. One of the village girls was heading up it, but she was barely able to keep her feet. Two of them men dropped what they were doing and hurried to her aid. One of them caught her as she fell, and carried her back to the village, where the older women shooed the men aside and took charge of the unfortunate girl. Out of curiosity, I had wandered across and could see she was covered in lacerations, mostly superficial, but that a large bruise was forming on one shoulder, and her arm was held at an angle that looked extremely uncomfortable.

"Sagoths," she gasped, opening her eyes and wincing from the pain. "Sagoths attacked us by the river."

We had heard nothing in the village, which was puzzling if the attack had occurred so close, because the river was only a hundred yards or so away. One of the older women understood what had happened, however, and elicited the fact that

Alaya had taken the girls a mile from the village, against the laws and all sense. Alaya and four girls had been captured, and this girl had barely managed to escape to run for help.

"What does this mean?" my uncle asked Halar. "What has happened to them?"

"The Mahars have taken the girls," the hunter replied, grimly.

"The Mahars?" I asked, confused. "But she mentioned some people named sag…"

"Sagoths," Halar explained. "They are not people—at least, not people like us. They are brutish and twisted, and they serve as the strong arms for the Mahars. Alaya and the others will be taken to their city."

This was all new to us, but my uncle managed to drag some information from the tribespeople. They feared speaking of the Mahars out of a superstitious belief that if they were spoken of, somehow the Mahars could know of it. This was why the villagers had spoken so little about these creatures. They were, we were told, utterly inhuman and evil, and lived in great and terrible cities all over Pellucidar. There was one not too far away from the village—they had no real measuring system, so "not too far" might mean a handful of miles or else a journey of a week. They did agree that the girls would be taken to the city, however, and that a rescue party must be mounted to try and intercept them. Once the women were in the city, escape would be impossible.

The rescue party would have to move swiftly, and it would be unwise to make it too large. "It is possible that this was done to lure the hunters away in order that the Sagoths might raid the unprotected village," Halar explained. "So we have to leave enough men with weapons here to defend our women and children in that event."

It was decided, then, that a party of six of us should suffice. Halar and Ned Land would lead. Hans and I would go along, as well as two more men from the village. We hastily grabbed our weapons and some dried meat—since we did not intend to stop to hunt for our meals—and said our farewells.

105

"Take care, my boy," my uncle said, warmly, clasping my hand. "Come back safely—and, hopefully, with the missing women."

"Don't worry about me, uncle," I told him. "I have Ned Land and Hans with me, as well as Halar. I shall be perfectly fine." I hefted my rifle. "No matter what kind of creatures these Sagoths might be, a bullet should stop them in their tracks."

And so we set off, hurrying down the path to the river. Halar was grim, clearly very concerned for his friends, and especially Alaya. Even Ned Land seemed subdued; clearly the savage girl meant a lot to him. We reached the kidnap point quite swiftly, and it was not hard to see evidence of the affair. Plants had been crushed on the bank of the river and there were small patches of blood. Halar bent to examine the disturbed ground and then looked up at us.

"They were taken in this direction," he said, pointing. "There are at least a dozen Sagoths in the raiding party. Let us hurry, for they cannot be too far ahead of us."

Silently, we followed him. A skilled hunter, he could see traces of the passage of the kidnappers invisible to my city-bred sight. We moved quickly up to where the trees began to grow farther apart, and there was grasslands favored by the thags. Here he stopped and scowled.

"Ah, we are too late after all," he said. "They have taken to *lidi* here." Even my untrained eyes could see that the ground was much disturbed and that there were prints of some large creature.

"What are *lidi*?" Ned Land asked.

"Huge lizards," Halar answered. "They are used as transport. They can walk for long periods of time, and it is not likely that we shall be able to catch up with them." He shook his head. "They will be able to return with our women to the Mahar city before we can reach with them. Our rescue attempts are doomed."

XIII: The Rulers of Pellucidar

This pessimistic outburst did not sit well with Ned Land—nor, truth be told, with me. I was in full agreement with the sailor when he gestured at the clear prints and said: "Even a blind man could follow that trail! Even Axel here!"

"Hey!" I exclaimed, annoyed at the insult.

Ned Land clapped me on the shoulder. "No offense, lad, but your tracking skills are somewhat lacking. Even you must agree to that." There was a certain amount of truth in what he said, no matter how much it stung. But in my defense I will say that he would make a terrible geologist. He turned back to Halar. "There is the trail—why should we not follow it? Do you not want the women back? Do you not want Alaya back?"

"Of course!" the hunter exclaimed angrily. "I have known them all my entire life. I do not wish to go back to their families and tell them we have lost them to the Mahars. But what other choice do I have? The sagoths will reach their city before us, and once they do, we cannot rescue the women. There is, then, no point in even trying to follow them."

"Why can't we rescue the women from the Mahars?" the sailor demanded.

"If you knew the Mahars, you would not need to ask that," Halar answered.

"But we *don't* know the Mahars," I said. "We've never seen them, and this is the first time any of you have even talked about them—and even now you are not being clear on the subject. Tell us about these Mahars and why they are so invincible."

The savage looked frustrated. "We do not talk about them," he said. "It is said that if you mention their names, they can hear it and listen to what you say."

"In that case," Ned Land growled, "they must already be listening in, because we've mentioned them an awful lot. So nothing you tell us now could draw their attention more, could it?"

Halar considered the point, and then nodded. "If they can listen, they are listening already," he agreed. His companions didn't like the sound of that, and they moved away from us as Halar finally deigned to explain matters to us. "The Mahars consider themselves the masters of Pellucidar, and with good reason. They have strange powers, many of which I do not understand."

"Which probably don't exist," Ned Land muttered under his breath.

"No!" the hunter exclaimed. "These powers exist. They are able to fly, for one thing, and to speak without using their voices. They are immensely old and wise, but very, very in-human. In appearance they are like the *thipdars*."

For the first time I started to get worried. We had seen *thipdars*—the native word for creatures we would call ptero-dactyls—and they were large and powerful hunters. It would explain how Mahars could fly, if they were related to these creatures. I exchanged a worried look with Ned Land.

"They live together in great cities throughout all Pellucidar," Halar continued. "The one closest to us, where these lidi are heading, is a hundred times the size of our vil-lage, and hundreds of Mahar live there. The Sagoths are their servants, but they take humans as slaves whenever they can. At least as slaves. The Mahar eat flesh, and it is said that they find humans quite tasty."

"Thundering seas!" Ned Land exclaimed. "Alaya and the other girls are destined for the dinner plate, and you won't lift a finger to save them? What kind of a man are you?"

"A practical one," Halar replied. "What is the point of going to the Mahar city only to be taken in our turn? It would help no one in that event."

"Then I am an impractical man!" the sailor vowed. "My friends and I have powers of our own that these Mahar have never encountered." He shook his rifle. As I have said, we had never used them in the presence of our savage friends in order to conserve our small supply of bullets. But here I was in full agreement with my companion that this was a cause in which some ammunition must be spent. Halar, of course, thought our rifles were simply wooden sticks—probably some sort of good-luck charms—and had no idea of the damage we could cause with them. "Whether or not you go with us, Halar, I am going along." He looked at me expectantly.

"I cannot abandon these women," I said, simply. "How could I ever face my sweet Gretchen again if I should have to tell her that I abandoned four of her fair sex to be slaughtered and devoured by reptiles?"

"Brave lad!" Ned Land said. He looked to Hans. Here there could have been a problem in communications because Hans only spoke Danish. He had the intellect to learn other languages, but it simply did not interest him. He was able to communicate with my uncle, and that was sufficient for him. To my surprise, then, he indicated that he would go along with us. He had evidently understood some at least of the conversation, though I could never be sure how much.

"Well, then," the sailor said, turning back to Halar, "the three of us are going along. If you are not, you'd better return to the village and let them know there what has happened."

Halar was clearly caught in a dilemma here. He was afraid to go on, convinced our quest was useless and our fates sealed. But he was clearly loathe to go back and abandon the woman he had hoped to marry and her companions. He squirmed, wrestling with this problem for several minutes before finally composing himself. "I shall accompany you to your deaths," he decided. "But my tribe can spare no others." He therefore ordered the other two hunters to return to the village and to let everyone there know what we were doing. "Tell them to hold a great funeral feast for all of us," he instructed.

"But not just yet," Ned Land snapped. "Give us the option to live first."

"Then when should they hold our funerary feast?" Halar asked.

Ned Land grinned broadly. "At the next full moon!"

I glared at him. "You know very well Pellucidar has no moon."

"Aye, lad, that I do," he agreed cheerfully. "So if they wait for it, it should give us quite sufficient time to rescue the women!"

I had to admire his optimism, as well as Halar's courage. We set off together, following the tracks of the *lidi*, despite the fact that he was marching off to his death. He could not have the confidence that we had in the power of our guns, but he accompanied us anyway. As it turned out, he was soon to be enlightened, though not through any event of our choosing.

The jungles of Pellucidar are thick and plentiful, probably owing to the warm climate that exists throughout this interior world. As there are no seasons, they are a profusion of color and growths. Ferns dating back to the Jurassic era rub fronds with flowering plants of far more recent periods. Likewise the fauna is just as mixed. I have mentioned the ferocious *tarags*, wiped out after the last Ice Age on the surface of our world, but their companions the cave bears also existed here, along with the Irish elk. From earlier epochs were the eohippus, the dog-sized ancestors of modern horses. Going further back in time were land creatures such as the *lidi*—which I was to discover looked very like reconstructions of the brontosaurus—and even small bird-like creatures that looked more like lizards with rudimentary feathers. In the seas and lakes there were the plesiosaurs I have mentioned, and in the skies were the great *thipdars*, pterosaurs of our world.

Along with these, of course, were some creatures that as far as science knows never existed upon the skin of our planet. The most obvious example, of course, would be the Mahars—intelligent and malevolent reptiles—along with their brutish servants the Sagoths—half-ape and half-human. Pellucidar was indeed a most strange environment. And, far too often, a very deadly one.

The *thipdars* are the hunters of the Pellucidarian airs. They take eagles on the wing and even sizeable beasts like small antelope from the ground. When they are hungry—

110

which is much of the time, as flying takes much energy—they will even attack and devour people. Some time into our journey, we became the objects of one such creature's attack.

It was Halar who spotted this, as we were still sufficiently new to Pellucidar not to think automatically of scanning the skies for trouble. We grew up in a world, after all, where the skies are perfectly cheerful and safe. Halar gave a cry, and pointed upward. We followed his gaze and saw one of the winged predators swooping down. We were caught in the open, crossing a river clearing, and there was no safety for us to rush to. We were forced, therefore, to stand and defend ourselves. Ned Land, Hans and I all raised our rifles, while Halar hefted his near-useless spear. I held my fire, knowing that my companions were better shots than I, and far more likely to hit the creature. I would wait until the last possible moment to use up any of my precious bullets.

It turned out to be unnecessary, as I had suspected. Hans, our best shot, fired first, when the great winged beast was little more than thirty feet from us. It was a brilliant shot, straight through one of the *thipdar*'s large eyes and into its brain. The beast was dead before it hit the ground before us. We were forced to dive aside as the immense creature tumbled to a bleeding halt.

Ned Land and I clapped Hans on the back, and our guide smile back modestly at us. Halar was completely shocked.

"How did you do that?" he cried in wonder. "Your wooden sticks threw thunder at the *thipdar*, and it died!" He shook his head, astounded. "For the first time, I begin to think that your magic may indeed match that of the Mahars." Now he had seen what a rifle could do—even though he could not understand *how* it worked—his mood improved immensely. He finally had confidence in us and our sound-throwing sticks. We did not inform him that we had only a small supply of ammunition. Now that he was optimistic again, we did not wish to destroy his hopes.

Ned Land drew his knife and eyed the dead *thipdar*. "It was going to eat us," he observed, "so it seems only fair that we should return the favor." He considered for a moment and then asked Halar: "Are *thipdars* good eating?"

"I do not know," the hunter answered. "No one I have ever heard of has ever killed one before."

The sailor laughed. "Then let us find out!" he exclaimed.

Thipdars, I might add, are excellent eating. They taste more like steak than chicken. We cut and cooked up a supply of the beast's meat, leaving the rest of the carcass for the roaming *jaloks* to find and scavenge.

We moved on. As I have said, it is almost impossible to estimate time in Pellucidar, with its endless day. We walked, following the ever-present *lidi* tracks, we ate and from time to time we slept. Sometimes we were attacked by the local animals, sometimes we attacked them for food. Time passed.

We entered another of the grassy plains that sometimes stretched for several miles at a time. But this time we knew immediately that there was something wrong. We could hear the snarls of *jaloks* ahead of us before we left the shelter of the last trees. They were clearly fighting over food, which meant something had killed another creature ahead of us. It might have been them, it might have been some other beasts, for *jaloks* are not above chasing off lesser animals and stealing their prey—or of simply scavenging what some greater killer had left behind. Normally we should simply have skirted a site like this, but it was clearly from directly ahead of us on the path we were following. We conferred on the matter for a brief moment, and decided we should be ready with our rifles in case of need, but that we should take a look at what was happening ahead.

We were quite unprepared for what we saw when we stepped from the trees. The *jaloks* were there, of course, and clearly scavenging what had been killed by one of the monsters that lived hereabouts.

It was a dead *lidi*, the first I had seen. Knowing that it was a brontosaurus was one thing, but seeing the immense beast laid out on its side, huge portions of its muscular body torn out, was quite another. It was a small mountain of flesh.

Impressive as it was in death, I could only imagine how majestic it must have appeared alive. Some great carnivore—perhaps a tyrannosaurus or one of its relatives—had slaughtered the beast and eaten its fill, leaving the carcass for the hyena-like *jaloks* to feast upon.

"Look!" Halar exclaimed, pointing at the corpse. I could see what he meant—there were the remains of some immense howdah beside the dead creature. And, as we looked closer, we could see, scattered about it, the corpses of several sagoths.

This was the *lidi* we had been following. It and its passengers had been slaughtered.

We were too late.

XIV: City of the Mahars

I stared at the scene of the massacre, stunned and depressed. After everything we had gone through, the savage land of Pellucidar had claimed more victims. Alaya and her friends were dead.

Then something penetrated through my shock and hopelessness. Halar was scouting about, and did not seem to be as depressed as I would have expected for a man who had lost his love. He was giving the feasting *jaloks* a wide berth—they were intent on their grizzly feasting, but spared us a glance and a heart-felt growl of warning from time to time—but he was clearly looking for something in the long grass.

"Poor Halar," I said to Ned Land. "He refuses to give up, even with the evidence before us that we have failed. He must truly have loved Alaya."

"I'm not so sure his brains are addled," the sailor said. "He seems sure of his purpose." He shook his head. "Though I cannot…" He broke off as something suddenly occurred to him. "Friend Axel, look at those corpses."

"I'd rather not," I confessed. I do not have a very weak stomach for such things. "I'd prefer not seeing Alaya and the others with their insides on their outsides."

"Nor will you," he said. "They are all without exception only Sagoths."

"What?" I turned to gaze of the scene of the massacre and saw that he was correct. Beside the dead *lidi*, the only victims in sight were the brutish forms of the ape-men. "Perhaps the *jaloks* ate the tenderer females first?" I suggested.

"They're not that tidy eaters," he replied. "There would be bits of the women left behind in that case, and I can see none."

At that moment, Halar gave a cry and gestured for us to join him. The *jaloks* growled at us again, but as we were moving further from their feast, they then ignored us. We hurried to join our friend the hunter, where he was pointing excitedly at the ground—and fresh *lidi* tracks.

"The second *lidi* escaped this fight," he explained. "Alaya and the others must have been on this one."

I was confused. "There was a second *lidi*?"

Halar laughed and clapped my arm. "Axel, my friend, you are a good companion, but probably the worst hunter I have ever known. Did you not know we were following a pair of *lidi*?"

I had to confess that I did not. My misapprehension was aided by the fact that the word "*lidi*" means both a single creature and multiple beasts. One *lidi*, two *lidi*, a herd of *lidi*... I felt such a fool, and my face must have shown it, for Ned Land laughed and slapped my back.

"Don't worry about your lack of tracking skills, lad," he said. "I didn't see the second set of tracks, either." He turned to Halar. "So we still have our trail?"

"Better than that, my friend," the hunter replied. "Look—there are signs of blood along the way. The second *lidi* escaped the attack, but it must have been wounded. It is walking slower now, and is undoubtedly carrying extra passengers. We now have a chance of catching up with it before it reaches the city of the Mahars."

That was good news indeed, and we hurried to follow the tracks, feeling of lighter heart now. Added to this good news was the fact that the bodies of the Sagoths left behind us meant that we also faced fewer foes than before. We moved faster than before, hope giving us extra strength. The *lidi* we were following was less steady upon its massive feet, and the trail of blood showed that it was probably getting weaker. Everything gave us encouragement.

And so we went. We stopped to eat at one point, but we refused to rest, sure our goal would be in sight beyond the next ridge, or through the next copse of trees. The blood trail that we followed had not coagulated, so clearly the *lidi* was not far ahead of us.

And finally we were correct—we came to the crest of a hill and there, at its base below us, lumbered the *lidi*. We had caught up with it—but not it time! It was approaching what was clearly the city of the Mahars.

And *city* is certainly the word for it. This was no village composed of wooden shelters such as those the tribe of the Sarak dwelt in. This was a sizeable community of stone-built houses, and towers. As Halar had informed us, it was clear that this was home to hundreds of creatures, not simply a few dozen. The stone had been hewn and lifted into place, creating structures that showed design skills. Though still far below the standards of a European city, this was the sign of the highest culture we had yet seen within the Earth. It was clear that these Mahars were as far above the Sarak culturally as those humans were above the *jaloks*.

There was one peculiarity that stood out about these buildings—the windows in the towers were huge, far larger than needed to simply allow in light. Then I saw a couple of flying creatures, larger than men but smaller than *thipdars*. They circled one of the towers and then came in to land on the ledge of the window. They waddled inside, and vanished from view.

They had obviously been two of the Mahars, since Halar had said they could fly, and the "windows" were actually their doorways into their buildings.

As we stared down at the city, the *lidi* we had been following arrived at a large pen area beside the closest buildings.
There were several other *lidi* stabled there, and I could make
out a mixture of humans and Sagoths in attendance upon the
beasts. I heard Halar give a growl of anger and pain and saw
that the brutal guards were forcing the four women they had
captured down from the *lidi*. Cuffing their prisoners about the
head, the Sagoths led them into the closest of the buildings.
The remainder of the Sagoths and their human slaves set about
removing the howdah from the *lidi* and then to examine and
tend its wounds.

"Just too late," Ned Land growled. "It will be difficult to
find the women in that maze of buildings."

"We cannot give up now," I objected. "Not when we are
so close."

"I wasn't proposing retreat, my friend," the sailor said.
"Merely bewailing our luck. But we don't know where the
women are being taken, not do we have a plan yet to rescue
them."

Halar gestured at the *lidi* pens. "The workers there will
know," he said simply. "We shall ask them."

"They work for the Mahars," I pointed out. "They may
betray us to the Sagoths."

"No man would work willingly for the Mahars," Halar
stated. "I am sure they will aid us if we ask it of them."

I have to confess that I was nowhere near certain of
this—and neither was Ned Land, judging from the skeptical
glance he gave me. But then he sighed. "We have no other real
choice," he agreed. "But I think we should single out just one
of the slaves—the less people who see us there, the better I
shall like it."

We conferred and finally agreed to a plan. We should
sneak down under cover of the rocks and trees until we should
be able to slip unseen into the compound. One of the slaves
had been left to feed the newly-arrived *lidi*, and we should
approach him while he was alone and speak to him. Because
he was human, we hoped he would help us, but if he tried to

raise an alarm, we were ready. Only three of us should appear at first, and Ned Land would make his way behind the man. If he gave any indication of intending to betray us, the sailor would jump him and subdue him.

We gave Ned Land a few moments to be on his way before Halar, Hans and I moved cautiously toward the *lidi* pens. Once we were close, we revealed ourselves to the startled slave.

The man jumped, and looked around quickly. "Are you insane?" he demanded. "The Sagoths are nearby. If they see you, you will be captured and enslaved as I am—or worse."

This did not sound like the speech of a man who intended to betray us to his masters, so I stepped forward. "We are here to rescue the women the Sagoths just brought in," I explained. "They are our friends, and we will not abandon them to their fate."

"More fools you, then," the slave growled.

"Do you know where they have been taken?" I asked him.

"To the Mahars, of course," he replied. "The Masters must decide the fate of all captives."

"Do you know how to get there?" I enquired. "Can you direct us?"

"I do know," he admitted. "But I cannot direct you—the way is winding and complex. Being strangers here, you would get lost—and then the Sagoths would capture you."

Ned Land stepped up close behind him, startling the man. "It sounds to me like you have many excuses for taking no action," he growled.

The slave looked from one of us to the next and then sighed. "You are right. I have been here a long time, and have accepted my slavery, not wishing worse." He looked up, and there was a new spark in his eyes. "But—enough! I will be a slave no longer. It may be that this is the time of my death, but even death is preferable to remaining a slave."

"That's the spirit!" Ned Land encouraged him. "You have become a man again, whatever befalls you."

"Come, then," the newly minted man replied. "I will take you to where you may see into the Great Hall of the Mahars. And if I die—I die in the company of men, and not of animals."

"What is your name, friend?" Halar asked him. "And of what tribe?"

"I am Siom, and I was once of the Dathar tribe."

"I have heard of the Dathar," Halar commented. "It is said that they raise great warriors. I am glad that you are with us, and am certain now that we will rescue our women." This little speech gave our new friend fresh pride and courage. Halar added to that by passing him a spare stone knife.

Our new friend led us quickly into the city. In moments, I had lost all sense of direction, but Siom seemed to know precisely where he was going. We had our weapons hidden from sight, but had no need to skulk in the shadows. The idea that any humans would invade the city of the Mahars was completely unthinkable, so any Sagoths who saw us assumed we were on some errand for the Masters, and completely ignored us. Their arrogance was working in our favor!

The Sagoths were huge brutes, more gorilla than men, though they had some rudimentary intelligence and could speak the common language of Pellucidar. There is nothing like them in our world, of course, but we sometimes found this to be true in this lost world. There were many relics of bygone eras still alive and thriving here, but there were also chimera, creatures the surface world has never seen—or, if once seen, they are long dead and science has discovered no trace of them so far.

Chief amongst these are the Mahars themselves. We caught our first glimpse of the Masters as we passed one of the houses. Inside were three of these creatures, all of them sleeping. They stood taller than a man, and in general form looked like smaller relatives of the great *thipdars*. But their heads were larger, to accommodate greater minds, and the claws on their wings possessed long and slender fingers that enabled them to manipulate objects as well as any man.

I do not know the origin of these creatures, but when I discussed the matter later with my uncle he agreed with me that these were somehow evolved from the *thipdars* over the long eons they had been isolated in Pellucidar, as men had once been shambling brutes like the apes. This was the only sense we could make of the matter, and we must let it rest unless we somehow discover further evidence.

Siom led us finally to the Great Hall. Herein were gathered hundreds of the Mahars, each on ledges in tiers, looking down to a stage in the center of the immense hall. We slipped in at a side entrance and were in time to catch the proceedings, though Siom cautioned us against taking any actions here. Not only were there hundreds of the Masters, but there were numerous Sagoths also. We were vastly out-numbered, and any attempts to free our women would surely lead to our own capture.

And our women were there—I could see Alaya, who stood tall and proud, despite the scratches and bruises that showed she had put up strong resistance to her capture. The other three women tried to emulate her, but they did not possess her haughty manner or her strength of spirit, and they looked cowed.

One of the eeriest things about the proceeding that followed was that none of the Mahars uttered a word. It seemed that they did not possess vocal chords, and could utter no audible sounds. Instead, Siom explained, they somehow communicated with each other directly, mind to mind, through some strange sense that they alone possessed. I wondered how they then could communicate their wishes, but soon discovered the answer to that.

One Sagoth, older and greyer than the rest, came forward. He was cloaked in an air of authority, and it was he who spoke for the Masters. It seemed that one in a thousand Sagoths possessed the sort of mind that could receive messages from the Mahars and understand them. As a result, this speaker was a valued member of the race, and most useful to his Masters.

"Gilaks," he said, solemnly. *Gilak* is the Mahar word for humans, but it means "beast", for the Mahar do not consider people to be intelligent, merely animals. They split all creation into Mahar and non-Mahar. I cannot say I do not understand this, for do we humans not do the same thing ourselves? It is because they consider humans on the same level as animals that they feel no guilt in enslaving them or eating them as they wish; no more than we should about devouring or domesticating a cow.

"Gilaks," the Sagoth repeated. "It is decided that no more slaves are needed at this time. You will therefore be taken to the Pits." It made a gesture and the Sagoth captors seized the women and dragged them from the hall. Other matters were to be taken up, it seemed, but they were of no interest to us.

"What are these Pits?" Ned Land demanded of Siom. "And where are they?"

The ex-slave shuddered. "The Pits lie below this building," he explained. "There Mahars who search for knowledge experiment upon captives. They wish to know all that there is to know about our world, so they study everything. Your women will be given over as subjects for study."

"They sound like scientists," I said. "They mean to examine the women?"

"Yes," Siom replied. "They will be taken apart to study their blood, their muscles, their hearts…"

Dissected! I fell horror rising within me. Given the level of culture I could see about me, I doubted that this would be done at all humanely. "We can't allow that to happen," I exclaimed.

"The paths to the Pits lie this way," Siom said, urgently. "If we move swiftly, we may be able to intercept them before they reach the depths." He looked at us earnestly. "Once they reach the Pits, we shall stand no chance of rescuing them—it is too well guarded."

"Then let's hurry, man!" Ned Land snapped.

We hurried indeed. Siom knew his way and he led us into the tunnels under the buildings. These were not well lit, but we had sufficient light to see what we needed—ahead of us were the three Sagoths carrying out their Masters' orders to take Alaya and the others to their fate.

Thankfully, Alaya was struggling, and she caught sight of us as we approached. Clever girl, she started screaming and kicking at her captors more than before, so that the three Sagoths' attentions were entirely on her. When we attacked them from behind, they suspected nothing until the last second, by which time it was too late, and then went down, clubbed unconscious.

Alaya laughed, and threw her arms about the sailor's neck. "Nedland!" she cried—she had never comprehended our strange custom of possessing two names, and always made his name a single word. "I knew you would rescue us!"

"You're not rescued yet, lass," he growled, disentangling himself from her clutches. "All of you, stay with us. Siom, lead us out of here!"

"With pleasure, my friend," the ex-slave said gladly. We headed back toward the surface, more than happy to leave those dark, unwholesome tunnels behind us. We were starting to feel optimistic about our chances when there came howls and cries from behind us.

Our victims had been discovered, and a hue and cry was raised!

We were still in the city of the Mahars, which was being roused to action against us.

XV: Pursuit!

"Hurry, man," Ned Land urged. "They must know where we are heading."

Siom nodded, and increased his pace. We followed, readying our weapons for the inevitable fight. Thankfully, so far the pursuit was behind us, so we were not cut off. We emerged at the surface again, and started to rush through the streets toward the safety of the waiting forest. However, our speed of flight roused the suspicions of the slaves and Sagoths in the city streets, even before they heard the sounds of alarm from behind us.

"We must make for the *lidi* pens," Siom called out, between gasps for breath. "It is our only chance!"

Trust ourselves to those mighty but slow-lumbering beasts? It didn't make sense to me, but what other choice did we have but to follow our new friend's lead? Accordingly, we sped along in his wake. Our path was not unhindered, but we did have surprise and desperation on our side. Halar's spear and Ned Land's harpoon soon tasted blood, and I used my rifle as a club, wishing to spare the bullets as much as possible. Even the women were no strangers to combat—they were, after all, savages, and unused to sitting idly by while their men fought. They snatched up weapons from the fallen Sagoths and laid about themselves, giving far more blows than they received.

But, in the end, there were only nine of us against a city full of foes, and there could only be one conclusion to this chase unless we could produce some miracle. Something did change then, but not in our favor.

The Mahars had been alerted to our rescue attempt by this point, and several of them leaped from their buildings and into the air in pursuit of us. As in ancient Rome, there were more slaves in the city than Masters, and the one thing that the Masters could not tolerate was a successful slave uprising. Our little escapade had to be cut short before it might inspire others to emulate us and fight for their own freedom. It was vital, then, that the Mahars crush us, and be seen to crush us.

Four of them were in the air when we spotted them, and they were swooping down toward us. It was clear that the time to conserve our ammunition had passed. "Stand and fire, my friends!" Ned Land called out, and Hans and I paused to obey. The sailor and the duck hunter were both superb shots, and even I managed to be more than passable. Our three shots plucked three of the Mahars instantly from the air. Hans fired a second time, this time with his revolver, and we gave a cheer as all four of the Mahars plunged to the ground. Two were dead instantly, both shot through their eyes. The other two died crashing into the walls of buildings as they fell.

Our actions produced a momentary lull in the chase. The Sagoths had no idea what we had done—all they knew was that we had made noises, and four of the Masters had mysteriously died. This event gave them pause, and I have no doubt they accredited us with supernatural powers. But, magic or not, they had been ordered to stop us, and they feared the wrath of the Mahars more than they feared our ability to throw invisible death. With a great roar, they charged after us again.

We fled onward, reloading as we ran.

The slaves took no part in the chase—they simply melted to one side out of our path. I do not think this was so much because they supported our actions as that they had been trained to fear, and would only act upon receiving orders. They were no longer true men or women, but beaten animals. We had truly been lucky to have stumbled across Siom, who had not had his will completely beaten from him yet. And it was he who saved us.

He had not paused while we had shot the Mahars but rushed ahead of us, reaching the pens of the *lidi*. Here he wrenched blazing torches from the stable walls and threw them to us.

"Fire the feed stalls!" he called out. "The *lidi* are terrified of fire and will panic." He laughed. "I have long been planning to escape this way myself, but lacked the courage to act alone." He immediately torched the foodstuffs closest to him. The rest of us, even the women, rushed about the pens, setting fires as swiftly as we could.

The Sagoths caught up with us then, and we were forced to use more of our few remaining bullets on them. By the time that the fires were blazing full strength, we were completely devoid of ammunition, but more than a dozen Sagoths lay dead. Now we were forced to rely on our stone spears and Ned Land's mighty iron-tipped harpoon.

But we had bought the fire the time it needed to take a firm root. Gushes of flame leapt all about us as we retreated toward the safety of the forest. And now the *lidi*—as Siom had predicted—began to scream and panic. They crashed from their stalls, and hurtled themselves in all directions, seeking to escape the flames. As a result, more Sagoths died beneath this huge feet, and several buildings collapsed, fanning and spreading the flames.

More Mahars had now arrived, along with the Sagoth speaker, but they were no longer interested in capturing and punishing runaway slaves—their entire city was being threatened by fire and the stampeding beasts. They were forced to order the Sagoths to fight the flames and to turn to recapturing or killing the crazed *lidi*. As a result, we were able to slip away unmolested at last, and into the jungle. As we hurried off, we could see the smoke from the blazing buildings behind us, and hear the cries and screams of the dying, as well as the bellowing of the *lidi*.

Siom was laughing and dancing with joy. "We have taught the Mahars a great lesson this day!" he crowed. "We men will not be enslaved forever!" I could not blame him for his enthusiasm, and, indeed, joined in his rejoicing.

"Save your breath," Ned Land advised. "As soon as they have extinguished the blaze and dealt with the *lidi*, they will be after us. We'd better be far, far away by that point!"

He was correct, of course, and so we hurried onward.

Finally, though, Hans indicated that we should rest, and we were all more than happy to concur with this. We were thoroughly exhausted from our adventures, and sank to the ground happy. After a short rest, though, Alaya sprang to her feet and threw her arms again around Ned Land's neck.

"You came for me, Nedland!" she cried, one eye cast in Halar's direction to see how the hunter was taking this. "I knew you would!"

"We *all* risked our lives for you and the other women," the sailor growled. "And it would not have been necessary if you had only been sensible and listened to the wise laws of your own people. Your selfish actions endangered not only the lives of your friends but those of your rescuers also."

Alaya didn't like the sound of that. "What are you saying?" she cried. "I am the daughter of a chief! I will do what I wish to do!"

"And that's the problem," Ned Land growled. Abruptly, he grabbed her and spun her round, pulling her face-down onto his lap. He then proceeded to give her a thorough spanking.

I did not know what to do. It disturbed me to see a young woman treated like a child, but if anyone had asked for trouble more than Alaya, I could not think who it might be. Halar was more troubled, for I could see that he loved the girl. Yet he did not wish to go against the will of the sailor in this matter, so he simply stood there, conflicted, waiting. The other women looked on, giggling and laughing to see Alaya spanked. They would probably have volunteered to help out if they were asked, as it was their lives she had so carelessly endangered. Hans, stoic as always, simply kept watch behind us for any signs of pursuit.

As for Alaya, she struggled and twisted and screamed, but it was impossible for her to break free of Ned Land's grip, and she was forced to endure the whaling that he applied. I do not know how much actual pain he inflicted—though I did not see her sit down or lie on her back for the rest of the journey home—but she certainly suffered indignities that she had never in her life known before. I suspect a good deal of her screaming was due to outrage, but eventually the sailor stopped and released her. Rubbing her tender portions, Alaya glared hatred at him.

"Nobody has ever treated me like that before!" she screamed.

"And that, I think, is the problem," Ned Land said, composed. "If your parents had applied a little correction like that to you when you were younger, perhaps you would not have grown up so spoiled."

"I hate you!" she yelled at him. "I hate you, and I shall be avenged!" Then she spun and glared at Halar. "And you! I hate you also, and will punish you for this!"

"But what did I do?" the hunter asked, helplessly.

"Nothing! That's what you did—nothing! When you could have stopped him at any time."

"To be honest," Halar said slowly, "I thought he had every right to do as he did. You endangered us all by your actions and needed punishing for your selfishness."

"You!" she spat at him. "On you I will have the greatest revenge of them all!" Then she spun on her heels and walked away. It would have been more effective if she wasn't limping for the pain of the spanking.

"Well," Ned Land said, brushing off his hands, "I think that's enough rest—on we go, my boys!"

And so we continued on our escape. There were no signs of pursuit, though Halar said that, sooner or later, it would come. I asked him if the Sagoths were likely to attack his village in retaliation.

"No," he replied. "The Sagoths are vicious, but they are cowardly at heart. They would not attack an armed village. But they will lurk close by for a while, hoping to take anyone foolish enough to venture out alone." He shrugged. "We shall simply have to take greater care for a while. Eventually the Sagoths will tire of waiting, or the Mahars will have something else for them to do."

That was something of a relief, for I had been worried that the Mahars would be so angered they would order an attack on the Sarak. Thankfully, it seemed that their reptilian minds didn't turn in the direction of vengeance.

Alaya, on the other hand, could think of little else. I suspect she was hurt more in her pride than in her flesh—but whichever hurt the most, her tongue barely stopped. She threatened Ned Land with all kinds of terrible vengeance when she returned to her father. And when she tired of abusing the sailor, she started in on poor Halar instead, vowing all sorts of repayment for his inaction. After a while I simply stopped listening to her litany of dire punishments. Ned Land paid her no mind, of course, but Halar looked very sad and downcast whenever she yelled at him.

Aside from the verbal abuse, the journey back was quite uneventful. I had along my compass, but it turned out not to be needed; the inhabitants of Pellucidar possess some strange ability to know exactly where they are in their world at any moment, and where their home lies. Halar set the pace and direction and we simply followed along. The trip was interesting enough, and I caught sight of many animals and plants I should dearly have loved to examine, but it was clearly better to press on, back to the safety of numbers at the Sarak village. I took notes, but could do little more.

Siom proved to be a good addition to our party. He was a skilled hunter, and joined with Halar and Hans in providing for our needs on the journey. His mood had much improved since he had escaped his captivity and he became an amiable companion. One of the rescued women seemed to find him quite appealing, so I took it upon myself to ask him his plans.

"My people, the Dathar, live a long journey from here," he said, exchanging a smile with the girl. "They have long since celebrated my death—I see no need for me to return from the dead. Halar has said that I would be welcome with his people..."

"And there is a certain appeal in that," I finished for him, with a laugh. "I understand the draw of a good woman." I sighed, thinking once again of my sweet Gretchen. "Siom, do your people know of any route that leads away from Pellucidar?"

He looked at me, puzzled. "Where is there but Pellucidar?" he asked. "He gestured, taking in the scope of the world we could see. "It is clearly all that exists."

So we were out of luck once again—nobody, it seemed, even dreamed of another world beyond Pellucidar. If there was an alternate route for us to escape from this inner Earth, it seemed that none of the locals would be of use in discovering it.

Finally, we reached the river bend close by the Sarak village from where Alaya and the others had been taken. Our pace quickened with the end of our journey now so close. I confess, I was eager to see my uncle again—yes, and the members of that savage tribe. I almost thought of their village as "home" myself. Alaya, of course, was ecstatic—she was within minutes of being able to get her father to punish her two would-be victims. Ned Land seemed unaffected by her repeated threats, but poor Halar—lost in his wretched love for her—looked downcast and beaten.

We hurried into the village and then slowed and finally halted. There was nobody in sight.

True, there was no way when anyone could possibly know when we were to return. There were probably men out hunting and women out gathering. But there was never a time when the entire village was left completely empty like this. Worried, we looked about, and called out for my uncle, for Tomak and for others, but there was no reply.

Ned Land was lost for an explanation. "The pots are ready for a meal," he said, pointing to one of the well-stoked fire pits. "Everything looks normal—and yet there are no people. What can have happened?"

I had to confess that it was a complete mystery to me. It looked as though everyone had been here just a short while ago, but there was no one here now. It was puzzling and very disturbing.

And then I saw movement, out of the corner of my eye. As I started to turn, a voice called out: "Gentlemen! It pleases my heart to see you again."

It was von Horst. He and one of his men held their rifles leveled, aimed directly at us.

XVI: The Second Serpent

"Von Horst," Ned Land breathed. "So, this is your doing?"

The officer inclined his head slightly, and gestured with his rifle. "You will carefully lay down all of your weapons," he instructed. "And instruct your savage companions to do the same." He was speaking German, of course, which none of the locals understood. I learned later that he had not bothered to even attempt to learn the Pellucidarian tongue. It was typical of his arrogance.

As we had no other choice, we obeyed his instructions. Our friends had seen the effects rifles could produce, of course, and understood the threat von Horst posed.

"Where is my uncle?" I asked him. "And the rest of the tribe?"

"They are in the jungle with the rest of my men," von Horst replied. "They will return when I instruct it. I didn't wish for you to cause trouble, and had them removed when my scout reported you were returning."

"So, what do you plan now?" Ned Land asked him.

"To complete my mission," the soldier said. "This is a fascinating land, and one that Herr Bismarck will no doubt wish to occupy. There are many resources here that Germany can use, and very little to stand in the way of our occupying it."

I could just imagine what Pellucidar would be like with a modern army marching through it. It was a savage land, but one also of great beauty. It did not belong to Germany or any other nation that might seek to expand its frontiers; it deserved to stay as it was, wild and free. I said as much to von Horst and he laughed.

"My dear Axel, you are so naïve! We may not have discovered our soldiers as yet, but I have seen some of the great beasts that live here. Imagine some of these dinosaurs turned loose on a battlefield! They would strike terror into the hearts of our foes. The armies of Germany would be invincible! And there is little here to prevent us from taking whatever we wish—merely a few half-naked savages armed with primitive stone weapons."

Sadly, what he said was perfectly true. We had brought a serpent with us into the strange paradise that was Pellucidar.

He pulled a whistle from his pocket and sounded a sharp blast upon it. A short while later, the people of the tribe began to filter back into the village from the trees. Amongst them was my uncle, looking older and more tired than I recalled. I hurried to his side to help him, and his face lit up at the sight of me.

"Axel, my dear boy—you are safe, and returned to me!"

"Yes, uncle," I agreed. "Safe—which is more than I can say of you, I'm afraid."

The Professor glared at their escort, two German soldiers with their modern weapons. "Yes, my boy. These ruffians descended upon us a short while ago, and have taken control of the village. They have killed three of the locals, including—I am sorry to say—Tomak. I was forced to tell them what had befallen you and your companions, and they have been waiting for your return ever since."

"And not to celebrate it, I'll be bound."

"Indeed not," he agreed. "That evil man has vile plans to exploit this land and its inhabitants. We are all that stand in his way—for the moment."

The villagers came together in the center of the village and slumped to the ground. They were frightened and their resistance had been shattered by the power of the Germans' guns. Von Horst indicated that Halar and the other natives should join them, and all but Alaya did so. She refused to leave our side and von Horst simply shrugged. "Let her stay—what can it matter?"

To my astonishment, Alaya answered him in perfectly acceptable German. "These men have insulted and injured me—I wish to see what happens to them."

"You can speak German?" I asked her, amazed.

She gazed at me in contempt. "You think only you are clever enough to listen and understand another tongue?" she asked me coldly. "I have been studying you as you studied us." And she had never let slip any of this before! My respect for her intelligence and my fears for her cunning rose both at the same time.

"Well," Ned Land said to our captor calmly, "are we to hear what you plan?"

Von Horst shrugged. "It is really very simple," he replied. "It is what I have been intending all along. Now that we are at the center of the Earth, we have no further use for you. Indeed, it has become clear that you do not stand with the glorious progress of Germany, and would interfere in any way you could with my aims. Therefore I intend to have you shot at dawn."

The sailor laughed heartily at this threat. "Well, you'll have a long wait, then," he gasped. "From what I understand from Professor Lidenbrock, there will never be another dawn here, for there won't ever be an end to this day."

"You are mistaken," the officer snapped. "Dawn will occur whenever I order it. The sun may not set or rise here, but the hours will follow good German order. I deem it now afternoon and once I have slept, it will be dawn, and you will be executed. Unless you would prefer to die now?" he offered.

"I'll take dawn," Ned Land decided.

"Good."

Alaya scowled. "You will kill him?" she asked.

"Indeed I shall," von Horst agreed. "Does this bother you?"

"Yes," she answered. "It will be a quick death, and I would prefer him to die slowly. He has insulted and offended me." She looked at the officer. "Give that one to me—and him," she added, pointing to Halar. "I will kill them for you, but it will not be quick."

Von Horst laughed. "Woman, I admire you. I am tempted to do as you request. It might be amusing to watch. But I have ordered these men shot, and shot they will be. My orders are to be followed implicitly. I am sorry if this upsets your pretty self, but you will simply have to live with it."

Alaya looked disappointed at this news. Then she pointed to Halar. "You ordered nothing to be done to him—let me have him, at least, and a knife."

That made the officer laugh again. "You are quite the bloodthirsty one, aren't you?" He stroked her face. "I'll tell you what—you come with me, and if you please me, I will grant you what you wish."

Alaya smiled happily. "And can I watch you have Nedland shot?" she asked, eagerly. "It will be too swift, but I should very much like to see him die."

"Persuade me," he said, suggestively. He turned to his men and then gestured to our small party. "Tie them up and keep them apart from the natives. Watch them closely. If any of them get away, you will be punished in their place." He put an arm around the willing Alaya and led her off.

The remaining Germans did as they were instructed, binding myself, my uncle, Ned Land and Hans. The sailor merely said to the man binding him: "Weren't there more of you when we left?"

"This cursed land has taken them," the man replied. "And soon it will take you, too." He and his companion moved off, and they took turns in watching us.

"Well, we're in a pretty kettle of fish now," my uncle said. "There may only be three of them left, but they are more than enough to help von Horst carry out his vicious plan. They have all of the guns and all of the ammunition. These poor locals have no chance against them."

"Perhaps one of us can get free?" I suggested.

"I'm afraid I've been tied rather expertly," Ned Land said. "But even if one of us could somehow break his bonds— then what? We can't wait for nightfall and escape under cover of darkness, for that may not happen for another million years." He inclined his head toward the soldiers. "If we try anything, one of those two will cheerfully shoot us."

"Then there is no hope for us?" I asked him, dismally.

"There is always hope," the sailor answered. "But, to be honest, I cannot at the moment see what it might be."

"And we have a greater problem," my uncle added.

"Greater than being killed?" Ned Land asked.

"You must learn to look beyond yourself," my uncle chided him. "Men of science understand that human lives are ephemeral, but the search for truth is eternal."

"If you'll excuse me, Professor," the sailor answered, "I'm not a man of science, I'm a man of harpoons, and at the moment I'd rather search for escape than truth."

"Pish-tosh," my uncle said, dismissively. "Did you not hear what von Horst said? He intends to return here with an army of occupation, and to enslave the population and exploit its animal life. That we cannot allow."

"That we cannot stop," the sailor argued. "We're to be his first victims, remember?"

"Then we must apply our intellects to the subject of escape," my uncle announced. "And, once that has been achieved, we must then decide how to stop his foolish plans. Mixing two environments that Nature has separated for millennia can only lead to disaster for both."

I must confess, I fell into a gloom. My bonds were too well tied for me to slip them, and it seemed to me that the soldiers had the upper hand. The thought that I should never see my sweet Gretchen or our child again occupied my thoughts far more than my impending death. I resolved that if we managed to get out of our dire straits somehow, I would press my uncle for an immediate return to our own world on the outside of our globe.

I do not know how long I was held a worse captive of my thoughts than I was of my bonds, but after a while, I felt Hans kicking me on my leg. At first I simply ignored him, wallowing in my loss, but he persisted, and I looked up to rebuke him. As I did so, I saw him nod in the direction of the guards and make a shushing noise.

Immediately, I saw what had caught his sharp eyes: beyond the two soldiers there was furtive movement. It took me a few seconds to realize that what I was seeing were three of the women of the village creeping up behind our guards. Then, with a sudden rush, they jumped the startled soldiers, who had been watching us and not the village. Each of the women carried clubs and they employed these in swift and deadly action. As soon as the guards were dispatched, the three women hurried across to free us with their stone knifes.

To my intense surprise, two of them were women we had freed from the Mahars. Their leader was none other than Alaya.

Even Ned Land was startled by this turn of events, especially when he was the first person Alaya cut free of his bonds. "What's this?" he exclaimed. "I thought you had defected to von Horst's side because you were so mad at us."

"I'm *still* mad at you, Nedland," she snapped. "But I am first and foremost of the Sarak tribe. I could not allow these wicked men to harm any of us—not even you or Halar. And they slew my father."

One of the other women had cut me free. "But I don't understand," I said. "You went off with the soldier."

Pah!" She spat on the ground. "He was a fool. He wished to lie with me, and thought I was a savage and a fool and would readily agree." She gave a rather wicked grin and held up her stone knife. I could see that there was blood on it. "I killed him. It was what he deserved."

"I'd be inclined to rather agree with you, my dear," my uncle said, shaking off his own severed bonds. "And those two guards?"

"Dead also," she said with pride. "They will never threaten us again."

"Which leaves just one man," Ned Land said, grimly. "I trust, Alaya, you'll leave this one for me?"

"You are a man," she replied. "I assume you wish to appear to be useful. You may have him. He is down by the river, watching over the rest of my people." She looked every inch the savage princess. "Now my father is dead, they *are* my people."

"Indeed they are, my dear," the Professor agreed. "And you have undoubtedly saved all of their lives by your courageous actions."

Ned Land slipped off, to finish off the last of the soldiers. Hans and I went to the two fallen men and confirmed that they were indeed dead. He and I stripped them of their weapons, but left them where they had fallen. We now had rifles and ammunition again, which made me feel a lot better. I returned to my uncle, offering him a revolver, which he took.

"Let us go and see to von Horst," he said.

"Come," Alaya said. She was getting quite used to giving orders. She led us to the modest dwelling where the soldier had taken her, and then stopped in shock. "He is gone!" she exclaimed.

It was true—von Horst was nowhere to be seen.

XVI: A Return From the Center of the Earth

I could see a pool of blood where the soldier must have been stabbed by Alaya, but evidently the blow had not been a fatal one. As soon as she had left to free us, von Horst must have seized his opportunity to escape.

There was no time to waste—as long as he was at liberty, we were still in grave danger. I pointed to the blood and said to Hans: "We must follow and stop him." Our guide nodded his comprehension. To my uncle I said: "Tell Ned Land when he returns what has happened and what we are doing." Then Hans and I set off at a trot on the trail of von Horst.

As I have said, I am not a great tracker, but even I could see the trail of blood left behind by the wounded man. He had headed for the river, probably to try and join his last surviving soldier and in the hopes that the two of them could somehow together turn the tables again. But his wound appeared to be severe, and he obviously wasn't traveling very swiftly.

The river came into sight, and we saw that the blood trail abruptly led off parallel to it. The reason for this was quite obvious—he had reached the river after Ned Land, and had seen the sailor freeing the tribe. Alone and wounded, he couldn't take on Ned Land, so he had fled.

We followed on, and after a short while we heard a cry from behind us. Ned Land and Halar joined us, the sailor armed with the dead German guard's rifle and revolver. We were now quite the war party, but the trail of blood was getting more difficult to see. The wound must be closing up, obviously. But we now had Hans, Ned Land and Halar, and von Horst's path was as clear as day to them.

We heard the sounds of crashing far ahead of us and paused a moment. Was some savage Pellucidarian beast hunting? Well, no matter—we had rifles and bullets again, and nothing this land could breed would stand up against those! We went on. In a matter of moments we reached the edge of the trees and promptly halted.

Something was indeed hunting—Sagoths! They had fallen upon von Horst, and in his weakened state he could not resist them. They were dragging him to where their *lidi* was waiting, clearly with the intent of taking him back with them to the Mahar city.

I raised my rifle, ready to shoot. To my surprise, Ned Land gripped the barrel and pushed it aside.

"What are you doing?" I asked him. "We must rescue him!"

"Why?" the sailor asked, simply. "This will solve all of our problems. If we attempt to rescue him then one or more of us might be injured or killed—and he is not worth that price. Besides, what would happen if we *did* rescue him? We should have to take him back to the village where Alaya would undoubtedly have him killed for murdering her father. Should we risk our lives for that?"

"But… to leave him with the Mahar!" I protested.

"As I said, a perfect solution. To them we are all *gilaks*, animals. I doubt they can tell that von Horst isn't one of us, so his capture and execution would probably satisfy them that they have paid us back for firing their city. They will be less inclined to harass the Sarak after this."

"They will send him to the pits." But my protests were growing weaker.

"I can think of no one who deserves such a fate more." Ned Land clapped a hand on my shoulder. "Your sentiments show you have a good heart, Axel, so allow me to offer you a ray of hope in this situation. The blood trail we have followed shows that von Horst was badly injured. It is quite likely that he will not survive the journey back to the Mahar city, and that the Masters will be left to dispense their idea of justice on a corpse. If it will make you feel better, believe this."

"He is right," Halar said. "Alaya can be quite... vengeful, as you know. The German would not be allowed to live in any event."

It had all become rather moot anyway, for the Sagoths and their captive had reached the *lidi* and were setting off on their return trip. It would now mean another lengthy pursuit if we were to attempt a rescue, and I could see that none of us had the heart for that—including me. "Very well," I agreed. "Let us return."

As can be imagined, there was much rejoicing when we returned. Alaya heard our story and let slip a curse.

"I wished to slay him myself," she growled. "I do not know how I failed the first time, but I should not have failed a second. Ah, well," she added, looking happier, "maybe he *will* survive the trip and the Mahars will kill him."

"In the meantime, my boy," my uncle said, "*we* can now plan our trip home."

"Home..." I repeated, happily. Gretchen!

"Yes indeed," he said. "The soldiers are all dead, and we have their weapons, so we can retrace our steps with ease just as soon as everyone is ready to go." As he said this, he looked pointedly at Ned Land.

The harpooner looked back and then laughed. "You think I'd want to stay here?" He shook his head. "Professor, I cannot wait to look upon a good, clear sky and an honest ocean again."

My uncle blinked in surprise and looked at Alaya. "I had thought..." he said, weakly.

Ned Land laughed again. "We sailors like to have a girl in every port and a home in none. Besides, Alaya is now the head of this tribe, and she will need a good, steady hunter beside her to help her."

"I need nobody," the savage said, coldly. Then her face softened. "But it may be that my heart will change and I will forgive Halar. *If* he tries hard…" I could see that she was enjoying the thought of tormenting our poor friend. But I suspected that with her as a prize at the end of it, Halar might endure.

And so we laid our plans to return to the surface of the Earth. The tribe insisted on a great feast to say goodbye to us, and we packed a good deal of food for our return journey. We had discovered the place where the soldiers had hidden their own supplies before they raided the village, and so we had our equipment and more than enough ammunition to last us on our return trek through Pellucidar.

Alaya, in her usual thoughtful mood stared at our guns with some lust in her heart. But then she sighed and said: "Those rifles of yours might be of help to us, but it is perhaps best that you take them. Sooner or later their supplies would run out and we could not replace them. I would not want my hunters to get too reliant on something they could not keep."

My uncle smiled. "I think you will make quite a wise ruler, Alaya."

"*If* you can control your temper," I could not resist adding.

She laughed. "If I could not control it, Axel, you would be leaving our village unable to sit down for the remainder of your journey."

We said goodbye to our friends with mixed feelings— but, in my case, mostly a longing to return to my wife and child. We were able to retrace our path with ease. The journey was—well, as this was Pellucidar it was hardly uneventful. But we won through, back to the passage that led back onward and downward—though, eventually, upward—to Iceland again.

As we took our last look at Pellucidar, my uncle called us all together. "This is a savage and often frightful land," he said. "But it has its own beauty and its own nobility." He held up his rifle. "Yet a few hundred well-armed men might be able to conquer this place and kill or enslave the inhabitants. They could turn it into another European colony, a slave-state run for the benefit of the rich and powerful of our world. My boy, my friends—I do not think that we should allow this to happen."

Ned Land nodded. "You think we should keep quiet about what we have found?"

"I do indeed. And I am sure that no one would doubt the word of Professor Lidenbrock and his nephew if we say that all we found were rocks and tunnels, and that there is nothing here of any value."

"And how are we to explain that von Horst and his men are no longer with us?" I asked him. "They will certainly be missed."

"Those brave souls were lost in a cave-in," my uncle said, with a slight smile. "We shall say they died heroically, saving our lives. That should satisfy everyone."

"Even Herr Bismarck?" I asked. "Surely he knew of von Horst's plans?"

"Even Herr Bismarck," my uncle assured me. "We do not know that he was aware of those plans. If he was not, then it is no problem. If he did—well, he could hardly admit to it, could he? Being a pragmatic politician, I am sure he will make the best of a bad situation. And even if he *did* plan to exploit the inhabitants of the underworld—he could do nothing without our help. And I think this time we shall all decide that we have had quite sufficient of our subterranean explorations."

I laughed. "I know that I, for one, have!"

And so we returned. To our surprise, our ship was still waiting for us. The Captain heard our story and sighed, but accepted it. We were quite astonished to discover that we had been missing only some six months. It had seemed to be so much longer—but, as I say, time plays strange tricks in Pellucidar. We said our farewells to Hans—who went off to see whether he still had a fiancée or not—and then to Ned Land, who was intent on finding berth on the next whaler he could board. He left us with a firm promise to visit the house in Koenigstrasse.

And about that—what can I say? I need not tell you of the great pleasure it was to see my dear Gretchen and our growing daughter again. I told her the true story of our adventures, of course—I cannot lie to my wife!—and then I set myself to write this account and to seal it for my daughter to read when she is old enough to understand and appreciate it. I shall leave it to her, then, whether to publish it or to pass it on to some child of her own.

There are just two further points to add. First, about a month after our return, my uncle received a note from Iceland. He beamed as he read it, and then showed it to me. It was written in careful, cramped Danish, which I could not read, of course. My uncle explained: "It is from Hans; it seems that his Habby was indeed a most sensible girl and waited for him. They are now married."

This was excellent news indeed.

The second point concerns the Gun Club of Baltimore. It was the story that they were attempting to reach the center of the Earth that impelled this entire adventure, but we had at no time seen them. The reason for that became clear—they had not, in fact, even set foot in Iceland. They had indeed gone to the Arctic Circle[2], but for entirely other reasons. What had therefore started our entire adventure off, then, was nothing more than unfounded gossip!

---

[2] If you wish to know why, you can find the story in *The Purchase of the North Pole* by Jules Verne.

This was the first of the adventures of the Shadowmen *that I wrote. Jean-Marc's brief for all of these stories was that they contain some character from French fiction that had fallen into the public domain. As I had recently finished reading* The Count Of Monte Cristo, *Edmund Dantes was a clear choice. A dashing hero, risking life and limb for truth, justice and the French way of life! I had also been reading the complete short stories of Edgar Allan Poe, and the few tales of literature's first detective—Dupin—and so a meeting of these two wonderful characters seemed to be called for.*

The Kind-Hearted Torturer

Paris, 1842

I have had occasion in the past to note down one or two of the singular affairs that my good friend C. Auguste Dupin has resolved, thanks to his strict interpretation and application of logical thinking. I have never considered myself a dull-witted man—nor have I been so thought by my acquaintances—but if I were to compare myself with Dupin, I should certainly appear almost Neanderthal in my thinking. He was frequently of great use to the official police, but there was one occasion when he was unable to help them solve a case.

We had been out smoking pipes and imbibing a moderate quantity of a rather fine Madeira and were on our way back to our rooms at an early hour of the morning. As is generally the case with Paris, we were far from alone on the city streets. In fact, due to the press of the crowds on the main routes, we slipped from them and into a maze of the back streets that Dupin somehow knew so well. I knew only that we were in the region of the église Ste-Mathilde—I could see her spire about the roofs ahead of us—but Dupin led the way without hesitation or doubt.

As we drew closer to the church, a figure turned from around the corner ahead of us. He was ambling rather than walking, but still almost collided with us. His hand flashed to the brim of his hat, and he nodded slightly. "I do beg your pardon," he said, in English. Then, he added: "*Pardonnez-moi.*" I was quite impressed with the Englishman's attempt at French—very few of them ever manage to get their tongues around the Gallic consonants correctly, and he had almost succeeded. I nodded back politely, noting that he was well dressed in expensive evening clothes, though without gloves, and carried a walking stick in his right hand of some dark wood, topped with a silver fleur-de-lys. He touched his hat again, and then walked on.

Dupin made no comment—he had spoken not a single word in this short encounter—but he had an abstracted look to his face that usually accompanied his attention being focused on some mystery or other. Since he had undertaken no such investigations, to the best of my knowledge, and since he had been most genial over our glasses and pipes, I came to the conclusion that I must have mistaken his glance. We moved on, only to encounter a crowd just two streets away, in front of Ste-Mathilde.

"It would appear that there is no one in their beds this night," I commented. "Perhaps we should find another way?"

"I think not," Dupin replied, his eyes feasting eagerly on the motions and sounds of the gathered crowd. "Observe—these people go nowhere—they instead crowd around something on the pavement. And, unless I am very much mistaken, that is Monsieur Couperin, of the Préfecture de Police attempting to move them along. It seems I was correct to suspect foul play."

I confess that I was puzzled by this remark, as I had seen nothing that had alerted me to the possibility of trouble. But Dupin was like a hound who has scented the fox, and hurried along to Couperin's side. The policeman appeared surprised to see my friend, but there are few in the Sûreté who do not know Dupin by both reputation and appearance.

"It would appear," Couperin said, jovially, "that you have a nose for blood. But there is little here to interest you, Dupin. It is merely an affair of honor that has ended tragically." He scowled. "Unless you know something of this case that I do not."

"I know very little about this case," Dupin replied. "I was not even aware that there *was* a case until moments ago. My friend and I were merely heading home after a pleasant evening. But, as I am here, and a dead man is here..." He shrugged.

Couperin considered for a moment, and then nodded. He turned to the three gendarmes who were with him, and who were attempting—without noticeable success—to disperse the onlookers. Parisiennes, it has been claimed, have seen everything—but, nevertheless, there would appear to be no lack of interest in seeing a dead body on the pavement. "Let us through," Couperin said, and the policemen motioned back the onlookers.

"This has only just occurred?" I asked him.

"Within the past ten minutes," Couperin confirmed. "There was a policemen in this street who heard cries, and then saw a man fall from the roof of the church. I happened to be close by also, on an entirely different case, and arrived just moments later.

"Then how is it that you allowed the murderer to escape?" Dupin asked. He was standing close to the body, and studying it, as was his habit, with minute attention.

"I am yet to be convinced that it *was* murder," Couperin said, somewhat stiffly. "It appears to me to have been a matter of honor."

"Indeed?" Dupin beckoned me forward. "And what is your opinion?" he asked me.

I bent to examine the corpse. It was of a thick-set man in his late 20s, I should judge. He wore no coat, and his clothing was otherwise tidy. His face looked heavy, not refined, and there was a deep wound in his right shoulder. It was clear that he had been the victim of a sword-thrust. Oddly, there was not as much blood about the wound as I would have expected, nor was there a great deal on the ground.

"There is not much that occurs to me," I confessed. "He was stabbed with a sword, obviously, but the blow did not kill him. It is not in a vital spot." I glanced upward—the roof of the church was some 40 meters high. "I imagine it was the fall that terminated his life."

Dupin turned to the policeman. "And on what do you base your ridiculous theory of an affair of honor?" he asked.

Couperin scowled. "On the *facts*," he replied. "Your friend is undoubtedly correct in saying that the fall killed the poor fellow. So, we must ask ourselves: what was he doing on the roof on the church in the first place? Note the sword wound—how could he have been given one? Through a duel, obviously. Why the roof? So that he and his opponent could fight without being disturbed. His coat has been removed, clearly so that he can have greater freedom in the fight. I imagine that he was startled by being run through the shoulder, and then lost his footing and fell to his death." He smiled, pleased with himself. "As I say, an affair of honor between two gentlemen—I admit I cannot deduce if it was over a point of honor or a woman—that resulted in the tragic death of this man. I do not believe that it was murder."

Dupin snorted. "You, like all policemen, see everything with the eyes—and nothing with the mind. Do not look so annoyed with me, Inspector—you did at least see all the relevant details. The problem is that you are a romantic. You come upon a man with a sword wound, and instantly imagine that he is a romantic, as you are. You decide that the whole business is an affair of honor, when it is clearly nothing of the sort. Have you been up to look at the roof of the church yet?" he asked.

The policeman was momentarily taken aback by the apparent change of subject. "I was just about to do so when you arrived," he said. He was still annoyed at Dupin's comments, clearly, but striving for politeness. "Would you care to accompany me?"

"No," Dupin said, carelessly. "I know precisely what you will discover up there. You will find this man's jacket, which is black. You will find a pair of discarded gloves, which are white, but covered with blood. You will find a pool of blood—more than a liter, I would imagine. What you will *not* find is the mythical sword that this man used in your imaginary duel." He waved one hand. "I will await you here. Ah, before you go, which is the policeman who was first on the scene and discovered the body?"

Couperin gestured to one of the trio, who stepped forward and saluted rather smartly. "I am going to examine the scene of the battle," he told the man. He gestured to Dupin. "Answer this man's questions as you would mine." He then stalked off, into the open door of the church, taking another policeman with him. Dupin turned to the policeman.

"You saw the man fall?" he asked.

"Yes, sir." The policeman had clearly been rehearsing his story in his mind, for he needed no further questioning to continue. "I was walking in this direction, and stood over there." He gestured to a spot some 20 meters further up the road. "I heard a cry from the roof of the church, and looked up. In the darkness, I saw some object fall and strike the ground. Hurrying forward, I saw it was the victim. People had already started to gather, and I sent one of them for Monsieur Couperin, whom I knew to be close by."

"I see." Dupin smiled slightly. "And you saw no one with a sword?"

"No one at all, sir. I should certainly have detained anyone with a weapon."

"I'm certain you would," Dupin agreed. "You seem to be a most conscientious fellow." There was a sparkle of amusement in his eyes. "Then where do you imagine that the Inspector's other duelist has vanished to?"

"I have no idea, sir," the policeman admitted. Then he looked startled. "You don't think he's still on the roof, do you? Monsieur Couperin—"

"Is in no danger at all," Dupin replied. "The murderer is quite some distance from here by this point."

The policeman looked confused, and then his puzzlement cleared. "You think he dropped his sword, then? I should have held everyone about here."

"You could hardly hold *everyone*," Dupin reassured the crestfallen policeman. He glanced at the crowd. "Though it would seem that almost nobody wishes to leave. Murder, it would appear, is something of a spectacle."

Couperin returned from the church, looking somewhat flushed. Part of this was no doubt due to the exertion of climbing and then descending the tower. The other part, I soon discovered, was from anger. "How the Devil did you know what we would find on the roof?" were his first words to Dupin.

"Because I understand what has happened here," my friend replied calmly. "You could find nothing other than I expected. Your problem, my friend, is that you are a kind person—you assume that others are like you, and give them too much credit for kindness. While this trait is admirable in the population at large, it is perhaps not the best characteristic for a policeman to possess. I, on the other hand, know the depredations that a person can sink into, and thus I expect nothing less. Sadly, perhaps, I all too frequently discover myself to be correct. I often wish that the human race did not lower itself to meet my expectations."

"All of which still does not inform me how you knew what I would find on the roof of the church," Couperin persisted, his annoyance still very evident.

"Very well," Dupin said. "Let us examine the evidence. You see a man with a sword-wound, and without a jacket. You assume from this that he had been fighting a duel of honor, and fell from the roof. Let us examine the possibility that you are right. First, look at this man. Note the heavy features, the coarse hands. Is this a man to whom honor might mean more than life itself? No, this is a man who would settle an argument not with a sword, but with a cudgel or a pistol. Is there a sword he might have used? No, you found no trace. And nor did your conscientious policeman find anyone who saw anyone carrying a sword in this vicinity."

"The other party might have hidden them," Couperin protested. But I did detect a lack of force in his words, as if he were already coming to believe my friend's objections.

Dupin waved his hand airily. "By all means, waste time searching," he said. "There was no duel. Allow me to explain what actually occurred, and I am certain that you will be able to follow my reasoning." His face took on the detached expression he always had when expounding his theories—if the word "theory" is not too light to be used concerning his mental processes. "This man's killer happened upon the man here. It was unlikely to be by chance, for the murderer clearly knew that Ste-Mathilde had a flat roof, and that it was accessible at this odd hour. Therefore, the killer knew this man, and had planned carefully for his arrival. When the victim reached the church, he was forced inside by his attacker—undoubtedly when the man brandished the weapon that produced the wound we have seen.

"He took the victim to the roof so that he might have a very private conversation with him. The wound was not inflicted in a moment of passion as two men fought—it was given calmly and deliberately. Its purpose was to induce the man to talk."

"How can you possibly say that?" the policeman asked.

"If you look at the wound," Dupin said, "you will observe that there are black threads driven into it by the point of the weapon. Since the man's shirt is white, clearly the threads had to have come from a black coat. Since the man was not wearing one, this was why I knew you would find one on the roof."

"That does not prove that the wound was given to make him talk," Couperin persisted.

Dupin sighed. "Again, look to the wound. There is remarkably little blood on the shirt, yet the wound is deep. It does not touch any vital spot, however, so it was not a killing thrust. And the man's jacket is missing. How to explain this? Obviously, the person who attacked the victim then thrust him down onto the roof on his hands and knees. The blood fell straight from the wound and onto the roof—and you discovered the pool of blood there, as I knew it must be."

"But why remove the jacket?" Couperin asked. His voice showed that he was considerably less sure of himself now.

"To restrain the man. Once he was on his hands and knees, gripping the collar of the jacket and pulling it down the arms is a very effective way of immobilizing a person. So, given that this is what must have happened, the only problem remaining is—why would the attacker act in such a fashion? The answer is apparent—the victim had some information that the killer wished to know. The attacker gave him the wound to torture him, to induce him to speak. The victim then told all. His attacker thereupon threw him from the roof. Why? For one of two reasons—to either silence the man, so that no one would know the information had been obtained. Or else... as a warning of our killer's earnest. He is a man not to be trifled with, and he takes this man's life as you or I would squash a bug."

"But how can you be sure that the attacker gained the information he needed?" asked the policeman. "Is it not possible that this man threw himself deliberately from the roof to avoid talking?"

Dupin smiled slightly. "If you wish to conduct an experiment, my friend, then perhaps you would get down on your hands and knees. I will then pull your jacket down over your arms to immobilize you. You may then see if you are able to struggle out of your jacket and throw yourself anywhere before I am able to prevent you. You would not succeed. No, the victim was thrown to his death by his torturer, who pulled off the jacket first and discarded it."

Couperin looked defeated, overwhelmed by Dupin's relentless array of logic. "And the gloves?" he asked, feebly. "How did you know I should find them?"

"Ah, there I have a confession to make," my friend admitted. "I was not absolutely certain that they would be there. It was a good guess, but by no means certain. They were stained with blood from the victim, so that the killer could not afford to be seen wearing them in public."

It was then that I realized the point that Dupin was making. "Great Heavens!" I exclaimed. "We passed by the killer!"

"Indeed we did," Dupin agreed. "And you and I both noted the oddity that such a well-dressed man was not wearing the gloves that would have completed his ensemble. That was what made me suspect they would have been left on the roof."

"You met the killer?" Couperin cried. "Why did you not say so at once? Perhaps there is still time to find him..." He looked ready to send off his policemen to search the city streets.

Dupin shook his head. "You will not find him," he assured the policeman. "He was disguised as an Englishman, and has undoubtedly discarded this disguise by now."

"Disguised?" I could scarcely agree. "Dupin, I would swear that man *was* English. His accent, his admirable attempt to speak good French..."

"My friend," Dupin said, smiling, "you heard what he wished you to witness. We are dealing with a most intelligent and dangerous man. But his accent, whilst superb, was not quite good enough to fool the ears of Dupin. He was a Frenchman, pretending a difficulty with our tongue, and that his native speech was English. I do not blame you for being deceived—very few people would not have been. Also, did you not notice the walking stick that the man carried? It had as a head the fleur-de-lys—a very French symbol, one that a true Englishman was unlikely to own. In fact, it was because of his attempt at disguise that I paid close attention to him. Why, I wondered, would this man pretend to be what he was not with two strangers who might never see him again? He was clearly

149

behaving oddly. And so I was prepared for some strange occurrence. That is why I moved toward, instead of away from, the gathered crowd here. And, in retrospect, is it not curious that while all other people were hurrying *toward* the scene of the crime, our false Englishman was walking slowly *away* from it?"

"This is all very logical," I was forced to admit. "But the man was not carrying a sword, and you do not expect to find one here. So, where is the weapon?"

"He *was* carrying it," Dupin argued. "Undoubtedly that walking stick of his concealed a sword cane. A most useful weapon that is simple to disguise."

Couperin looked quite exhausted. "But what was this man killed for?" he asked. "What information? And how can you be certain that your fake Englishman obtained what he sought?"

"If he had not, he would not have been so pleased with himself when he ran into us," Dupin explained. "As to what that information was—I cannot yet say. Whatever it was, though it was of sufficient importance to cost a man his life, it was not of great urgency, otherwise the killer would have been hurrying away instead of walking quite casually. No, whatever it was that he learned, it is not something he will be able to make use of for several hours yet, at least." Abruptly, he yawned. "So I believe we all have sufficient time to go home and get some rest. If you will excuse us?" Then he paused. "Perhaps you would be kind enough to let us know any further facts you might unearth, my friend?" he asked the policeman. "You have our address, I trust? Just in case, please write it down—I would not wish you to mistake the house." He dictated the address where we stayed to Couperin, and then had the audacity to force the policeman to read it back so Dupin could ascertain that it had been taken correctly. I was not surprised that Couperin looked distinctly annoyed at this lack of trust. In fact, once we had taken our leave of the poor fellow, I berated Dupin for humiliating him so.

"Did I really?" he asked, showing little concern. "I am sure that I will be forgiven. But I had to be certain that the man listening to all that was said heard it quite distinctly."

"Man?" I asked, astonished. "What man?"

"You did not notice him?" Dupin asked. "He was attempting to pretend to be one of the crowd, but was paying inordinate attention to our conversation with the Inspector."

"A journalist, perhaps?" I ventured.

"I think not." Dupin shook his head. "The killer of this unfortunate is a most cunning and intelligent man. It seems to me that he may well have left an agent behind to ascertain what the police might discover from the corpse of his victim. I trust that when he receives the report, my deductions will unnerve him."

"Good Heavens!" I said. "And what will he do then?"

"Come and call upon us, I hope," Dupin replied. "Why else should I have made certain that he will get our address? I do not believe that we are in danger from this man, my friend, but it might be as well if you slept with a loaded pistol close at hand."

Thankfully, despite Dupin's warning, the rest of the night was uneventful. We had just finished a late breakfast—it might even have passed for a late lunch—when our visitor was announced. Dupin glanced to me to ascertain that I had my pistol within reach, though concealed from view, before allowing the man in.

Thanks to Dupin's assurance that this was our fake Englishman who passed us in the night, I paid careful attention to the stranger. Though he was certainly as tall and muscular as the "Englishman," had I not been forewarned that it was the same man, I would never have guessed. It wasn't so much that his features had changed, but that his complete attitude had altered, making him appear so very different. This morning he was without a single doubt a Frenchman born and bred. And, from the style and cut of his immaculate clothing, one of rare breeding and wealth. I have heard it said that great actors are able to change their appearance through nothing more than their attitude and mannerisms, but never before had I ever seen it done.

"Chevalier Dupin," the man said, bowing politely. "I trust I have not arrived too early for our appointment?"

"Not at all," my friend replied, equally politely and calmly. "Though I confess a small hesitation in knowing how to address you. Should I be addressing Lord Wilmore, Edmond Dantès or the self-appointed Count of Monte-Cristo?"

A slight shock passed fleetingly over the features of our guest. "I see that you have discovered who I am," he murmured. "May I sit down?"

"Excuse my bad manners," Dupin replied. "Of course, please take a seat." He gestured to one facing the both of us. A slight smile crossed the man's face, and I understood that he knew he would be covered by a brace of pistols.

"I assure you," he said gently, "that you have no need to fear violence from me. Had I wished it, you would both be dead by now. But I have nothing against either of you—save that you might cause me a small inconvenience in my plans."

"I assure you, Monsieur le Comte," Dupin answered, somewhat offended, "that any inconvenience I might cause you would be by no means small."

Our visitor laughed. "No, you are correct—you could cause me a major inconvenience by simply telling the police my name. Which raises the interesting question of why you haven't—and how you happened upon it."

"I did not happen upon it," Dupin replied. "I attended the details of your case with interest as it happened. I know that you were born Edmond Dantès, and were unjustly committed to the Château d'If for life. That you somehow escaped, took upon yourself the identity of the fictitious Count of Monte-Cristo and subsequently brought justice to the men who had wronged you and others. I confess, I was much impressed by your methods. I noted that in the course of your actions you adopted a number of disguises, including that of an aristocratic Englishman, Lord Wilmore. When you ran across us last night in this disguise, the details of your case sprang back to the forefront of my mind, and I was certain that I was dealing with none other than the much-wronged Edmond Dantès. It was solely because of the regard I held you in that I did not immediately pass along your name to the police. However, that is an oversight that can be corrected at any time."

"And your invitation for me to visit you was for the purpose of deciding whether to do just that, I take it?"

"You are correct," Dupin agreed. "I am willing to hear you out as to the reason you committed torture and cold-blooded murder this last night. If I am not convinced by your explanation, then I am afraid that I shall have to call in my friend Inspector Couperin and hand you over to him."

Dantès—Monte-Cristo—whatever the man was called, he was cool. "And you feel that the odds of two against one will enable you to take me captive?"

"Two armed with pistols against one who is not," Dupin corrected him.

"Ah, yes, I had almost forgotten the pistols," Monte-Cristo said. He snapped his fingers, and the door to our breakfast room burst open. Two large men entered, both with pistols of their own. Our visitor held up a hand. "No violence, please," he requested. "Simply relieve these two men of their weapons, and then leave us alone." The two men did so, leaving me, at least, feeling humiliated and rather naked. "I merely removed the pistols to prevent accidents," Monte-Cristo assured us. "Now I believe I do owe you at least my story as to the events of last night. After that... well, we shall see." He settled back, apparently quite at ease, and commenced his tale.

"After I had achieved my aim of justice against those men who had wronged me, I left France with every intention of never returning. I had a bride whom I was learning to love, and had left matters completely settled—or so I believed. My house on the Champs-Elysées I had left to the son of my old master and friend, Maximilien Morel. He had wed Valentine de Villefort, and their life promised to be one of happiness.

"However, this was not to be. Two weeks ago, I received an urgent missive from Morel, telling me that his wife had been kidnapped, and was being held for ransom. He feared greatly for her safety, and begged assistance. Even if I were not moved by compassion and friendship to agree, my wife, Haydée, would have forced me into it, for she and Valentine were great friends. Accordingly, we returned as swiftly as possible. Yesterday, I met with Morel, who is a broken man after the abduction of his beloved wife, and learned the details of the story. She had been taken on the street in broad daylight, and her maid assaulted. It was clear that this was the work of the Black Coats." He paused. "I take it you know of the association?"

Dupin nodded and smiled. "I have caused that organization more than a small amount of inconvenience. I should relish causing them more."

"So would I," Monte-Cristo answered fervently. "As I say, it was swiftly apparent that they were behind the kidnapping and ransom of poor Valentine."

"They have demanded money for her return, then?" I asked.

"They have." He named a considerable sum, more than Dupin or I would make in ten years.

"There is a problem with paying this amount, then?" I asked him.

"The amount? No." He waved a hand. "Morel or I could—and would—pay ten times that figure for Valentine's safe return. The problem is not financial, but a matter of trust."

Dupin saw that I did not understand, so he elucidated. "The Black Coats will require the ransom to be delivered before the lady is returned. However, once they have the money *and* the lady, what is the likelihood that they will set the lady free? In many cases, the victim may be considered to have seen too much."

I understood. "You think it likely, then," I questioned the Count, "that they will take the money and kill the lady instead of fulfilling their bargain and setting her free?"

"It is more than likely," he replied. "But, even if they do allow her to go free—once they know Morel will pay, what is to stop them from abducting her again and forcing the family through this torture a second or third time?"

Dupin nodded. "Given the habits of the Black Coats, I believe your assessment of their likely strategy to be a sound one. I take it, then, that you have a different plan?"

"Indeed." Monte-Cristo resumed his tale. "It was the work of a few short hours to learn that the man whose body you examined last night was a lieutenant in the Black Coats. It was a simple matter to divert him, and his fate you know, of course."

I believed I now understood. "Ah! So you tortured him to make him tell you the whereabouts of the unfortunate Madame Morel!"

"Had he known them, it would have been a great help," the Count replied. "But the Black Coat organization is large, and he did not know who was responsible for the kidnapping. I thought it unlikely that he would."

"You had a different aim in mind, then?" Dupin asked. I could tell that the case intrigued him. He hated boredom more than anything, and this case was proving to be of the greatest interest.

"Yes—an exchange of prisoners. If I could take as hostage someone that the Black Coats valued, then this person might be exchanged for Valentine. It would ensure the safety of my friend's wife, and also stand the Black Coats on notice that any further attempt on her person would be met by serious reprisals."

"Which is why you felt no compunction about killing the man last night?" Dupin hazarded a guess.

"They had to be shown that they were dealing with someone who would have no single hesitation in doing whatever he said," Monte-Cristo amplified. "Also, as he is dead, they can have no idea who my target within their organization is, and cannot defend that person."

"So you propose to kidnap one of their higher functionaries and then effect an exchange?" Dupin summarized.

"This afternoon." He withdrew a watch from his pocket and glanced at it. "In two hours, to be precise. Always assuming, of course, that you decide not to… inconvenience me." He looked at Dupin expectantly.

Dupin didn't need to look to me for confirmation. "Not only will we not inconvenience you," he vowed, "but I'll wager that you might be able to find the use for two stout fellows—with pistols, if you'll return them."

"Capital!" the Count exclaimed, leaping to his feet. "Your assistance in this matter will be gratefully accepted." He opened the door, and called in his companions, instructing them to return to us our pistols. Thus armed once again, we accompanied him outside to a waiting carriage. This took us to a section of the Rue de Bois—affluent, without being too ostentatious.

"The person we await will be arriving at No. 17 shortly," he informed us. "There will be a small guard, naturally, whom we shall have to overcome. This is why I am so glad of your assistance. Jacopo, Michel and I might have managed the task alone, but with the two of you as well…" He smiled his thanks.

During the wait, I could not but wonder what adventure we were in for. As Dupin had remarked, he had encountered the Black Coats once or twice, always to their detriment. They were a secretive band of law-breakers, who were willing to undertake any enterprise that might fill their coffers, no matter how vile or anti-social. Dupin had cut off a couple of their minor heads through his detection, but more seemed to constantly spring up. France, it would seem, might sometimes find itself in want of good artists or composers, but never of criminals. The same is undoubtedly true of any center of enterprise in our modern world.

"Softly," Monte-Cristo murmured a short while later, dashing me from my reverie. "The carriage approaches." From where we sat on the road opposite the target house, we could peer through the curtains of our own conveyance and see the small enclosed carriage that drew up. Along with the driver, there were two other riders on the outside.

"I am sure there must be at least one other guard within the coach," the Count said softly.

"We shall take the more obvious ones," Dupin said. "You and your men take the others."

We waited a moment, until the two guards began to disembark. At a signal from the Count, we then sprang from our own carriage. I raised my pistol instantly. At the sight and sound of our approach, the two men whirled, drawing pistols of their own. The same instant, the driver attempted to whip his horses into motion again.

I fired first, and had the satisfaction of hearing my target howl and fall, clutching his shoulder. Blood was pulsing from a wound there as I sprang across the road and seized his unfired pistol, thus rearming myself. Dupin, I noted, had also taken down his man, and was procuring his weapon also. The servant named Jacopo had leapt atop the carriage, and prevented the driver from moving it, while Monte-Cristo and his remaining retainer threw open the door of the vehicle.

There was a gunshot at that instant, and Monte-Cristo fell. I thought for a horrified second that he had been injured or killed, but he pounced onto the man who was now drawing a sword and dragged him from the carriage. In his own hand, I saw the cane flicker, and then became a sword also—the weapon that had been used to wound the man the previous evening. The Count and his opponent set to fighting with a will, as Michel, Dupin and I surrounded the coach. I confess to being startled.

I had been expecting some evil-looking man, a human spider used to spinning webs of treachery and deceit, to be within. Instead, I saw, calm and refined, one of the most beautiful women I have met. She was tall, elegant and dignified. Had we, after all, made some terrible mistake?

Thankfully not. Dupin smiled slightly. "The Countess of Clare," he murmured. "I had long suspected that there was a link between you and the Black Coats."

"Chevalier Dupin," she replied, inclining her shapely head slightly. "I have long been expecting you. This trap of yours is admirably well set."

"Not mine, Madame," Dupin answered, gesturing toward the Count. "I merely assist."

Monte-Cristo had his man by now. The guard was skilled, but the Count much better. With a final flick of his wrist, he disarmed his opponent, and then plunged the blade into the man's shoulder. The man cried, clasped his wound and fell back.

"Tell your colleagues," the Count cried, "that the Countess is captive and hostage. She will be kept alive as long as Madame Morel is in good health. If you wish the lady returned to you, I will exchange her for my friend. The exchange is to take place at six precisely at the Bois de Boulogne." He mentioned a place. "If Madame Morel is not there at that time, or if she is at all harmed, you will receive the Countess back in small pieces. And then we shall take another of your elite and attempt the exchange again." He did not bother to ask if his terms were understood. Instead he strode to the lady's carriage. "If you will accompany me?" he asked, politely but firmly, extending a hand.

"How can I refuse?" the Countess replied. She accompanied us back to our own carriage. Jacopo then whipped the horses, and we sprang off through the streets of Paris. The Countess surveyed us without apparent fear. No doubt she felt protected by virtue of her feminine sex and her beauty, though in her situation few women would have been so poised. "I fear, gentlemen, that you are being naive. There is a rule in the Black Coats—*coupez la branche*—cut off the limb—that the fallen are to be left behind. I am afraid that they are more likely to abandon me than to exchange me."

"I think not, in this case," Monte-Cristo countered. "They will recognize that your abductor is the same man who tortured one of their number last night and killed him. They will fear that I shall torture you to obtain your secrets. They may not want you back, but they will desire to safeguard what you know."

"I fear you overestimate their fears."

"For your sake, my lady, let us hope not."

Nothing more was said for the remainder of the ride. Eventually, we drew up outside a house in a section of the city not far from the woods. The Count led the way inside, where we were met by a young woman whose beauty surpassed even that of the Countess. There was the suggestion of the Near East about her countenance, and a definite suggestion of ferocity within her dark eyes.

"My wife," the Count introduced her.

This fresh Countess faced our captive one. Her eyes were blazing with suppressed anger. "My lady, you are no doubt feeling yourself safe from harm from these gentlemen. You are no doubt considering that you are a beautiful woman, and they clearly men who respect the sanctity of the female. You are thinking to yourself that they would not be able to bring themselves to harm you in any way." She shrugged her shapely shoulders. "And it is possible that you are correct. However, I am also a woman, and it is my friend that your scoundrels are holding to ransom. Believe me when I say that, to save her life, there is no degradation or torture I would not offer you—and with joy in my heart the whole time."

For the first time, the Countess of Clare looked concerned. She did not answer, but turned her head slightly away. I could not help looking in some small horror at the Count's wife. I, for one, had no doubt at all that the woman would cheerfully keep her promise. All the determination a man may possess is as nothing when compared to the ferocity a female may offer.

"An interesting lady, my friend," Dupin remarked. "And one I should by no means like to offend."

"That is unlikely," Monte-Cristo replied with a short laugh. "Haydée is by inclination the gentlest of women. But like a she-bear, she is ferocious in her defense of those she loves. Come, let us take refreshment as we wait the approach of our appointment."

He played the most urbane of hosts, and, it is to be confessed, his fare was more than adequate. As befitted a man of his wealth, he was able to offer us delicate pastries and a more than pleasant port. My own appetite was a little reduced due to our circumstances, but Dupin plunged in with a will.

In the eventuality, we departed for the rendezvous a shade after five. The Count showed the first hint of concern I had noticed upon his countenance. "I cannot but suspect that there will be treachery attempted," he confessed. "These Black Coats deal in dishonesty as a matter of course, and I cannot believe that they will abandon it now."

"Nor I," Dupin agreed. "You have a plan?"

"Such as it is." He gestured for his wife to take the coach, along with our captive. Jacopo and Michel accompanied her. A second coach arrived for the three of us. "I dislike placing Haydée in jeopardy," he admitted, "but she would not remain out of this. Valentine is her friend, and she will not rest until that friend is restored safely to her husband. But Jacopo and Michel will protect her with their lives, should the need arise."

"It is our task, then," Dupin remarked, "to ensure that the need does *not* arise." We took the coach to the edge of the woods. The Bois de Boulogne is a public park, and there were pedestrians strolling the grounds. Monte-Cristo's rendezvous point, however, was a little off the main thoroughfare.

"I thought that the Black Coats might be more circumspect in a semi-public place," he explained. "But perhaps we had better conceal ourselves and await their coming. Haydée and the others will arrive shortly, and I should like to be well hidden by then." So saying, he handed Dupin and myself two spare pistols, already loaded and primed. We already had our own at the ready, along with knives, should any fighting be at close quarters. We would be able to face a small party—but what would happen if the Black Coats came out in force?

We slipped from the carriage, which the driver then removed from sight, as the three of us found solid hiding places overlooking the point where the exchange would take place. It was then merely a matter of waiting, and trying to quell the doubts that my feverish mind kept raising. Had we planned well enough? Would there be sufficient of us? What might the villains arrange? Since there was no way of deducing the answers to any of these questions until the moment of truth arrived, speculation was pointless—but still my troubled mind insisted on making it.

And then the two carriages slowly approached from opposite directions. I knew ours because of the figure of Jacopo, acting the part of the driver. Michel, then, was inside the coach with his mistress. The carriage of the Black Coats had two men on the outside—and who knew how many more within. Both conveyances drew to a rest some 40 meters apart. There was a brief moment of inactivity as both sides regarded the other—and we three in hiding regarded both sides. I was concealed in bushes some 50 meters from the Black Coats' coach, and had an excellent view of what was to transpire.

The door to our coach opened, and the Countess stepped down. Haydée was as close as her shadow, and a flash of light at the Countess's throat showed that Haydée had her knife at the ready. I watched the other vehicle intently, praying that this was not some treachery. The door opened, and an unfamiliar, yet beautiful young woman stepped down, followed closely by a man with a pistol at the ready. This, I assumed, was Valentine Morel. She looked shaken and haggard, but otherwise unhurt.

"We will both release our prisoners," the man called out. "They will then walk toward each other."

"Agreed," I heard Haydée reply, her voice firm and resolute. She took the knife from the neck of the Countess, and prodded her forward with the point. Valentine, also, began to walk steadily away from her captor.

I kept flickering my eyes all about, though I wished to follow the drama occurring before me. If there was to be treachery, this was the moment. As the two women's paths crossed, the Countess suddenly sprang forward, her arm wrapping about Valentine, attempting to make her a captive once again.

There was a rush of movement as Monte-Cristo leaped from his hiding place, and he rushed to where the two women had begun to struggle. Madame Morel might be a sweet flower, but she was determined not to fall into the hands of the gang again. As the Count dashed forward, the man by the Black Coat coach whirled, his pistol at the ready. There was a flicker of movement from the carriage also, and two more armed men dropped to the ground.

I ran from concealment, the first of my pistols in my hand and ready to fire. Out of the corner of my eye, I saw that Dupin had done the same. The Black Coat men caught sight of us, and held their fire for a second, unsure where the greatest threat lay. I fired my pistol, not expecting at this range to hit anyone, but to draw their attention to me and away from the struggling women.

My ruse worked, fortunately for them, but not so for me. The man at the coach spun about and discharged his pistol at me. The bullet went as wide as mine had, but then he ran toward me, drawing a second weapon. I discarded my spent pistol and drew the second. Now that battle was joined, I would have to be more careful. I heard two further shots, but dared not break my concentration to see what was happening elsewhere. My attacker fired his second shot, and this time I heard the bullet whistle past my ear, and felt the breeze of its passage. Dropping to one knee, I steadied my pistol across my left arm, and fired carefully.

The man leaped into the air as if startled, and then fell to the ground, bleeding copiously from a wound high in his chest. I did not dare see what I had done, but came to my feet again, throwing aside the pistol and taking my last fresh weapon in hand. I looked for further targets, but there were none. Both men beside the coach were down, either dead or severely wounded. One had been shot by Dupin, the other had a knife in his stomach, clearly thrown by Jacopo, who was reclaiming it and wiping the blood from it.

Monte-Cristo had reached the struggling women, and immediately struck down the Countess with the butt of his unfired pistol. The villainous beauty collapsed with a cry, and Valentine finally broke free. She ran with a gasp of relief to clutch at her friend Haydée, and the two women hugged and greeted one another.

Panting somewhat, I reached the Count at about the same instant as Dupin. We looked down at the Countess, who was dazed, but conscious. "Shall we take her again?" I asked Monte-Cristo.

He shook his head. "I promised to exchange her for Valentine," he said, "and I always keep my word. I know she attempted to break the deal, but I hold myself to higher standards."

"So I note," Dupin said, a wry smile on his lips. He glanced about the battlefield. "It might be as well to depart now, before the police arrive. The Countess may have some difficulty explaining the situation, and I have no desire to see the inside of the Sûreté from the point of view of a suspect."

Monte-Cristo nodded. "Gentlemen, you have my thanks for your assistance in this matter. I will return this lady to her husband. My other carriage is at your convenience. Know that you have made yourself a friend today who will go to great lengths should you ever have need of his services." He held out his hand to both of us, and we shook it.

"It seems to me," Dupin remarked, "that we may have the better part of the bargain. You have shown what your friendship means quite graphically."

The coach we had taken to reach the woods had now returned, and Dupin and I hastened into it, and away from the scene. I looked back, and saw that the other coach, driven by Jacopo, also departed.

"It might have been a mistake to allow the Countess to go free," I remarked to Dupin.

"What else could we do with her?" he inquired. "We could not hold her captive, and we have no evidence to offer the police of her guilt in anything. She was, after all, out of town when the kidnapping occurred. No, a woman like that will get herself into further trouble, and we may be able to deal with her at such a time." He was lost in thought for a few moments, and then sighed. "Well, my friend, there is only one small task left for us to do." He rapped on the roof of the carriage, and called up to our driver: "To the Sûreté, if you please!"

Once there, we were ushered into the office of our acquaintance, Inspector Couperin. He glanced up from paperwork he was completing, and then motioned us to take seats and await him. As he finished his work, he laid down his pen and regarded us. "You have further information on the murder at Ste-Mathilde?" he asked.

"Not exactly," Dupin replied. "In fact, I have come to tell you that I now feel I can agree with you, and that I may have been mistaken."

Couperin preened himself. "Indeed?"

"Yes. I believe that you were quite correct—the whole business was over the honor of a lady. And I do not think that you will uncover the identity of the other party."

The Inspector was almost bursting with pleasure. "Well, Dupin," he said generously. "It takes a big man to admit that he may have been wrong. So it would seem that, at least on occasion, the romantic view of life might be right."

"It would seem so," Dupin agreed. He rose and shook the policeman's hand. "Good day, Inspector."

As we left, I frowned at my friend. "That was most duplicitous of you, Dupin."

"Was it?" he asked, casually. "I told him no lies. And I do not believe that Couperin will uncover the name of the man who threw that villain from the tower."

"You allowed him to believe that he was right and you were wrong," I protested.

"Let matters lie as they will," he said, unconcerned. "I have not so feeble an ego that I must be proven right every time. Besides, those who are important know the truth. And there is something else that I know."

"What is that?"

"That there are pipes and glasses of a fine amontillado awaiting us at the house of Monsieur Grunet. Let us not keep him waiting, my friend!"

Part of the fun of writing the Shadowmen *stories is that Jean-Marc often suggested characters for me to use that I'd never heard of before. As a result, I would go off and read adventures that were completely fresh to me. Jean-Marc was astute enough to know which characters were likely to appeal to me, so I found myself engrossed in Joseph Rouletabille, Gaston Leroux's idiosyncratic detective (*The Mystery Of The Yellow Room *is available for Black Coat Press). Mix this with a few real historical characters, the premiere of Stravinsky's* The Firebird, *and stir in a corpse...*

The Incomplete Assassin

Paris, 1910

The premiere of any new form of art in Paris is always an occasion for extravagance and celebration, and that of the 1910 season of the celebrated *Ballets Russes* was certainly no exception. As the grand evening dawned, I considered myself quite fortunate in having a friend who had secured us tickets for this new production, but as the evening drew on and the fresh corpse turned up, I was no longer as certain of my good luck.

Nothing of this will be found in the official accounts of the premiere, for reasons that will shortly become apparent. Not even a hint of it can be delved from the report delivered by my good friend Joseph Rouletabille, reporter, who was the prime mover in resolving the strange mystery.

I had known my peculiar friend some ten years before these events, and had never noted in him any particular love of music. Oh, on an evening in Maxim's, he would enjoy a gypsy violinist, or a performance of the can-can, but they can hardly be considered serious music—more frivolity than virtuosity. So when he mentioned to me that he had two tickets, and asked me to accompany him, I was both pleased and surprised. Naturally, I questioned his motives, and he smiled at me over his freshly-lit briarwood pipe.

"Music is always interesting," he explained. "Though I am not certain that I quite like the trends some composers are taking. But this performance is reputed to be something quite special. As you know, in their first season, the *Ballets Russes* took Paris by storm, so the second is a highly anticipated event, which in itself makes for news. Add to that the fact that this production, *The Firebird*, is their first with freshly-composed music, and it becomes more important. And since most of the people, including the composer, are still young, my editor felt that a young man's opinions on the night's performance would be of interest. And I am to be allowed backstage after the performance to conduct interviews, which I felt you might enjoy." He laughed. "There really is no mystery in this at all, my friend."

In that prediction, he was to be proven quite incorrect.

It seemed that everyone who was anyone in Paris was at the Théâtre du Châtelet. Though not as well-known as the Opera House—or as infamous, as the celebrated case of the Phantom of the Opera has shown—it is to my mind one of the most pleasing of the city's many temples of culture. Set a little back from the Seine, it is perhaps a trifle square and straightforward by day. But at night, illuminated from within and without, it captivates the senses. The main entrance, through five arched doorways surmounted by five equally-large arched windows, greets with warmth and a promise of the grandeur within. Pass the steps crowded with the elite of Paris society, festooned in jewels, perfumes and expensive clothing. Go through the throng in the lobby indulging in their last cigarettes before taking their seats, and into the sumptuous hall— well, it raises the excitement level, and hones the anticipation of a grand evening.

And such it proved to be. It was perhaps a trifle *avant-garde* for my tastes, but the staging could not be faulted. Parisiennes have become accustomed to horses upon their stages, and the *Ballets* used theirs sparingly. But at the point when the magician's spells are broken, and the long-frozen, gray, cobweb-festooned statues came to life, a collective gasp sped through the audience. Michel Fokine, the young choreographer, also danced superbly. I was a trifle disappointed that it was not the prodigy Nijinsky who was dancing—as, too, were many of the women in the audience. Anna Pavlova, my companion informed me, had been intended to dance the title role, but had refused, claiming the music to be undanceable. True, the music I found a trifle grating, but the main themes were certainly harmonious enough. Pavlova was replaced by Tamara Karsavina, who may not have had the same reputation, but who clearly did not find the ballet unperformable. At the end of the performance, the audience gave vent to its pleasure, and Rouletabille and I cheerfully joined in the applause.

"What do you think, Sainclair?" my companion asked me.

"Another triumph, of course," I replied.

"But not quite your taste, I take it?"

"I'm not as young as you, my friend," I replied honestly. "And consequently, I am a little stuck in my ways. Tschaikovsky is about as advanced as I can thoroughly enjoy these days." We had seen a performance of *Swan Lake* by the Kirov whilst on a recent adventure in Russia, and that still lingered favorably in my memory.

Rouletabille laughed. "And this upstart Stravinsky simply will not do, eh? Well, shall we go and hear what the upstart has to say about his success?" He led me through the maze of corridors out of the public areas of the theater and into the performers' and managers' sections. To my surprise, we were not challenged by any of the attendants whose task it was to prevent the over-zealous from mobbing Nijinsky or any of the other performers. As had happened before, it seemed that the staff here knew my companion by sight. Naturally, Rouletabille did not explain, and I knew that questioning him would be fruitless. Doubtless he had performed some service here in the past.

Champagne was flowing in the performers' rooms. Laughter, ribaldry and other slightly-coarse comments were also flowing. I had once discovered that the artistic community tends to flout accepted behavior, sometimes quite scandalously. Diaghilev himself, the manager of the *corps*, made very little secret of his own passion for his leading man, and Nijinsky made little secret of his passions for almost anyone. It must be difficult for a young man, not yet out of his teens, who is the toast of Paris, to restrain his impulses, so I do not judge him—I merely observe.

The composer, it turned out, was a smallish man, with nervous habits and a penetrating glare. He responded readily to my companion's request for a few words about the successful performance.

"This is merely the start of a revolution," he declared. "I envision more and greater ballets that will take Paris—nay, the world—by storm. I will overthrow the old, and bring in a new era." He went on in such a vein for quite some time before Rouletabille and I could make our excuses and go in search of Diaghilev for his opinions.

"What do you make of our young composer?" Rouletabille asked me, a twinkle in his eyes, as we elbowed through a crowd of stage hands. "Is he capable of such a revolution?"

"It seems to me that far too many Russians are trying to foment revolutions in too many spheres," I replied. "That young man may succeed in starting something, but whether it will ever catch on is another matter." After a moment's consideration, I added: "He is a shortish man, and I have noted that many such people like to make up for their lack of stature by seeking to make a large impact in the world."

"The Napoleon of music, eh?" Rouletabille laughed again. "I suspect he will be one of the voices of the future, my friend. Whether for good or ill—who can say?"

The crowds seemed to be thinning out, finally, as the house was getting packed back into trunks and boxes ready for the following day's performance. Dancers, now without makeup and in their normal attire, had started to filter out into the Paris streets. No doubt the crowds were also on their way for nightcaps, or a late-night meal. Things were winding down—or so I imagined. One's imagination can be so often very wrong.

Movement in the corridor ahead of us caught my eye. An elderly gentleman, quite distinguished-looking and dressed with modest but excellent taste, stopped walking when he caught sight of us. It was clear from his manner that he was expecting us to come to him, and we did not disappoint him.

"Monsieur Rouletabille, I believe?" the gentleman asked. "I have been looking for you."

"It appears that you have found me, Monsieur..."

"Strogoff," the man replied, with a formal bow that my companion returned. "I have two favors to ask of you—though it may seem presumptuous of me to ask any, since we have not been formally introduced."

Rouletabille laughed. "It is hardly necessary for Michel Strogoff to introduce himself," he commented. "Knowing your name, I also know that you are the Tsar's man, and that, if you seek me out, it is so that I may perform another service for Tsar Nicholas. I should be more than happy to offer such services."

Strogoff smiled back. "It would appear that your reputation is deserved, Monsieur." He glanced at me, clearly weighing me up. "I think I will be able to find something to occupy your companion in the meanwhile," he offered. "Some of the ballerinas have not yet departed..." It was a wonderfully polite way of saying that he could not be sure that he could trust me to hear whatever he wished to tell my friend.

Rouletabille shook his head. "It will not be necessary to trouble the young ladies—though I am sure they would be, as you say, his glass of tea. Monsieur Sainclair is a longtime friend and companion of mine, and can be relied upon utterly—as I have often done."

The Russian nodded. "If you vouch for him, then I, too, shall trust his discretion. If you gentlemen would be so kind as to follow me..."

He led us through the corridors with their thinning crowds, and into the backstage area of the theater. Here, I noticed, there were more people concentrated, and one man standing outside a closed door was clearly performing guard duty. He moved aside as we approached, and allowed Monsieur Strogoff to open the door and usher us inside.

Diaghilev himself was there, tall, distinguished and resplendent in his tails. We were in some sort of scenery storage room, and there were several of the stage hands about. There was also one corpse laid out on a long table. Rouletabille, knowing now why he had been summoned, rushed forward to examine the body. I was a trifle more reluctant, but went to do my duty as my friend's observer.

The victim was in his late twenties and dressed as a stage hand. He had been shot, once, in the chest, the bullet puncturing a lung, but narrowly missing the heart. I observed blood on the table, but there was a pool of it on the floor, closer to the door, clearly where he had been shot. There were drag marks made in the blood from the original spot behind the door, to the table, which was in the center of the room. I could tell nothing else from the body, but the smile that flickered on my friend's face told me that, as ever, it educated him far more.

He turned to Strogoff. "What can you tell me of this event?" he asked.

"Little enough, I am afraid," the Russian replied. "He was shot and killed perhaps 20 minutes ago. He lingered a short while, being found on the verge of death by the other stage hands. One of them was dispatched to find me, and the others, intelligently, barred further entry to this room. He died shortly after I arrived."

"This is a disaster," Diaghilev wailed. "When news of this reaches the newspapers, this production will become a scandal."

"It is my desire that such an event will not happen," Strogoff said, firmly. He looked at Rouletabille. "For the first of those favors I mentioned, can I ask that this even be treated as if it had never happened? The *Ballets Russes* represents the Tsar and our country, and a scandal such as murder would not help our diplomatic mission here in Paris."

Rouletabille smiled slightly. "I am not certain that I agree with you there," he said. "I suspect that if all of Paris knew of this killing, it would induce many more people to flock here for the ballet. Parisiennes can be drawn by the ghoulish. Nevertheless, I understand your request, and I am willing to abide by it. The killing will need to be reported to the Police, of course, but I can suggest a few names of those who will be willing to be most discrete."

"That would be acceptable," Strogoff agreed. He turned to the impresario. "Your reputation will be unharmed, and your performances will continue unhindered—at least, by any breath of *this* scandal."

"Thank you!" Diaghilev exclaimed, delightedly shaking my friend's hand. "Now, I must be off—if Diaghilev does not party this night, some tragedy will be suspected. I shall force myself to be witty and gay." He rushed from the room.

Rouletabille smiled at me. "I suspect he will not need to force himself too strenuously," he observed. Then he turned to Strogoff. "And the second favor you wish of me?"

The Russian gestured at the table. "To uncover who did this deed—and why. I have always been more of a man of action than a man of deliberation, I must confess, and I can see nothing here to help me understand this tragedy."

"Each to his own *métier*," my companion said. "I shall see what effects my own small skills may have." He turned to the stage hands. "This man was one of your company?" he asked. "But it is clear that he has been with you only a short while."

"Barely two months," one of the others agreed. "His name is Zhadikov. But how could you know that?"

"His hands," Rouletabille said, casually. "I see that the four of you have calluses from your work; this man is barely starting to form them. Hence, he joined you recently. Also, he clearly did little manual work before this, which would be odd in a man as old as this."

"He spoke little of his background," a second man offered. "Nor did he socialize with us."

"That is understandable, since he did not come here to find work."

Strogoff looked curiously at my companion. "How can you be so certain of that?"

"His hands, once again, Monsieur," Rouletabille said. "Always examine the extremities, for they will tell you much about a man. In this instance, if you look at the hands of these good workers, you will see that their fingernails are broken, due to the work they perform." He held up the left hand of the dead man. "Zhadikov, by contrast, has hands that were clearly manicured recently, as his nails are unbroken and filed. Hence, he is a man with his own income, and therefore he did not come here because he needed work. Rather, he came here because there was something here for him." He looked at the workers again. "Did he speak at all before he died?"

"A little," the first stage hand said. "But he was delirious, and his words made no sense. I asked him who had done this to him, and he replied, simply, *More...*" The man shrugged. "He was having great difficulty breathing, and spoke no further."

"That is understandable." My companion considered for a moment, and then looked at Strogoff. "I take it that these four good men may be relied upon to say nothing of what they have witnessed?"

"They may be French and not Russian, but they are reliable," Strogoff replied.

"Good. Then all that needs be done now, I think, is to summon an ambulance."

Strogoff looked astonished, as well he might—he did not have the advantage I had of knowing my friend often made suggestions that at first might appear more than a trifle odd, but that, eventually, would make perfect sense. "An ambulance?" he repeated. "But this man is dead."

"Perhaps he is," Rouletabille agreed, examining the body once again. "*But he may not necessarily remain that way*—at least, not to the murderer. He is a young, well-built man. If you can aid me with a little of the stage makeup here and a wig, I imagine that I might be mistaken for him, especially at this time of night."

Strogoff's eyes sparkled. "Ah! You are laying a trap?"

"Indeed I am." Rouletabille smiled. "I must confess that I am, from time to time, a lazy man. I don't see why I should race all over Paris searching for the man when I can force him to come to me." He turned to the four workmen and myself. "Now, I require of you all to be consistent in this story. When the ambulance arrives, it will cause some curiosity in passersby outside the theater. If anyone should ask you, tell them merely that a stage hand has been injured, and is being taken for emergency medical aid. If asked for further details, say only that the man is expected to recover fully. Then say no more."

I nodded. "You expect, of course, that we shall be asked."

"I rely upon it. And if I understand the murderer correctly, it is inevitable." He clapped me on the shoulder. "Stay at the theater here no more than a quarter-hour after the ambulance leaves. Then hurry at once to the hospital. Dr. Génessier is on duty tonight, and I believe I can rely on his skills to ensure that I—as the injured stage hand—will make a surprisingly wonderful recovery."

Most of the audience and the performers had left the theater by the time that the ambulance arrived. It departed a few moments later, with my friend on a stretcher in the back. A small crowd only had gathered, mostly of the well-dressed in no hurry to return to their homes after an evening out. As Rouletabille had predicted, several of them wondered aloud what was happening. As per my instructions, I said only that a stage hand had been somewhat injured.

A well-dressed young man asked casually how this could have happened.

I shrugged. "I know few details," I said. "Only that his wound is apparently not severe, and that the medical attendants believe he will recover after surgery at the local hospital." I tipped my hat. "Now, really, I must be off. A glass of cognac will steady my nerves." I hurried away, and three blocks later I hailed a cab.

It deposited me at the hospital a few minutes later. I hurried to the admitting station, and discovered that a M. Zhadikov had been rushed into surgery, and that Dr. Génessier was operating. After this, he should be taken to room 301. I would be allowed to wait there, as Dr. Génessier had already approved this.

Hurrying to the room, I found that there was already a patient in the bed—my friend Rouletabille, naturally. The room was dimly-lit, and with a wig and a little applied makeup, he did bear a passing resemblance to the murdered man. There was with him an elderly attendant, arranging water and flowers beside the bed.

"Sainclair, excellent," my friend said, happily. "Everything went as expected?" he asked me.

"Indeed," I agreed. "I was questioned after I left the theater by a group of onlookers, and then left to come here and join you." I knew his methods well by this time, and yet I could not help but wonder how he could be so certain that the murderer would follow along. But there was little point in questioning him—Rouletabille explained what he wished only when he wanted.

"Good. Then come, sit by my bedside as if you were some concerned relative, and we shall await events." He glanced at the attendant. "I think that will be all."

"As you wish," the old man said, and he left the room, closing the door behind him.

"Turn down the light a trifle, if you would," Rouletabille suggested. "Shadows are our friends when we are in such a rough disguise as this."

We sat quietly together, and listened, whilst pretending to do nothing of the sort. It was by now past midnight, and the hospital was fairly quiet. From time to time footsteps approached the room, and we both tensed. But on each occasion, they passed on by. We had sat there almost an hour when we heard further footsteps—only these stopped outside the door instead of moving on.

I glanced around as the door opened. It was difficult to make out details, as we were in such gloom, but I could see our visitor was the well-dressed young man I had spoken to outside the theater.

"So," he said, harshly, "despite my efforts, you still thwart me, Zhadikov. But no more!" He raised his right hand, which held a pistol. "This time, farewell!"

The events of the next few seconds were quite confused. I launched myself from my chair, hoping to intercept the man before he could fire, despite the distance between us. Rouletabille, with his customary agility, threw himself from the bed toward the floor. And the elderly attendant sprang onto the assassin from behind.

The bullet passed over my head, and impacted in the now-vacant bed. With surprising skill and strength, the old attendant wrestled the pistol from the young man's grip, and then Rouletabille and I helped to subdue the now crazed and screaming man. A few moments later, several strong policemen joined in the struggle, and the howling assassin was dragged off to a cell. Rouletabille promised to be along shortly to explain the charges against him, and the corridor was soon almost empty again.

"Dr. Génessier has, as I instructed, kept the hospital staff from this area," Rouletabille explained to me.

"Except this attendant," I said, "who proved to be of such valuable assistance."

The attendant laughed, and drew off his own wig, and wiped his face. I saw with surprise that under the makeup it was none other than Michel Strogoff. "It has been a long time since my duties have been quite so physical," he admitted. "And I am sure I shall pay for it by waking aching in the morning. But it has been worth it." He reached out a hand to my friend. "Monsieur Rouletabille, your aid has been invaluable. But perhaps you would now explain how you knew that this would happen?"

"By all means," he agreed. "But it was all quite obvious from the scene of the murder—if only you knew how to interpret the facts."

Strogoff looked at me in astonishment. "You are his colleague—do you know what he means?"

"Rarely ever," I confessed, with a smile. "Until he expounds, and then you wonder how you could have missed it all along."

Rouletabille laughed. "Come, Sainclair, you are an intelligent man—was all of this truly baffling to you?"

"It was, as you know it always is," I responded. "I cannot see the link between the theater and here—save for the obvious. You made the killer believe that his murder had not be accomplished, and so forced him to try a second time. But how could you know that he would do so? After all, it might have been a crime of the moment—that Zhadikov had stumbled over the killer committing some crime and been killed for it."

"No, the facts did not admit to that as a possibility," my friend replied. "Though the murder *was*, indeed, a crime of sudden intent. The first clue was the dying man's last word."

"He said only *More*," I protested. "That means very little."

"It means everything. Zhadikov was Russian, and the stage hands who found him were French. What he wished to say had to be translated for them to understand. As you know, there are a number of revolutionary groups involved in Russia politics at the moment. Many feel that their country needs a change in rulership, often through violence. Zhadikov, a wealthy man, joined this company here in Paris as a stage hand? Why? Clearly because here he had contacts with people allowed to travel freely to and from Russia. I am certain that it will be found that Zhadikov—under another name—was on a list of known activists, and would not be allowed there himself. Here, at the *Ballets Russes*, he could work unknown and meet his contacts for intelligences.

"Our assassin, attending the *Ballets* himself, must have seen and recognized Zhadikov. How and why? Just seven years ago, the Russian Social Democratic Labor Party split on matters of policy. One branch became known as the Bolsheviks, the other as the Menshehviks. No love has been lost between the two factions. Bolshehvik, of course, means *more*, because they demanded more; Menshevik means *less* because they are less extreme."

The matter was starting to become clearer. "So!" I exclaimed. "Both men were revolutionaries, but on opposite sides of the issue."

"Quite so. And their chance meeting here led our killer to a swift decision. Seeing Zhadikov in the theater, he knew he had stumbled onto a spy ring belonging to his opponents. The only one he recognized was Zhadikov, so he would have to act to close down the ring. How? By making the others think they might become his next victims. He followed Zhadikov into the backstage change room and killed him. It then became important that Zhadikov be discovered swiftly, and his death become a warning."

I frowned. "But why was the shot itself not heard?"

"The backstage areas are well soundproofed," Strogoff interjected. "It would not do to have activities there heard on the stage." That I could understand.

"But you no doubt noticed that the place where Zhadikov had been killed was behind the door," Rouletabille said. "That did not suit our killer's purpose—it was always possible that in the bustle and confusion of a premiere that the body might not be found immediately. He needed to strike instant horror into his quarry, so the body *must* be found before the end of the evening. So he dragged the dying man across the room and then positioned him on the table—in clear view of anyone who opened the door."

"But how did you know it was the killer who dragged the poor man, and not the stage hands?" I objected.

Rouletabille smiled. "My friend, they are four strong men, used to moving heavy pieces of stage equipment. If they had stumbled across the dying body of their friend, they would not have *dragged* it—they would have picked it up and carried it to the table. So, no, the killer moved the body, and clearly so that it would be seen. Most killers *hide* their victims—this one did the opposite, so it obviously was in order that the corpse should serve as a warning."

Strogoff smiled. "And, of course, you made the killer think that his plan had come apart, and that the victim was still alive. He then *had* to follow, and attempt the murder again—and so we have him." The Russian shook his head. "I cannot believe that we saw the same things as you, and yet understood so little."

"As I remarked before," my companion said, "each of us to his own *métier*. Fortunately for you, you had on hand the one man in all of Paris who would be able to resolve your mystery. If you will allow me to intrude just a fraction on your profession, though, I would suggest that you begin to search through the personnel of the *Ballets* to discover Zhadikov's co-conspirators."

"Indeed I shall," Strogoff agreed. "And I should like to meet with both of you gentlemen again, to discuss the thanks my Tsar will undoubtedly wish passed along to you." He bowed formally to us both, and left.

I turned to Rouletabille, who had by now shed his disguise and recovered his evening clothes. "Well, my friend—now what?"

He examined his pocket watch. "Well, with a little luck, the crowds may have started to thin. Perhaps we might do well to see if either of us has sufficient influence to get a table at

Maxim's? All of this mental activity has left me quite famished."

Another of Jean-Marc's suggestions was Isidore Beautrelet, created by Maurice Leblanc. He appears in The Hollow Needle *(available from Black Coat Press), along with Arsene Lupin and Sherlock Holmes – a thoroughly grand read. All I needed, then, was a one-time assistant for him – so it was time to head back to W.E. Johns. Any boy growing up in England in the Fifties and Sixties inevitably read Johns. His most famous creation was Biggles, the pilot hero of World War 1. Johns continually updated (and rejuvenated) him over the decades in dozens of action adventures. He was, perhaps, the very essence of the* Boy's Own *adventures, so, naturally, I had to use him. Oh, and stay tuned – he will be back...*

The Successful Failure

Fontainebleau, 1913

The Police were still buzzing about the Musée du Château de Fontainebleau when Isidore Beautrelet ambled up to the entrance. Most of the men appeared bored, but were attempting to seem active. Beautrelet could tell, however, that they were studiously doing nothing of any importance. While he knew that sometimes persons entered the Police force with low aims, it was a trifle puzzling that so many of them should be concentrated in such a small area. It was even more puzzling when he discovered that they were there in the company of Commissaire Guichard, an efficient and uncommonly able officer whom Beautrelet had once had occasion to assist. It was not like him to tolerate such obvious inefficiency in his men. They were, however, efficient enough to refuse entry to Beautrelet, but sent word to the Commissioner.

"Beautrelet!" the Policeman called out a few moments later, hurrying to greet the young student. "I don't know how you managed to hear of this so quickly, but I am sorry to say that there can be nothing in this minor mystery that could possibly be of interest to you."

Beautrelet spread his hands. "In all innocence, Commissaire," he vowed, "I was not even aware that there *was* any mystery."

"Indeed? Then why does your arrival coincide with a bungled burglary attempt?"

Beautrelet smiled. "Simple chance," he said. "I am currently occupied at university with the study of art, and the Musée de Fontainebleau has an exceptionally fine collection of medieval icons. I am here purely as a member of the public, hoping to broaden my grasp on the finer points of such masterpieces."

"I must confess I am relieved," Guichard said. "For one ghastly moment, when I saw you striding up the pathway, I was certain that there was some dreadful crime that I was completely overlooking, and which you were already well upon your way to solving."

The young man laughed. "Nothing like that, at all. As I said, I had no idea that any crime had been committed."

"Technically, one hasn't," the Commissioner said. "The would-be thieves were disturbed and left the premises empty-handed. I am here merely in the attempt to see if they left any clues as to their identity behind. But the search has been unsuccessful—they were too professional to make such mistakes."

"Indeed?" Beautrelet now understood why so many Policemen were attempting to look useful without actually working—there was nothing to find, so little need to exert oneself. "Then I am sorry I caused you any consternation. Do you have any notion when the Museum will be opened to the public again? I have made a fairly strenuous trip out here, and would hate to be turned away without seeing the remarkable triptychs they possess."

Guichard shrugged, a gesture that involved moving much of his upper body; it was most expressive. "The general public—I do not know. But for you, I am sure I can arrange something. Come with me." He led the way inside the neo-Gothic building, where two worried-looking gentlemen were pacing impatiently. The Museum Director, an older man, with thinning grey hair slicked and precisely combed back, rushed with as much dignity as he was able to meet them.

"Commissaire," he said, urgently, "nothing was stolen, nothing was harmed. How much longer must we be inconvenienced by all of these brutish bluecoats clomping about my premises?"

"Monsieur Voisin," the Policeman said politely, "we are completing our investigation and will shortly be leaving. In the meantime, may I be permitted to introduce you to Monsieur Isidore Beautrelet? He is a student of art, and I would ask you to be kind enough to allow him to study whatever he wishes."

The second man had arrived by now, and at the name his eyebrows shot up. "Isidore Beautrelet?" he asked. "The celebrated young detective? You have called him in to consult upon this minor case?"

Guichard shook his head. "No, Monsieur Poitevin, he is not here in any capacity save that as a student of art. He wishes to examine your triptychs to aid him in his studies in school. I merely introduce him to you gentlemen in the hopes that you will be kind enough to extend him courtesies beyond that of the average member of the public."

"But of course, Commissaire," Poitevin agreed. "We would be most pleased." He turned to Beautrelet. "In fact, you have timed your visit just right—for today we are packaging the triptychs in seven cases for shipment to the Louvre Museum tomorrow morning, where they will be on display for several months."

"This is all very well," the Director complained to the Commissioner. "But when may we get back to normal? And when will you remove your suspect?"

"Suspect?" Beautrelet's eyes sparkled. "Come, Inspector, you made no mention of having seized a villain!"

"Hardly that," Guichard laughed. "He is merely a young boy who cannot account for his activities too well. I would not even call him a suspect—merely suspicious. He's a young Englishman who speaks remarkably good French, but who appears to me to be a trifle lunatic."

"You intrigue me," Beautrelet confessed. "A crime that is not a crime, and a suspect who is not a suspect? It seems a shame that there is no real mystery here then, all things considered."

"There's nothing to get your fertile little brain overly interested," the Policeman insisted.

"Quite," Poitevin agreed. "It was merely a botched robbery, and the thieves managed to steal absolutely nothing. The young Englishman was merely lurking about and unable to account for himself. I'm sure he's merely a simpleton, like so many of that island race."

Beautrelet sighed. "Then it is perhaps a bad thing that all of this non-mystery has excited my perhaps overly-active imagination. Might I be permitted to learn the facts of this non-case?"

"They are simply told," Guichard replied. "At 2 a.m., the night guards made their rounds and found nothing amiss. They retraced their steps precisely on schedule at 2:27 a.m., and discovered a door ajar. One of the guards sounded the alarm, and three men promptly fled through the gardens. The guards telephoned the police, the Director and Monsieur Poitevin. We all arrived here roughly together. While these two gentlemen examined for any missing objects, I and my men searched for clues. But the thieves were obviously professionals, and had left nothing to be discovered."

"And my assistant and I checked the collection thoroughly," Monsieur Voisin added. "We soon ascertained that nothing had been stolen. The thieves were obviously interrupted before they could steal anything."

The Commissioner nodded. "And one of my men, searching the general area, came across a young English boy who was not able to explain his presence here with any clarity, so he was apprehended."

"Interesting," Beautrelet commented. "There is nothing missing, and the guards say that the men were carrying nothing?"

"Nothing," Voisin confirmed.

"Might I perhaps be allowed to see the room in which they were disturbed?" Beautrelet asked the Director. After a moment, the older man shrugged.

"The Police have thoroughly investigated, but I can see no reason to refuse such a simple request. If you would follow me?" He led the way from the entrance hall into a side room.

Beautrelet noted that the walls were lined with paintings, none of which were of great value or of interest—minor works for the most part by French landscape painters. There were also some small statues on pedestals, including two which even his untrained eye could see were Greek originals, dating back to at least 300 BC. They appeared to be quite fine. "Curious," he commented.

"What is?" asked Director Voisin, frowning.

"Assume for a moment, if you are able, that you are an art thief. You determine to break into the Musée de Fontainebleau. What among the collection would you steal?"

"Why..." The older man spluttered a moment, and then scowled. "I would take the icons, I imagine."

"So, too, would I," Beautrelet agreed. "Yet, if I recall the floor plans for this Museum correctly, the icons are housed upstairs, are they not?"

"Yes," Poitevin agreed. "I imagine that the thieves intended to head there, but were startled and fled instead."

"Yes, I think most people would imagine that," Beautrelet agreed. "Is it not odd, then, that they took nothing?" He gestured toward the two statues. "Even if I were fleeing in fear from the guards, I think I would have the presence of mind to help myself to those rather valuable objects."

"Perhaps the thieves did not realize how valuable they are?" Poitevin suggested.

"That is always possible," Beautrelet agreed. "But you would imagine that anyone attempting to rob an art museum would know the value of what they are stealing."

"Unless they were focused in on stealing a certain set of items," Guichard offered. "They may have been specialists."

"Again, it is possible." The young man rubbed his hands together. "Now, what about your suspect? Pardon me, your non-suspect?"

The Commissioner laughed. "Whatever he is, I think you'll find him interesting."

He led his friend to a door marked *Privé*, and they passed into a rather crowded office. There was a desk and a set of filing cabinets, but a large portion of the room was taken up with a number of packing cases. Into what small space was left were crowded a bored-looking policeman and a teenaged boy who looked decidedly cross.

He was fair-haired, and appeared to be about 14—though, as he was small, Beautrelet decided he might just be a little older. He stood straight, and controlled his temper with obvious difficulty. Guichard gestured toward the youth. "This is Mr. James Big… Big…" He stumbled over the name and finally gave up, shrugging. "One of those impossible, unpronounceable English names."

"No matter," Beautrelet decided. "James will do nicely." He smiled at the youth, receiving another scowl in return. "Now, perhaps you can explain why you are found so close to a spectacularly unsuccessful robbery?"

"I know nothing about any robbery," the young man growled. "I was merely coming to the Museum to talk to the Director about his cousin."

"My cousin?" Voisin spluttered, confused. "Do you know him?"

"Not at all," James replied. "But I should like to. Is he not the man who, partnered with the redoubtable Monsieur Blériot, who constructed aircraft until quite recently?"

"Oh, that folly!" The Director sighed. "Yes, I'm afraid he is. It's all nonsense, you know. It will never catch on."

The youth glared at him. "This? This from a man whose country has invented the aerial show? It would seem that your career of glorifying the past has left you dwelling there also— the *airoplane* is the coming thing," he pronounced. "It will shape our very future. Mankind will no longer be bound by the shackles of the ground, but will soar to wherever his imagination can take him. And I aim to be in the forefront of those so soaring."

Beautrelet couldn't help chuckling at this statement, which earned him another of the boy's dark glares. "You are evidently an aero enthusiast," the young detective commented. "I find it difficult to believe you had anything at all to do with this robbery."

"That's what I've been trying to tell these idiotic Policemen for more than an hour now," James growled. "But they refuse to listen."

"We have listened now," Commissaire Guichard pointed out. He turned to Beautrelet. "My friend, I cannot simply release this youth until my investigations are complete. Perhaps I could impose upon you to keep an eye on him for me, and so free up the energies of my men?"

Beautrelet considered the proposal. There was something in this stiff-backed and stiff-necked young man that he found appealing. Truth be told, James reminded him of himself, but a few years back. And it might not be a bad idea if he had a hand in what he was already starting to plan... "Very well, Commissaire," he agreed. "If James is agreeable, I will happily take him into my custody."

"Are you another of these damnable Policemen?" the young man demanded.

"No; like you, I am a student. I merely dabble in detection as a sideline." He held out a hand. "My name is Isidore Beautrelet."

"James Bigglesworth," the other replied. After a moment's hesitation, he shook the offered hand.

Beautrelet could see why Guichard had faced problems attempting to pronounce such a surname! "Well, James," he said, "perhaps you'd be kind enough to accompany me? While the Commissaire clears up what details he can, I should like to have a chance to examine the triptychs I came to see, before they are packaged and shipped away. We do not have much time, it would seem."

The young man's face fell—he clearly had little interest in art, and wished only to get into his beloved aerial craft. Beautrelet had a little pity for the youth, but a little art education could hardly hurt James. Monsieur Poitevin took them up the wide marble stairs to the room where the icons were stored in cases that, he noted, were wired for an electrical alarm. James attended rather sullenly, but Beautrelet found immense pleasure in examining the exquisite workmanship. From time to time, he pointed out details to the young man—the subtle workmanship of the gold leaf on one piece, the enameling on a second, or the subtle placement of jewels to enhance the scene on a third. Despite his initial sullen response, James soon began pointing out details without being prompted.

"You enjoy the artwork after all," Beautrelet commented with a slight smile.

"It's not as good at the work Monsieur Blériot manages on his rotary engines," James answered, "but there is skill of a kind here, and they are rather pleasing to the eye." He considered for a moment. "Are they very valuable, then?"

Beautrelet nodded. "I hesitate to use the word *priceless*, for each does have a price, but they are certainly irreplaceable—and much desired. There are collectors who would love to have these in their own hands, even if theft were involved."

"But the thieves apparently mucked the whole thing up," James said.

"So the Police believe," agreed the detective.

James didn't misunderstand the comment. "But you do not?" he asked, finally showing a little life.

"I do not," Beautrelet agreed. "The thieves, as the Police agree, were professionals. And yet they managed such a gross mistake as to not know the times the Museum guards made their rounds? Does that not sound like a contradiction in terms?"

"Yes," James agreed, thoughtfully. "If I were going to rob this place, that's one of the first things I'd want to discover. I'd need to know how long I had to swipe the stuff."

"And yet the Police would have us believe that these criminals were not as smart as two scholars, eh?" Beautrelet grinned. "Now, I don't know about you, but I find myself growing famished. Why do we not talk further over a plate in the local café?" And he steadfastly refused to be drawn on the subject of the robbery attempt until they were both seated and dining on a rather pleasant dish of chicken.

"Right," James said, his mouth rather full, "you don't buy this theory that the robbery was unsuccessful, then?"

"Not quite," Beautrelet answered. "I do not believe that it should be termed a robbery at all. The aim was never to steal anything."

James halted, his next fork load close to his mouth. "Then why break into the Museum at all?"

"Precisely!" Beautrelet beamed. "The Police, assuming the purpose to be robbery, do not consider any other possibility. I, on the other hand, approach the matter in my own way."

"You mean, you work like Mr. Sherlock Holmes— search out clues, and add them together to solve the mystery?" said James.

"I do not," Beautrelet replied, somewhat primly. "That sort of thing is all very well for Mr. Holmes, but it has little bearing on my methods. What I do is to examine the crime. I then form a theory as to how it is committed, and why, and then I go in search of the evidence necessary to prove me either correct or incorrect. Once I am certain I know how the crime has been committed, then I know what evidence must be there for my theory to be true. So!" He sat back from his meal and steepled his fingers together. "I begin with the idea that the thieves—we may as well call them that, even though they stole nothing—yet!—accomplished their purpose in breaking into the museum. Knowing the timetable the guards must follow, they allowed themselves to be seen and chased, empty-handed, from the premises. If they did not *take* anything from the museum, then, logically, their mission was to bring something *into* the place."

"Something in?" James was clearly confused. "Why would they want to do that?"

"That is the very essence of the problem," Beautrelet said, with some satisfaction. "When we know the answer to that, then we shall uncover the whole plot. So—their aim was not to steal, but to plant something in the Museum. Something that will make their intended target simpler to steal later, clearly. Their target *must* be the icons—aside from the fact that they are the most valuable items that the museum owns, we know that many of them are soon to be sent to the Louvre on loan for several months. The matter of the timing can hardly be coincidental. Now, as well-guarded as this museum is, the Louvre is so much more defended. Since the theft of the *Mona Lisa* from there two years ago, security has been increased and improved. The chance of stealing the icons from there must be minuscule. So, they are to be taken here."

"But they weren't taken," James argued.

"No, and why not? For the first reason, because it would take time to steal them. You were in that room with me, and saw the exhibits. All of the items are under glass, and there are electrical alarms affixed the cases. No doubt a moderately skillful thief could get around this problem, but it would take time. And time is what our criminals do not have. The guards make their rounds in such a fashion that the rooms are examined every seven minutes. That is clearly not enough time to steal the icons, no matter how expeditious the thief is."

"I see," James nodded. "But you said this was only the first reason; there are more?"

"One other," Beautrelet informed him. "Let us assume that the thieves did somehow manage to steal the icons and make their getaway. The alarm would be raised within minutes. Sleepy as the Police are in this town, even they would be able to respond in time, perhaps, to intercept the fleeing villains. And, in any case, even if the thieves escaped, everyone would know that the icons were missing, and a watch would be set for them. The icons are indeed beautiful and valuable, but there are not many places where they could be sold. Oh, the jewels and gold in them would be intrinsically valuable, but it is as complete works of art that they would fetch the most money—and once word of the theft was issued, the market for the icons would close."

James considered these points. "But you are making a case *against* stealing the treasures," he objected.

"Indeed I am," beamed Beautrelet. "And, in fact, the icons were *not* taken!"

"I must confess, I am getting extremely confused," James said with a frown. "You are arguing that no crime has been committed."

Beautrelet shrugged. "Well, there is the matter of breaking and entering, and criminal trespass—but, other than that, no crime *has* been committed—*yet*. What has occurred is merely the setting for the real crime—and a rather cunning one at that."

"But I'm blowed if I can see what the crime is yet!" James exclaimed in exasperation.

"That is because you were not present when the final clue was uttered," the detective consoled him. "I, however, was. Director Voisin mentioned that the icons would be sent to the Louvre in the morning, in seven packing cases."

James blinked. "Seven? But there were *eight* cases in the room." He smiled depreciatingly. "I don't normally count such things, but I was in there a while, and had little else to occupy my mind."

Beautrelet chuckled. "Yet you did note the one salient fact—seven cases are being sent out, but there are eight awaiting pickup." He examined his new friend with curiosity—did the English boy have the brains to work the rest out for himself?

After a moment, James's face lit up. "Of course!" he exclaimed. "The thieves brought in the extra crate… filled with replicas of the icons they wished to steal, no doubt. This crate must be marked in some way, so that they can tell it apart from the crate with the *real* icons… Then, when the crates are removed, the thieves will intercept the van carrying them and steal the crate that they want." He considered a moment further, then nodded with conviction. "They will set the raid up, like the raid on the Museum, so it will look as though they have failed again. There will, after all, still be *seven* packaging crates on the truck when they leave. The fakes will go on display at the Louvre. Sooner or later, someone will spot the deception, but by that point, the real icons will have been sold to collectors and the thieves long vanished."

Beautrelet beamed. "James, I do believe you have followed my thought processes almost exactly. We shall make a detective of you yet."

"Right," James said, putting down his utensils. "So we now tell the Police?"

"No, we do not," Beautrelet said sharply. "And that for two reasons. Firstly, because it is clear that there is someone on the inside working with the gang. This person must have supplied them with precise descriptions and photographs of the icons so that replicas could be forged, and must, clearly, be the one who is watching over the shipment. I do not have enough evidence to accuse any specific individual, so if the Police strike now, the truly guilty man will go free."

James nodded, understanding this. "And the second reason?"

"The Police have the same facts that we have; if they are not bright enough to follow them to the same conclusion we have, then I do not see why they should have the credit for the arrest of the thieves. Let the glory come to those who have worked for it."

The English boy's face lit up. "You propose that *we* capture the gang ourselves?"

"I do indeed."

James looked worried again. "Just the two of us? There may be many of them, and they may well be armed."

"Are you any good with a pistol?" Beautrelet asked him, casually.

"I'm a decent shot," James assured him. "I've had plenty of practice—I grew up in India, and did a lot of hunting."

"Fine. Then you shall carry my spare pistol, and I shall have one also. But I do not aim to get into a fight—I am sorry to have to say it, but I am not a terribly bold man. I prefer the cerebral arts to fisticuffs, and usually leave that side of things to the Police. No, I propose we arm ourselves simply in case of the unexpected. I propose also that we follow the delivery van, unseen, and then wait for the robbery. Once it is accomplished, we must then follow the thieves back to their hiding place, and the alert the local constabulary. They are professionals, and I am happy to leave the actual capture to them. I have, however, one small problem yet to overcome in my plan."

"And that is?" James prompted.

"How we shall be able to follow the thieves without being observed doing so by them. I shall have to think about it for a while."

James shook his head. "No, I do believe that I can work something out," he said. "The only problem is that what I have in mind isn't exactly legal."

Beautrelet made an airy gesture. "We shall be preventing a major crime—I should think my standing with the Police is good enough that bending the rules a trifle will be overlooked." He regarded James with amusement. "What do you have in mind?"

The English youth shook his head. "Let me plan it out before I tell you," he suggested. "Meanwhile, do you think we could manage some sort of disguise? It might be a good idea."

Beautrelet beamed; if there was one thing he enjoyed, it was in assuming a really convincing disguise. "I imagine that something of the sort might be arranged."

"It would help if you could make me look a trifle older," James suggested.

"A fake beard and moustache should do admirably," the detective decided. "And I shall become an itinerant painter—there are some sights hereabouts well worth a canvas or two, if I were only skilled enough."

"Right," James said, happily. "Then let's finish eating, and get to work." He lay down his utensils.

Beautrelet smiled at his eager young friend. "I think we have time for a little pastry first..."

The following morning found Beautrelet at his easel two blocks from the Château, watching carefully whilst sketching the building. A large, noisy truck had drawn up earlier, and four workmen were engaged in loading the crates aboard. They were being watched carefully by several Policemen under the personal supervision of Commissaire Guichard. The good Commissioner had glanced over at Beautrelet several times with evident suspicion, but the disguise the detective wore—a goatee beard, a monocle and painter's smocks—served to hide his true identity from his friend.

All that was missing was James. The young man had vanished yesterday afternoon for a while in his own disguise, and had reappeared at supper time evidently rather proud of himself. He refused to explain how he had arranged for the truck to be followed, merely promising that they would not be observed. Then he had vanished after breakfast, and failed to reappear.

The rear of the truck was closed up, and there was a round of paperwork that was signed. Beautrelet was getting quite alarmed that his companion was still missing. It was starting to look as though his plans would crash and burn.

"Sorry I'm late," James apologized, hurrying up. "But I had the devil of a time getting petrol. Some of your country-men are lazy beggars at this time in the morning. Am I too late?"

"No," Beautrelet informed him, considerably relieved. He gestured, though carefully—he did not wish to draw attention. "They are just about ready to leave."

"Then perhaps we should also," James said. "I'll give you a hand with your art supplies, if you like." Together, they packed everything away. They stopped at the café on their way, slipping the materials just inside the door, and then James led the way out of the town and into a large field.

Beautrelet stopped dead in his tracks, his face ashen. "What is that contraption?"

James laughed easily. "That *contraption*, as you call it, is one of the most advanced *airoplanes* in the world—the Morane-Saulnier Type L. There are only a half-dozen yet constructed, and I was lucky indeed to be able to borrow it. It isn't likely to be missed for a couple of hours yet."

"An aircraft?" the detective spluttered. "You propose that we use that... monstrosity to follow the van?"

"It's the best idea," James said, airily. "Those thieves will be looking behind them on the road for pursuit—not hundreds of feet over their heads."

"But... but... that machine must be very noisy!" Beautrelet protested.

"They won't hear a thing over the racket their own motor is making," James answered. "Besides, we'll be pretty high up—at least a thousand feet."

"A thousand feet?" the detective said, weakly. "In the air? My friend, you are insane! I told you before, I am not the most courageous of men, and I much prefer that my feet stay planted firmly on the ground. Besides, I do not trust these airplanes—they have a great tendency to crash."

"Not this beauty," James said happily, stroking the fabric of the fuselage. "It's got a very reliable Gnome Lambda 7 cylinder rotary engine, and it flies like a dream. I know—I had to fly it here this morning. Come on, you'll love it."

"I would hate it—if I were to try it, which I shall not!" The detective shook his head. "I am not getting into that death trap for anything this world has to offer!"

James sighed. "Well, then, I guess the crooks will get the better of us, because there's no other way to follow them without their knowledge." He sighed heavily. "I guess I'll just have to live with failure, then—the knowledge that they have beaten us."

Beautrelet was no fool, and could see immediately James's aim. But, at the same time, he had to confess his hand was well-played. If there was one thing Beautrelet would never allow, it was defeat. He knew it was stubborn pride and a touch of arrogance in his own character, and no doubt a flaw. But he would never allow himself to be beaten. Swallowing hard, he screwed up every last little bit of courage he possessed—and, as he had confessed, it was not a large supply—and he set his hand to the fragile craft.

"Help me aboard," he said through gritted teeth.

James helped him into the second seat, and then hopped cheerfully into the pilot's seat. "Engine's still warm and we shouldn't have much problem," he announced. The beastly machine roared to frightening life, and it took every gram of will-power the detective possessed not to leap, screaming, from the machine and back to the safety of the dear Earth.

Then James let out the throttle, and the plane taxied across the field, gathering speed as it went. It had to be going far faster than Beautrelet had ever traveled before—certainly more than 50 kph—and then it somehow managed to stagger into the air. Beautrelet was wishing sincerely he had not breakfasted so well.

The ground fell away below him, and he fought back panic that threatened to overwhelm his reason.

"This is the life, eh?" James laughed, his voice snatched away by the wind through the struts.

Life? This looked like death to Beautrelet! They were being suspended in the air only by the strength of a noisy, smelly engine and a large wing above their heads. At any second the whole insane contraption might fail, and they would plunge to their inevitable and grisly deaths... He strove to force this ghastly image from his mind.

James maneuvered the craft around, and a moment later he called out: "There's the road to Paris, and I can see the truck on its way. Take a look."

"You must be insane," Beautrelet complained. "I have no intention of staring over the side of this machine. I shall merely sit here and suffer."

"Oh, chin up, old man," James said cheerfully. "You'll get to love this in no time at all."

"You are quite correct," the detective agreed. "At no time at all will I get to love this. Keep your attention on the road, and I shall sit quietly here and panic until we are on the ground once again."

The journey was an absolute misery. Beautrelet sat as still as he was able, eyes screwed shut, attempting to breath regularly. Fear almost overwhelmed him, and it was only by shutting out the thought of what they were doing that he was able to remain seated. He allowed James to do the work, being updated by the young man from time to time.

"Ah!" James called, finally. "The truck has stopped! Some kind of a blockade." Beautrelet's stomach almost exited his mouth as the mad English youth dropped the plane down for a closer look. "A tree has been felled, which has forced the truck to stop. Ah, here's a second truck, blocking retreat— obviously the crooks we've been expecting. They have guns held on the workmen, and have started to unfasten the back of the truck. A couple of the men have gone in... and they're bringing out one crate and transferring it now... The workmen are being held in the cab, so they haven't seen it go... And here now comes the Police escort. They've seen the crooks, but the crate has been hidden."

"Naturally," said Beautrelet. "Now the thieves will allow themselves to be chased away, and when the shipping truck is examined seven crates will still remain. Once again, a successful failure on the part of these villains!"

"Right," James agreed, swooped their plane around again. "I'm now following the thieves' truck. This is all rather exciting, isn't it?"

"It will be if and when we return to the Earth safely," Beautrelet assured him. He was not at all assured that this was likely. He could picture any number of things going wrong with their flimsy craft, and see it spinning from the sky in his mind's eye and crashing back to the solid Earth, killing them both... He was on the verge of fainting from hysteria when he heard James call out again.

"The van's stopped at a large old house," he yelled over the howl of the wind and the pounding of the engine. "It's on the outskirts of this small town. I think we had best alert the Police now."

"And how do you propose to do that?" Beautrelet. "This infernal device is not fitted with a telephone."

"Drop a message," James said cheerily. "I wrote one before we started, and put it into a small pouch. We simply drop down low enough and lob it at the first Policeman that we find. It alerts him to follow us, and call in reinforcements."

Beautrelet had to admit that James was performing well in his detective duties. But the most important thing, to him, was their imminent landing, and his successful return to Earth. As soon as James had located a Policeman and dropped the message, he flew slowly back toward the house where the thieves had holed up. Then he looked for a field large enough to land in.

"Hang on tight," he called over his shoulder. "The landing's always the trickiest part."

"But you have done it before?" Beautrelet howled.

"Well—just the once. I've never been allowed in a plane on my own before this morning."

"What?" Beautrelet almost did faint that time. "This is the first time you have flown this craft?"

"The second—the first was when I borrowed it. In fact, it's only the second time I've flown *any* airoplane. But it's jolly easy, really—I haven't had any problems, have I?"

"He's insane," the detective muttered to himself. But it was probably a good thing he had not known this information earlier—if he had, nothing would have induced him to clamber into this Hellish contraption!

James took the plane down, and Beautrelet felt a distinct thump as the wheels touched the ground, bounced once, and then settled back. James cut the speed, and the craft gradually came to a halt. Beautrelet, with a cry halfway between thanks and terror, leaped from the craft, and fell onto his knees, kissing the ground.

"Never," he vowed, "never will I step into one of those Devil's devices again!"

"Buck up," James said, laughing, as he jumped lightly down. "That was the most awful fun. And we're safe and all in one piece."

"You are a maniac!" Beautrelet swore. He shuddered and pulled the tattered remnants of his courage together. "But now, let us meet the Police and go and capture the thieves."

That part of the adventure, at least, was simply effected. The local gendarmes, happy to show their big-city rivals how efficient they could be, raided the large house and captured the art thieves without a shot being fired. An hour later, Commissioner Guichard arrived, a surprised look on his face.

"But... there was no robbery!" he exclaimed.

Beautrelet, having regained his equanimity at last, laughed. "That's what they wished everyone to believe. But James and I knew otherwise."

Guichard gazed at the art treasures, half-unpacked from the shipping crate. "I shall have these returned to the Museum at once," he said.

"Not yet, please, Commissaire," Bernardine suggested. "We still need to capture the ring-leader of this little plot. He glanced at his pocket watch. "In an hour or so, the villain should arrive."

"How can you be so certain?" the Policeman asked.

"Because this is the half-day for the Château de Fontainebleau," Beautrelet explained. "And our mastermind will hurry here once it is closed to examine his haul. So, we have your men hide, and allow everything to look normal. And then we wait for our trap to be sprung." He glanced over at James, who was sleeping soundly in a comfortable chair. "Ah, the resilience of youth. You would hardly know, Commissaire, that only a short while ago, he and I were in peril of our lives a thousand feet above this house."

"I'm surprised he managed to get you into a plane," the Commissioner commented.

"No more than I am. But now—we wait."

Sixty eight minutes later, the front door opened and closed. A man's voice called out, and Beautrelet and Guichard both stiffened. James sprang suddenly awake, the loaned pistol in his hand.

The door to the room opened, and Monsieur Poitevin stepped through—and stopped, stunned, as three pistols were leveled in his face. "What does this mean?" he cried in shock.

"It means, my dear chap," James informed him, "that you've been well and truly nabbed."

Beautrelet beamed. "I could hardly have phrased it better myself. Commissaire, here is the ringleader of this gang." He turned to Poitevin and bowed slightly. "My congratulations, Monsieur—a very accomplished and creative crime. Unfortunately for you, it attracted my attention—otherwise, I am sure it would have been carried through most successfully."

He tipped his hat as the humbled man was led off by the Police. Then he turned to James. "Despite the affair of the aircraft, I wish to thank you for your assistance. You were of great help. And you have convinced me to keep my feet firmly planted on the ground in the future!"

"You'll be missing a lot of fun," James informed him. He handed back the borrowed pistol, and then held out his hand. "Well, Monsieur Beautrelet—thank you for a grand adventure!"

"And my thanks to you also, Mr. Biggles... Biggles..." He stumbled over the pronunciation of the foreign name.

James laughed. "Biggles will do just fine!"

This is perhaps the most significant story in this collection. Not necessarily the best, of course, merely the one that has had the most consequences. Jean-Marc had suggested that I read his adaptation of Arnould Galopin's long-forgotten novel Doctor Omega. *(He can be quite evil sometimes, and he knew what the character would do to my imagination!) As a result, I came up with this short story, and thought little more of it at the time, though I did bring the good Doctor back for a few more adventures in the* Tales of the Shadowmen. *It turned out that I wasn't the only person to be captivated by the madcap scientist. I was approached by Chris Pederson some time later to write a short story for his take on the character. (More on that in the second volume.) And, more recently, artist Andrew Skilleter evolved his version of the character and invited me to pen several novels based on this. As a result, I found myself writing no less than three completely different incarnations of Doctor Omega... Any resemblance between him and a certain BBC time traveler are purely coincidental, of course – Galopin created his character in 1906! And this tale is probably also the closest I've come to date to bringing Sherlock Holmes into my stories.*

The Dynamics of an Asteroid

Space, 1908

Since I had thrown my lot in with Doctor Omega, straining whatever small quantity of bravery I might by nature possess, I had faced many dangers. My name is Denis Borel, and my limited claim to fame before this was to fall heir to a medium-sized fortune and to be sufficiently gifted on the violin as to be an accepted amateur player at an occasional *soirée*. However, once I joined my rustic neighbor for dinner one

201

evening, all manner of strange, calamitous and life-threatening events had ensued.

He had been engaged in the building and test flight of a craft capable of traversing both space and time. Together we had embarked on a perilous journey to the planet Mars at a time when it still possessed life—sentient, malevolent reptilian creatures bent on our destruction. All save one, that is, a scientist named Tiziraou. When the Doctor, his hulking assistant, Fred, and I had escaped Mars, this worthy had accompanied us back to Earth—which he found as fascinating as the Doctor's neighbors found *him*.

I mention all of this as preface to explaining why I discovered myself one day perched on the side of a waterfall, waiting for a man to fall into my lap. Nothing in my life previous to meeting the good Doctor would have ever led me to such a dangerous predicament—but since meeting him!... Well, it seemed almost perfectly natural, in a very unnerving manner.

These were the Reichenbach Falls, one of the tallest such in Europe. Near the pleasant town of Meiringen in Switzerland, they descend (perilously) some 250 meters to a large pool below. A good deal of steam is thrown up by the descent, often completely obscuring the pool if one stands at the head of the falls. The rocks, as I discovered by personal experience, are quite slippery as a result, and it seemed to me quite likely that a man could plunge to his death—in this case, myself and my own demise.

"Why must I do this?" I asked the Doctor before venturing out onto the rocks with Fred, who had already begun to affix a safety net—though not intended for us!—in place.

"I have already explained twice," the Doctor replied in his usual gruff manner. "I can hardly balance like a mountain goat on those rocks at my age. And Tiziraou is hardly adapted to life with this amount of moisture in the air. Besides which, anyone seeing him here might well expire from shock, and we are attempting to save a life and not destroy one. Therefore, it must be you who helps Fred. Now, off you go, and stop complaining." He made sweeping gestures with his hands and I, most reluctantly, stepped from the safety of the cabin of the *Cosmos* and onto the slippery rocks of Reichenbach Falls.

Fred held out a strong hand to help steady me, and then passed me a rope to tie off. As he and I worked, straining carefully not to lose our precarious footing, the Doctor glanced at his watch from the safety of the ship.

"Do hurry it up," he called above the roar of the falls. "It is almost time. May 4, 1891—a most momentous occasion." It was typical of the Doctor that we were risking our necks, and all that concerned him was his chronometer. He had planned this rescue down to almost the exact second. This was understandable, because as soon as anything happened, there would be only seconds in which we could act.

I strained to see anything in the mists above us, but visibility was extremely limited—no doubt a good thing, since otherwise the *Cosmos* would have been visible to the two men even now making their way along the upper falls. I hesitate to imagine what would have happened if either man had caught a glimpse of the ship. History might well have been changed had one or both men turned from their assigned fates to investigate.

Doctor Omega had explained several times, with great care, that we had to be very certain that we did not affect the natural flow of the timeline at all with our interference. The body of the man we were attempting to save had never been found, so there was no actual proof that he had died. Saving him and whisking him away, then, would alter nothing. But if the combatants were to be distracted from their fatal encounter, then history would have been altered, and there would be no way to know how this might have affected our own time.

"And I mean that quite literally!" the Doctor had snapped, emphasizing his point by wagging a bony finger under the noses of both Fred and myself. "If the past were to be changed in any way, then *our* pasts would change with it. And that change would become part of our memories, and we would believe that history had always been like that. But such changes, no matter how minor, might result in, say, one of us never being born. And I'm certain that people even with your limited intellects can see how unpleasant that might be. So— no changing of any details in the past, no matter how trifling! I trust that this is quite clear!"

It was, of course. I had no desire for my entire life to evaporate like a puff of smoke—no matter how inconsequential I might be to the history of the human race, I still feel myself to be somewhat essential, even if only to myself. As a result, I was taking great care with the placing of the safety net. Fred and I were barely finished with our chore when the Doctor announced urgently: "It is time!"

Clinging to the rocks, Fred and I stared upward, striving to see something—anything—in those wretched mists. I strained my ears in an attempt to hear some signal of the fight that was even now taking place almost 200 meters above our heads. But through the mists and over the roar of the falling waters, nothing could be discerned. We might as well have been blind and deaf.

And then, in an instant, a body came crashing down through the mists, and into our net. The lean, angular form bounced, and then almost broke free before Fred and I both managed to grasp a limb apiece and haul the badly shaken man from the net. He was stunned and incoherent, unable to stand or aid in his own rescue. Fred thrust him toward the open door of the waiting *Cosmos*, and Doctor Omega gripped the man's hands and pulled him within.

"Now," he barked, "cut free the net! We must leave no trace of this man's salvation!"

Fred pulled an axe from his ample waist-band and chopped at the ropes securing the net in place. As soon as he had severed the ropes close to him, he passed me the axe so that I might do the same to the ones on my side. Let me tell you, it is no simple matter to chop at soaked ropes on slippery rocks with one hand whilst holding on for grim life with the other.

Needless to say, I received no sympathy from the Doctor. "Hurry it up, man!" he cried. "We must be gone from here before anyone can investigate!"

As swiftly as we could, Fred and I finished the chore of disposing of all traces of the netting. We hurried back inside the ship, and the Doctor sealed the door, and then set the *Cosmos* into temporal flight. If anyone in 1891 were looking at us, the ship would simply have seemed to vanish.

Shaking from both the exertion and the strain on my nerves, I staggered to one of the chairs in the main cabin and all but collapsed into it. Fred, in his usual cheerful manner, seemed unaffected by our feat, and joined the Doctor at the controls. I glanced around and saw that the man we had rescued was sitting in another of the chairs, but he was not relaxing, or even recovering from his ordeal. He was staring fixedly at Tiziraou.

I cannot blame him, for anyone seeing the Martian for the first time would stare. He was only about two feet high, with a large head and unblinking red eyes. His skin had a greenish cast to it, betraying his reptilian ancestry. He was seated in a specially-built chair and pouring over the controls, ignoring the rescued man.

As I was the only person close to him, our guest leaned over to me, and gestured. "What manner of creature is that?" he asked. "I had believed myself cognizant of all classes and phylum of terrestrial life."

"Perhaps you are," I rejoined. "It is not reflection on your learning—our companion is a Martian."

"Ah." The lean man nodded, pressing his hands together almost as if in prayer. "That would explain matters at least, a few. Now, of greater importance—why have you risked your lives to rescue me?"

Doctor Omega, though apparently deep in study of the ship's controls, had clearly been listening to our conversation. He turned toward up, his right hand gripping the lapel of his frock coat. "May I take it that I am addressing Professor James Moriarty?"

"You may indeed, sir—though you have the advantage of me. To the best of my recollection—and it is inevitably accurate—I have never met any of you before. I repeat then—why have you risked your lives to rescue me?"

The Doctor chuckled. "It is hardly likely that you would have either met or heard of us, Professor—though you are well known to us through the memoirs of Dr. John H. Watson."

"Watson?" Moriarty snorted. "That third-rate scribbler of the so-called deductions of Sherlock Holmes!"

"I fully understand your animosity toward both men," the Doctor said. "But please place your personal feelings aside for the moment, and I will explain our purposes here. According to the writings of Dr. Watson, you and Sherlock Holmes faced one another at the Reichenbach Falls, where you both appeared to perish."

"Appeared?" Moriarty's forehead creased. "Do you mean to say that Holmes survived also?"

"Indeed."

The Professor gave a cry of rage, and thumped his clenched fist down on the chair arm with sufficient force to crack the wood. "Damnation! I would gladly have perished if it meant the end of Holmes also."

Fred's eyebrows rose. "You'd have been happy to die if you killed him too?"

Moriarty had recovered his spirits by now, and stood up. "My pride is everything," he said, simply. "Holmes inconvenienced me, and I allow no man to do that with impunity. My death would have been a small price to pay to destroy him."

I found it difficult to understand the man. "I have long been taught," I replied, "that pride is the first and greatest of sins. It was the sin that caused Lucifer to be cast from Heaven."

"Sin?" Moriarty looked offended. "An unimaginative response from someone barely qualified to be called *homo sapiens*. A man's pride is what raises him above the animals. A man who has no pride in his achievements *has* no achievements."

"Yes, yes," the Doctor replied impatiently, "be that as it may, it has no bearing on why you are here. Allow me to continue, if you would be so kind. My friends and I are from France in the year 1905—14 years after your supposed death. This is why you could not have known us, though we know you."

Moriarty's eyes sparkled. "Then this... craft in which I find myself is some kind of device that travels between the ages? A chronic yacht, shall we say?"

"Yes and no, not precisely," the Doctor answered. He appeared to be pleased that our guest had worked this out for himself. "It is mainly capable of space travel—the temporal portion of our journeys are mostly a side-effect, but often a most useful one, as in this case."

"I begin to understand." The Professor bent forward, the index finger of his right hand touching the tip of his nose. "Thanks to the memoirs of Dr. Watson, you knew the date and place of my demise."

"*Supposed* demise," the Doctor corrected. "Had your body been recovered, we could never have attempted a rescue. Changing the course of even a single event known to have occurred might have disastrous effects."

Moriarty nodded. "I can see the logic in that," he agreed. "Alteration of the skein of time could lead to the unweaving of the past as you conceive it, and the future as far as I am concerned."

"Precisely." Doctor Omega beamed. "It is so pleasant to be able to confer with a man who follows my points without all sorts of silly arguing." I felt that the glance he spared me at that point was quite unwarranted.

"So, then," Moriarty continued, "we have established the *how* of my rescue. All that remains is the *why*. I find it difficult to believe that your actions were motivated by simple compassion, else you would spend eternity hopping about like a flea in time, saving all manner of unfortunate souls."

"Well, in fact," Doctor Omega replied with a chuckle, "we are engaged in a purpose something along those lines—

though we hope to be able to save a considerably number of lives with only one of your hypothetical flea-jumps."

He was quite enjoying teasing the Professor, clearly hoping that Moriarty would work as much as possible out on his own. The Doctor was enjoying having another articulate man of science about the *Cosmos*. Much as he appeared to enjoy the company of Fred and myself, we were hardly in his intellectual league. And while Tiziraou was in the same intellectual stratosphere as the Doctor, his alienness made true companionship with him extremely difficult. In Moriarty, Doctor Omega had discovered a virtual intellectual equal, and he was exploiting the situation.

"The reason we rescued you is because of that scientific volume you wrote." As he spoke, he drew the book in question, *The Dynamics of an Asteroid*, from the shelf behind him.

Moriarty's eyes sparkled, and he inclined his head slight. "I am to understand that you have read it?"

The Doctor nodded, a smile on his lips.

"And comprehended it?

Again the nod and smile.

Moriarty sprang forward, his hand extended. "There cannot be three people in all of England who can say the same," he commented. "In your case, I do believe that you speak the truth in your claim, given the evidence to my senses." He waved a hand about the cabin. "So, then, the reason you rescued me has become clear. Given the evidence of my rather abstruse work in conjunction with a yacht to sail the reaches of space, I can only conclude that you have discovered an asteroid that is of some problem to you. And since you mentioned the saving of a quantity of lives, I can further only assume that the asteroid in question is on a collision path with the Earth."

"Splendid, my dear Professor, splendid!" the Doctor cried, clapping his hands in approbation, for all the world as if this were some student examination at a University, and the pupil had just managed to defend his thesis with a measure of success.

"My dear Doctor," I said, unable to restrain myself further, "you might simply have told him, instead of playing these games."

"My dear Borel," he replied, somewhat sharply, "it was necessary for me to try the Professor and ascertain that his reputation was not based on some fraud. And I find, to the contrary, that his mental abilities are almost as sharp as my own. I do therefore believe we have enlisted the aid of the right person in our quest."

Moriarty inclined his head at the praise. "I take it, then," he said, "that your aim is to somehow divert this asteroid in order that the impending collision will no longer occur?"

"Precisely," Doctor Omega agreed.

"And you require me to perform the calculations to ensure that the object will indeed miss the Earth."

"Correct again," the Doctor agreed.

"Then I have only one further question," the Professor said. "What specific force will you be utilizing in order to divert this aerial rock?"

"That," Doctor Omega replied, "you shall find out very shortly, as we are now on our way to collect the final member of our daring band of adventurers."

I had to confess that I had not taken too well to Professor Moriarty. An intellectual genius he might be, but his egotism was worse than that of Doctor Omega—and he was by no means a modest man! Also, I could not forget that Sherlock Holmes himself had called the man the "Napoleon of Crime." Trusting him appeared to me to be a very foolish mistake. I had, of course, said as much to the Doctor when he had broached his daring plan to avert catastrophe, but he had, rather typically, simply waved away my fears by stating that nobody would ever get the better of Doctor Omega.

It would have done no good to have reminded him of all the people who had, in fact, gotten the better of him—even if only on a temporary basis. And none of *them* had ever been considered a genius.

So, as you may imagine, I was not altogether sanguine about this entire enterprise. And my confidence sagged even further as Doctor Omega brought the *Cosmos* in for a stealthy landing in the Bois de Boulogne in the early evening, when there was less chance of our being observed. Moriarty elected to remain in the ship, along with Tiziraou and Fred, while I accompanied the Doctor to retrieve the final member of our band from his lodgings in the Rue Cassette.

The Widow Thibault—who owned the building following the death of her husband, and who let out rooms to one singular individual—met us at the door. "Oh," she said, in her usual surly fashion. "It's you two gentlemen again. I hope you've come to take him away. All that banging about upstairs, and me a poor widow whose nerves can't stomach all of these to-ings and fro-ings such as he indulges in, and returning with all manner of oddments and assortments."

"He has been busy, then?" Doctor Omega asked, cheerfully.

"I'll say he has!" The elderly lady looked indignant. "Can't you hear him even now?"

We listened, and heard nothing. I ventured to say as much, and in return received a ferocious scowl that would have intimidated even one of the greater cats.

"It's just stopped," she said. "I dare say it'll start up again shortly."

"I doubt that, my good woman," the Doctor replied, making for the stairs, "for we are indeed here to take him away."

"Well, mind he comes back in one piece!" Widow Thibault snapped. "I don't want to have to go looking for a new lodger at my time of life."

"We shall have him back in no time," Doctor Omega promised.

"Perhaps literally," I added, but under my breath. I did not wish to have to explain myself to the Widow. I followed the Doctor up the stairs, and waited as he hammered loudly on the lodger's door.

A moment later, it was opened by a veritable wreck of a fellow. Tall, disheveled, and remarkably ugly, Zephyrin Xirdal was always a shock to look at. He always appeared to have dressed in the dark, with one arm tied behind his back. Nothing he wore matched, and none of it was freshly pressed or worn entirely straight. His mismatched socks were twisted—one inside a boot, the other encased in a slipper. His trousers looked as if they had been slept in—and perhaps had, as Xirdal did not always remember to change clothes before retiring—and his shirt was only half-buttoned, and most of those buttons in incorrect holes.

He blinked at us both, as if struggling to recall who we were, even though (in his measurement of time) he had seen us only three days before when we had approached him with our proposal. He raised a finger, which wavered in the air uncertainly. "And you are here for...?" he asked, vaguely.

As I believe I have already mentioned, my confidence of success in our venture was rapidly approaching zero. Xirdal was another of those eccentric geniuses I seemed to be constantly stumbling across. Like both Doctor Omega and Professor Moriarty, he had a terribly high opinion of his own abilities, but, unlike them, his mind was so restless as to be unable to settle upon a single track and remain on it. The slightest, strayest thought might distract him and set his feverish imagination off in a completely unpredictable direction. Doctor Omega had required Xirdal to reconstruct a machine he had once created—a task the inventor claimed was child's play (before going off on a tangent and trying to invent a new game for the younger generation). Indeed, given his apparent intellect, it might well have been—but only if he had managed to recall just what it was that he was supposed to be building.

"Your rectilinear generator," the Doctor prompted.

Xirdal's vast expanse of brow creased as he struggled to recall. "Didn't I use that to move the golden meteor?" he asked. "I believe it was destroyed then."

"Indeed it was," the Doctor replied. "And I requested that you rebuild it, if you recall."

"You did?" Xirdal shrugged. "If you say so. I have been busy on a new invention, you know, and—"

My heart sank. It was as I feared—the pitiable fool had become distracted, and instead of building the device we needed in order to save the Earth, he had manufactured instead perhaps some device for removing the skin from rice pudding.

"We might as well give up now," I said to the Doctor. "We are defeated without his device."

"Don't be so swift to despair, my boy!" Doctor Omega replied. "True, Monsieur Xirdal is easily distracted, and apt to be a trifle forgetful—but he *did* commence the work for me, if you recall." He turned back to the puzzled inventor and smiled. "Might we just glance at what you have done?" he asked.

"By all means," Xirdal agreed, amiably. "You might find this new idea of mine most interesting. I was walking down the street this morning, and it occurred to me that we waste a great deal of our time in our daily toiletries. So I thought it would be most helpful if we had some devices that could aid us in them." He had led his way into his cluttered apartment. Did I say "cluttered?" That is too mild a word for it! There were piles of papers all over, save for a small space before the room's single window. The leaning tower of Pisa could hardly have appeared more precariously balanced that many of the stacks that lay about the room. Yet Xirdal insisted that, if the need arose, he could find any article or note at a moment's notice. The table was reasonably clear—at least of papers, as there were the remains of breakfast scattered upon it. Aside from that, and a small path to walk upon, the room was almost literally overflowing.

In the small space beneath the window stood two odd-looking constructions. One of them appeared to be all armatures, belts and small motors, and it was to this that the inventor headed. "My automatic shaving device," he explained. "I intend to mount it on the arm of a chair, you see. The head fits within this area here—" he indicated the place in the middle of what looked like an apparatus more suited to a torture chamber that a bathroom "—and then the machine will proceed to shave him while he reads the morning paper."

I examined the machine closer, and saw that there was indeed a straight razor attached to one armature. "Good Heavens!" I exclaimed. "I wouldn't trust that machine not to cut my throat! Thank you, but I prefer someone considerably more human wielding a razor near my throat!"

"Stuff and nonsense!" Xirdal replied. "My device is perfectly safe. Well, will be, once I adjust it." That did not inspire confidence.

"Excuse me," Doctor Omega broke in, indicating the second machine in the small space. "And what, pray, might this be for?"

I followed his gaze, and saw a machine even odder than the probably-lethal automatic shaver. It was a black box, surmounted by a reflective mirror on some sort of universal joint that would allow it to be positioned at any possible angle. There were a few small knobs and switches on the side, but nothing to indicate its function.

"That?" Xirdal waved a hand airily. "That's a duplicate of my helicoidal and rectilinear generator."

"The same one I was just inquiring about?" the Doctor persisted.

"Most likely," Xirdal agreed. "But to return to—"

"And is it completed?" the Doctor growled.

"Completed?" The inventor bent to examine it. "Yes, I would say so. It certainly appears to be. Why do you ask?"

Doctor Omega turned to me. "Grab one of his arms, my boy," he said, gaily. "I shall bring the generator. We must return to the *Cosmos* immediately."

I did as I was bid, and dragged the puzzled, protesting inventor along with us as we raced down the stairs. Xirdal protested weakly, but neither the Doctor nor I paid him much heed. Nor did we really listen to the Widow as she yelled: "One piece, mind you! One piece!" as we left.

We managed to secure a cab, and sent it racing toward the Bois de Boulogne and our comrades. I was now able to pause and breathe. Xirdal had completed his machine for us—and then promptly forgotten about it, lost in the plans for his later device. But we were saved—and, hopefully, the rest on Mankind along with us!

"Where are we going?" the inventor finally asked. "I do not have my coat on."

"I'll lend you one of mine," the Doctor assured him. "We are on our way to outer space."

"Outer space?" Xirdal blinked. "It's terribly cold out there—I shall require an overcoat as well."

We managed to get him back to the ship without drawing too much undue attention to ourselves, and then we were off, leaving fair Paris behind and heading into the cold darkness of outer space.

I can only leave it to your imagination to picture the wild conversations flung about the cabin as we traveled. With one alien mastermind and three human geniuses, neither Fred nor I could make out more than one word in ten, and could understand even less. Xirdal was entranced by the *Cosmos*, and immediately perceived several ways to improve upon its design. Doctor Omega vacillated between feeling insulted that anyone had the temerity to imagine they could improve upon anything he had constructed and curiosity and admiration for the suggestions that Xirdal let slip. I cannot tell how much of this Moriarty understood, but he was paying very careful attention to everything—suspiciously so in my mind, though I could get no one else to share my suspicions. Even Fred, who I felt the closest to, simply shrugged.

"If he's planning any treachery, I'm sure the Doctor has plans well in hand." How could you argue with such faith? Especially when the object of his faith wouldn't comment on the matter beyond a tetchy "Bah!" before plunging back into his animated conversations.

Thankfully, even the longest of journeys must finally come to an end, and we reached our target—the unnamed asteroid on its way to collide with our fair home planet. As we neared it, Fred and I gazed out of the observation windows at it.

It is almost impossible to successfully describe the scene we beheld—the depth of the blackness of space itself, the glimmer of billions of lights, each a pinprick of a star. Even the Sun itself, ruler of all our days on Earth, was a mere speck of light at this distance. And there, growing before us, the asteroid, our target. We seemed to be so far from the Earth that the rock surely would pose no threat. I mentioned this to the Doctor, but it was Moriarty who chose to reply.

"Bah! You cannot comprehend the beautiful intricacies of mathematical formulae! Celestial mechanics are fixed and unswerving, their elegant designs predictable to the nth degree. I have checked and rechecked the Doctor's calculations, and I concur completely—this asteroid will indeed impact upon the Earth, with catastrophic results."

"Thank you, my dear Professor," the Doctor said, with a smug glance in my direction, as if daring me to challenge his theories further. "In 12 years, humanity will face almost certain destruction."

"Shortly after 7 a.m. on June 30, 1908," Moriarty amplified. "It will strike in Russia, and the impact will be so immense that it will alter the composition of the atmosphere, and raise so much debris and dust that the face of the Earth will be completely cut off from the benevolent rays of the Sun."

"All growing plants will die as a result," Xirdal added. "And, as a consequence, any animal life that survived the initial impact will face slow starvation. In a matter of months, virtually all life on Earth will become extinct."

"Unless we prevent it," the Doctor said, completing their thoughts.

"But why here? Why now?" I objected. "Surely there is plenty of time to act, and millions of kilometers in which to pursue this would-be killer."

Xirdal sighed. "As this asteroid is pulled into the center of our Solar System," he explained, "it will speed up. By the time it reaches the Earth, it will be traveling at an immense speed. The farther from the Earth we affect its course, the easier it will be to ensure that its path avoids that of our planet entirely. A small force applied here and now will be most efficacious—were we to attempt this closer to the Earth, then a much greater force would be required." He gestured to the box and parabolic dish we had brought with us from his crowded flat. "My machine is very efficient, but even this would not be powerful enough to affect the path of the asteroid if we were to attempt to deflect it closer to the Earth."

I nodded my understanding. Xirdal had previously attempted to explain how his machine worked, but it was quite beyond my grasp. All I knew was that in some strange—yet thoroughly scientific!—manner, the machine was able to produce a force that acted upon remote objects. Once planted upon the surface of the asteroid and switched into operation, it would somehow reach out across space to Jupiter, that giant among planets. It would then latch onto the gravity of this world and using this force, create an attraction that would cause the asteroid to adjust its path slightly. Slightly, true—but sufficient to ensure that the asteroid would completely miss the Earth. And if reversed, the machine would repel other objects.

At least, that was the idea. I could only hope and pray that our small herd of geniuses knew whereof they spoke—because Fred and I were completely lost! And why, you may wonder, were we there? We whose intellect was so far below that of the Doctor, the Professor and the inventor? Why else, but to do the actual work involved.

Doctor Omega fiddled with the controls of the *Cosmos* as intently and furiously as I fingered the strings of my violin during a Caprice by Paganini. His digits flew across the controls—twisting here, turning there, tweaking everywhere—until at last he interlaced the fingers of both hands together and announced with a certain amount of self-satisfaction: "Well, gentlemen—and Tiziraou—we have arrived!"

I must confess that it was something of a disappointment. The asteroid looked like nothing so much as a rather oversized baked potato. It was covered in small craters, rather like the surface of the Moon, but there was nothing else to see. No mountains, nor rivers, or anything else. "It's rather dull," I observed.

"Perhaps now," agreed the Doctor. "But once it reaches the Earth, it will be far from such. Now, we must position the helicoidal rectilinear device on the surface and then set the timer precisely. Obviously, my dear Xirdal, you must accompany us—as will Fred and Denis."

"Me?" I objected. "I don't see what is so obvious about that!"

"Come now, my dear Borel, this is something of a unique experience—to be amongst the first humans ever to set foot on an asteroid! Surely you would not even think about passing up the chance?" He did not give me the opportunity to reply that I most certainly would, but plunged ahead. "On which point, I must caution you all. This asteroid has virtually no gravity, such as we are used to on Earth or even Mars. We shall need to fasten a safety line to enable us to move about, and you must all be careful to remain attached to it at all times. If you were to kick too hard, you would go flying off into space, and we should have to attempt to rescue you."

"What of the cold?" Xirdal asked. "I did not bring a coat, you may recall."

"Hang the cold!" Fred objected. "What about the insufficiency of air to breath? That's far more urgent."

"Actually, both items are equally important," Doctor Omega replied. "Either one would kill you in an instant."

"You're hardly making this little stroll of yours sound very appealing," I said. "It makes remaining behind more and more attractive."

"Courage, my friend, courage!" The Doctor slapped me on the arm heartily. It stung. "I have carefully considered the issue, and settled the matter. Using the *Cosmos*, I ventured forward in time a century or so and... borrowed several special sets of clothing from the future. Come along, all of you, and I shall see about getting you prepared for your perambulation."

"I shall, of course, remain with the ship," Tiziraou said. "I doubt you have protective clothing in my size."

"And I shall, if you've no objection, remain with him," Moriarty said. He glanced out of the observation window and shuddered. "Having experienced falling to my death once already today, I am not anxious to repeat the experience. I must confess it makes me a trifle nauseous simply to glance outside the ship."

"As you wish," the Doctor replied. "Then that leaves the four of us, my friends!" He seemed to have ignored my desires to remain behind. I attempted to reiterate them, but he brushed my protests aside, and I found myself swept along with the others into the store room.

Here stood four sets of the strangest clothing I had ever seen. They were a pure, almost dazzling, white, and looked a little like diving equipment, down to the helmets that rested beside each suit. They were large and cumbersome, and appeared to be very uncomfortable. Each one had a curious emblem on the arm bearing the letters NASA. I assumed that this was some sort of a ship from which the Doctor had stolen the suits.

"These are designed to protect you from the deadly environment out there," the Doctor explained. "We must each don one, and then check that there are no leaks—which would be lethal. There is no air on the asteroid at all."

"No air?" Xirdal had been examining his suit intently—no doubt thinking of a thousand and one ways in which he could improve upon it. "Then how are we to communicate with one another?"

"Each suit has a Marconi device implanted within, at a preset frequency. It enables us to converse with one another, and with a similar device I have implanted in the control room, and which Tiziraou will operate. We shall be in constant communication in case of difficulties."

"Remarkable!" the inventor exclaimed. "I'll just take a quick look at it, and—"

"First things first!" Doctor Omega replied. "After we have adjusted the trajectory of the asteroid, there will be ample time for you to indulge your whims." Xirdal wasn't happy about being derailed and set back on his original course, but he subsided and condescended to don the suits, along with the Doctor, Fred and myself.

Yes, myself! Despite all of my protests, I somehow found myself inside one of those infernal contraptions!

We moved through the ship to the exit. Here Doctor Omega handed Fred a harpoon, to which was attached a long, coiled rope. He then opened the outer door. There was a hiss as all of the air within the small room was sucked outside. "The natural force of a vacuum," the Doctor explained. He then pointed a gloved hand at a small hillock. "Fred, if you would be so kind as to throw that harpoon and embed it in that mound, we shall have an anchor point."

Fred eyed the distance dubiously. "That's some throw, sir," he finally said.

"There is very little gravity, my boy," was the reply. "You'll discover that it is a comparatively simply toss when you try it."

Fred looked by no means as certain of this claim as was his employer, but he hefted the harpoon and threw. I watched with interest; I have always known that Fred was strong, but that throw was astounding—the harpoon slipped through the air as if fired from a cannon. In moments, it was indeed deeply embedded in the stony side of the hillock. Fred gave the rope an experimental tug and pronounced it safe to use. The near end was tied to a stanchion on the ship just outside the exit door, and we all attached cords from the belts of our extravehicular suits to it.

"Now, remember," The Doctor cautioned, "there is minimal gravity, so there is no need to press down hard with your feet. If you do so, you will literally step off this world and float away. Take very small steps to begin with until you are comfortable moving about. Xirdal, you have your device?

Good. Now, then, gentlemen—let us be the first to step upon the surface of this strange world."

Despite my trepidation, and a mild feeling of claustrophobia from being encased in my mechanical suit, I found the experience novel and even stimulating. As Doctor Omega had said, even a tiny step was akin to a stride wearing the legendary seven-league boots. It was extremely difficult staying close to the surface of the asteroid, and without the restraining ropes, we should all have certainly floated off into space, perhaps to be lost forever. Or, at least, until our air supply was depleted. However, there was a certain exhilaration in being able to leap about unfettered by the ties of gravity that bind us to our Earth, and after a short while I began to actually feel glad I had agreed—however reluctantly—to go along on this strange excursion.

After a short while, Doctor Omega recalled to us that there was a purpose to our expedition, and we set off, more or less together, to find a good place to plant Xirdal's strange device. The inventor and the Doctor conferred and eventually selected a small depression about 30 meters from the ship. The two of them set about playing with the controls, until they were happy with the settings.

Fred and I, meanwhile, simply looked around. I cannot convey the absolute desolation of the asteroid. There was nothing living, and nothing of any color save a slate gray that varied only slightly from place to place. The horizon was astonishing close, and even a few steps in any direction would bring fresh vistas to be seen. Of course, these vistas looked entirely the same as the one we already could see, so there was no variety at all. The sky was uniformly black, punctuated by the brilliant lights that were stars. It was not a place one could love.

Suddenly, Fred gave a warning cry: "Doctor!" I turned to see what had startled him, and found myself rising from the surface. A quick grab by Fred located my foot, and he pulled me gently back to—well, not Earth, but Asteroid, I suppose I should say. But I did see what had startled him.

The farther end of our safety rope, the one attached to the *Cosmos*, had come unfastened. It was floating in the sky. If it had not been for the other end, anchored in the hillock, we should also have been floating in the sky.

"Professor," Doctor Omega called. "The safety line appears to have come detached from the ship."

"I know that," came the Professor's voice. "For I am the one who detached it."

"What is the meaning of this?" the Doctor cried.

"Mutiny, my dear Doctor," Moriarty answered. "This ship of yours is far too valuable and intriguing a device for me to allow it to remain in your hands. I therefore propose to take it for myself and utilize its capabilities to aid my life of crime."

"And what is to happen to us?" the Doctor asked, his voice gravely quiet.

"You will perish, I am afraid," Moriarty replied. "But you may go to your Maker in the knowledge that you have died saving the Earth. Not many people can claim so much."

The staggering enormity of what Moriarty was saying was not lost on me. "He aims to kill us!" I cried.

"Not I," the Professor said, emphatically. "It is merely circumstance that dictates you must perish. I had to seize my opportunity while so many of you were missing that taking over the ship was simple."

"And Tiziraou?" the Doctor asked, anxiously.

"He is safe, but incapacitated," Moriarty replied. "I look forward to immensely entertaining discussions with the Martian."

"Good," the Doctor said. He did not sound at all bothered by what was going on.

I could not be as calm. "I warned you that he was treacherous!" I cried. "And you ignored me! As a result, we are going to die."

"On the contrary," the Doctor said. "I agreed with your estimation of the Professor's character from the start—that he could not be trusted."

I was confused. "Then why did you allow him to take over the ship and strand us here?" I asked, bewildered.

"Because I cannot condemn a man for what he *might* do, only for what he *does* do. I was certain Moriarty would betray us, but I might have been wrong. He deserved the chance, and he has used it to show his true colors."

"I don't understand," I had to confess. "You *wanted* him to seize the ship?"

"Wanted? No. Expected? Yes. And I was certain he would not harm Tiziraou—but I could not say the same about you, my boy. That was why I insisted, against all of your wishes, that you accompany us on this expedition. I wanted you safe outside the ship if the Professor betrayed us."

"Safe? Outside?" I felt like screaming. "Doctor, we will *perish* out here. Our only safety lies inside the ship."

"The young man is correct," Moriarty said. "And, I am sorry to say, that safety is now about to leave you. Farewell, my friends, and my sincere thanks for this gift to aid me in my future career."

"I only *appeared* to dismiss your warnings, my boy," Doctor Omega continued, as if we were not about to be abandoned to die in the cold depths of space. "I am afraid I slightly misled you. I knew that Moriarty might expect that Zephyrin and I, as men of science, might be somewhat unrealistic in accounting for human nature, and Fred he would dismiss as some simpleton employed only for his strength. But you—you, my boy, he would have been very suspicious if *you* had not suspected him of malicious intent. So we had to keep our plans from you in order that your most natural outcries against the Professor were not stifled."

I was commencing to understand what the Doctor was saying. "You *planned* all of this? And left me unknowing?"

"Precisely, my boy." He sounded smug and unrepentant.

"Then I have been worrying all of this time for nothing?" I cried.

"There was no other option. My dear Denis, you have many talents, but play-acting is not one of them. If we had told you of our plans, then you would never have been able to convince Moriarty that he was safe in his machinations."

"But he has the *Cosmos*!" I pointed out. "And we are to die here."

"No. To both points."

At that instant, there was a cry of frustrated rage from over the Marconi connection. "What have you done?" Moriarty cried. "Why will the ship not move?"

Xirdal cleared his throat. "That would be my doing," he replied. "I have used the helicoidal forces to anchor the *Cosmos* to this asteroid. It will not be able to depart until I adjust my machine—and that will not be until you return control of the ship to the Doctor." He turned to me. "My machine can either repel or attract matter," he explained. "At the moment, it is set to attract—but only specifically the ship. That is why we are not affected by its forces."

There was a moment's silence, and then, of a sudden, the asteroid beneath our feet began to shake. "What is happening?" I cried.

"It's the ship," the Doctor said. "Moriarty is boosting the power, hoping to shake free of the holding force. Grab a hold of the rope, everyone!" We all did so as the asteroid trembled beneath our feet. I glimpsed the Doctor's face within his helmet, and for the first time he appeared to be showing concern. "I confess, I had not anticipated this exact eventuality."

He hadn't expected the Professor to attempt to break free? How foolish!

Like a dog shaking itself to attempt to free himself of fleas, the rock beneath our feet quivered and cracked. I could see fissures commencing to open, all in a terrible silence. The foundations of the asteroid were being torn apart by the two opposing forces of Xirdal's machine and the mighty engines of the *Cosmos*. I could see that it scarcely mattered which won—all of us on the surface of the asteroid would be the losers. The anchor rope we depended upon for our lives would be of little use if the rock broke apart. We would be attached to the rope, but the rope would be attached to nothing.

"Cease this foolishness!" the Doctor cried. "You cannot break free of the machine, and if you cause our deaths, yours will shortly follow. Even now, the engines must be overheating. Turn them off, and allow us to return to the ship if you wish to live."

For long moments, it appeared that his appeal to reason was unavailing. Portions of the asteroid continued to shudder and break free, floating apart from the main body of the rock. In moments it looked as if we might have a strange experience of rain—instead of water falling downwards, that of rocks, pebbles and dust falling upwards. Then, of a sudden, the shaking stopped.

"Very well," came Moriarty's voice. "I am in your hands."

As we recovered our equilibrium, Doctor Omega called out: "Tiziraou—is he telling the truth?"

"Yes," came the Martian's flat reply. He sounded as if nothing that had happened was of any consequence—and possibly, to him, it was not. It was always difficult to discern his emotions—if he possessed them at all.

"Then we are returning to the ship. Kindly open the outer door."

I cannot convey the tremendous relief I felt when we re-entered the ship. I, who had been certain I was on the brink of death, was alive again! Relief flooded through me as we all—save for Xirdal—divested ourselves of the cumbersome suits and then returned to the control room. The inventor remained behind. Our Martian companion was seated at the controls, and Moriarty was standing, hunched, head bowed, to one side.

"Fred," Doctor Omega said with grim satisfaction, "perhaps you would be good enough to lock the Professor within the store-room?"

"Fine," Fred agreed, with a wide grin. "Come on, you." He gripped the Professor's arm and led him off to be imprisoned.

Doctor Omega turned to the Marconi device on the main panel. "Zephyrin, my friend," he said, "you may now go outside and turn your splendid machine off. It is of no further use." Xirdal acknowledged the order, and he left the ship again on his quest.

"No further use?" I asked. As usual with the Doctor, I was at a loss again. "I thought it was needed to steer the asteroid away from the Earth?"

"That was merely what I wished the Professor to believe," the Doctor answered. "I desperately needed Moriarty to confirm all of my calculations concerning the asteroid—which was the reason for this whole charade. Normally, I would have trusted my reasoning implicitly—but with the fate of the human race at stake, I could not take such a chance. Moriarty, for all of his faults, is indeed a mathematical genius, and I knew I could rely on his calculations. The Earth was never in any peril all along."

I suppose I shall one day get accustomed to the feelings of confusion and futility I inevitably feel around the Doctor, but I have not yet risen to such heights. "Then all of this was for nothing?"

"Far from it!" Doctor Omega answered, clapping me on the shoulder. "If we had not intervened, then the Earth would certainly have experienced the catastrophe I described. But I knew that we *must* have intervened, since history shows that humanity faced no such disaster. Remember, I have stressed that we cannot alter history in any way! Since the human race was not to perish, then, clearly, my scheme to save is must have worked."

"But the asteroid is still on a collision course with the Earth," I protested. "And it will still strike Russia in 1908."

"As indeed history said it did," he replied. "It will cause great devastation—but only over a small area in Siberia. Our activities have shaken the rock apart, so that most of it will no longer impact on the Earth, and much of the rest will be small enough to burn up from friction. Only the central core of the asteroid will survive entry into Earth's atmosphere, and it will cause the explosion known to historians of the future as the Tunguska Event. So you see, my boy, our actions were both absolutely critical and absolutely inevitable. We did what we had to do, what we *must* have done, and the Earth is saved and history is conserved. We do, however, have one small matter to resolve."

"And that is?" I asked.

"What we are to do with the Professor."

I smiled. "I would suggest we do to him as he would have done to us—leave him on the surface of the asteroid as we depart."

Fred shook his head. "Why don't we take him back to when we found him and toss him out, so that he can complete his interrupted journey down the Falls?"

"Gentlemen, I am surprised at you," the Doctor answered—though there was a twinkle in his eye. "Both suggestions would make murderers of us."

"He was doomed to die anyway," Fred objected. "We would only be allowing history to run its natural course."

"And you have said that there is no future record of him," I argued. "So he cannot be set free."

"On the contrary, I think that we must indeed allow him to go free," the Doctor answered. "It is simply a matter of finding a suitable prison for him where he can no longer affect events. And I have the perfect solution—Pitcairn Island."

"Pitcairn Island?" I asked.

"A small island in the Pacific far from any shipping lanes. The mutineers from the *HMS Bounty* ended up there in 1790, and the island was uninhabited at the time. So I suggest we drop the Professor off there in 1750—he is an elderly man already, and he can live out the rest of his natural life there without being able to cause any trouble for anyone else again."

Fred and I glanced at one another. Despite our blood-thirsty suggestions, neither of us really wished to be the cause of death for even such as Moriarty. "Very well," I agreed. "Pitcairn Island it is."

"Splendid." Doctor Omega rubbed his hands together in glee. "As soon as Xirdal is back aboard, we'll head there directly. And after that, my friends—who knows? Who indeed?"

226

I can remember very clearly my first encounter with Doc Savage. Being born and raised in England, I didn't know of his pulp magazine adventures. When I was 15 I discovered a wonderful second-hand book store a mere 20 minute walk from my house. It was a treasure house for me. Besides the books, the owner had piles of old comics. I spent a considerable amount of time and money there, as you can probably imagine. He had a display of some of his latest acquisitions in a large window, and one day I saw something completely irresistible: James Bama's stunning cover for Doc Savage #37: Hex. *I didn't know (then) it was by Bama. I didn't know who the heck Doc Savage was. And I didn't care that it was book 37 in a series – with a cover like that, I had to buy it. And every other one I could find... From that moment on, I wanted to write a Doc Savage story. And couldn't: he's copyrighted. However, Jean-Marc to the rescue – he introduced me to Guy d'Armen's awfully similar character, Doc Ardan. And so, I very nearly achieved my ambition, because the two Docs were clearly (possibly; maybe) the same man in two different disguises... Mix in a little Jules Verne and Conan Doyle, and I had a rather fun yarn, I think.*

The Biggest Guns

The Western Front, March 1918

Francis Ardan Jr. first realized the trouble he was in when a burst of bullets slammed into the fuselage of his Sopwith Camel F.1. He banked to the left instantly to get out of the line of fire, and then scanned the skies for his opponent. He was near the operational ceiling for his plane—20,000 feet—and there weren't many enemy craft capable of catching him at this height. He was annoyed with himself for thinking he had been safe.

There—from the Sun! The enemy was instantly recognizable. A blood-red Fokker Dr.1 triplane, its twin Spandaus blazing, was screaming toward him. Only one person flew such a craft—Rittmeister Hans Von Hammer. Ardan knew the man's reputation; a total number of kills was hard to come by, but the ace had certainly shot down more than 50 allied aircraft.

It looked as if he was going to boost the Rittmeister's score today. He'd been caught badly by surprise, and Von Hammer had the height advantage. Still, Ardan was no novice in a cockpit and, as his friend Biggles had said often enough, "If you can fly a Sopwith Camel, you can fly anything." The aircraft took considerable skill, and had killed a number of over-confident or unwary trainees, but it repaid attention with amazing abilities. It was better than virtually any aircraft either side had in the air, at least in an even fight.

But this wasn't even. Ardan was skilled, and he managed to weave out of the next burst of gunfire, but Von Hammer was second only to Richthofen as an ace, and he wasn't about to allow his prey to escape.

Ardan twisted and rolled the Camel, trying to coax just a little more speed from the Clerget engine powering the craft. The Fokker was almost the match of the Camel in airspeed, but Ardan's plane had the slight edge in rate of climb. And the Camel had a slightly greater ceiling than the Fokker. If the young man could just push it enough to get above Von Hammer, he'd be safe.

He never got the chance. The enemy pilot was no fool, and he had clearly anticipated Ardan's reaction. With a sudden twist, the Fokker was aligned once more with the Camel, and the Spandaus chattered out death.

Ardan managed to spin to one side so that the bullets missed the cockpit, but they slammed instead into the Clerget. The engine started spitting smoke, and then fire. One of the fuel lines had clearly been severed, and the fire would be sucked back to the tank in a matter of seconds.

There was only one thing to do. The young adventurer grabbed the plate from the camera strapped to the side of the Camel and quickly slipped it inside his shirt. It was cold against his skin, but it should be relatively safe there. Then he stood up, and kicked himself free from the doomed aircraft. There was a rush of air, and he was thrown clear as the Sopwith lurched and fell. Barely five seconds later, it exploded in a smoky fireball.

Ardan was some 18,000 feet in the air and falling. He glanced around and saw the Fokker. Von Hammer tipped its wings in salute to his enemy, and then turned away to hunt more targets. Ardan was lucky that his opponent had been the Rittmeister, because many German pilots would also riddle the pilot, even if he appeared doomed. Von Hammer went only for the aircraft.

Besides, no one had ever fallen from 20,000 feet and survived, so leaving a man to die was barely a kindness. Many Allied pilots took their revolvers along on missions to shoot themselves in situations like this. A bullet in the brain was just as certain a death—and less drawn-out and terrifying.

One day, Ardan was convinced, parachutes would be packed into planes to enable men to fall safely to the earth. Experiments had shown that descents from balloons were possible using such devices, and even an aircraft or two. The Germans were reported to be experimenting with such devices.

Which was why the young man had done the same.

Ardan saw that the ground was approaching quite rapidly, despite his initial height. He could certainly pick out a great number of details on the farm below him. Wind resistance had stopped his acceleration, but he was falling quite swiftly. If he hit the ground—or even the pond he could clearly see—at this speed, he'd shatter every bone in his body. The important thing was to slow his descent, and that could only be accomplished by manipulating wind resistance. To do that, he needed to make himself larger.

He shed his flight jacket—a heavy leather garment that kept him warm but added to his mass. The wind chilled him, but briefly. He forced his trained body to ignore the cold, at least for the moment. Then he snapped the releases on his clothing.

His shirt and pants had been carefully constructed to his design by a French seamstress he knew. They were not a single layer of clothing, but several. Once the restraints were released, his shirt and pants blossomed out, like a flower unfolding. The strong cloth caught the wind, and he could feel that he was slowing down. The extra surface area was working! He spread his arms and legs, maximizing his cross-section as he fell, and the air resistance built up.

If only the stitching was strong enough to hold up under this terrible strain... This was his trial run of this new method, and he sincerely hoped it was successful enough to allow him future refinements...

Air ripped at him and his clothing. He glanced at the exposed seams. They appeared to be holding, but for how long? Well, there was nothing he could do now—if the threads failed, he would die—it was that simple. He had to assume that they would hold and give him a chance of surviving. He examined the ground that was drawing ever closer.

The pond was out. He was slowing as he fell, but at this speed, hitting the surface of the water would have pretty much the same effect as hitting a brick wall. It wouldn't be the wall that broke. What he needed was something compressible. That meant avoiding the farmhouse and the out-buildings, and the ground itself, of course. That left him only one possible target...

He wished that he had managed to invent some way of steering his fall. The only effect he could have on direction was to draw in or extend one of his limbs. It worked to a degree, but it was hardly very effective. That was something to consider for the next trial. Still, by using his limbs, he did manage to control his fall enough to head for the largest of the haystacks below.

And then, time ran out on him. He barely had time to hope for the best before he slammed into the hay.

It didn't kill him.

It did hurt. Quite a lot. His right ankle felt as if it was sprained, and he knew he would have extensive bruising over all of the front of his body. But he was alive, and had broken nothing. Not even the photographic plate he had risked his life to obtain.

As soon as he could breathe again, he rolled onto his back. Pain flared up all over, but that was a good sign—it meant that he was still alive, and hadn't broken his neck or spine. He moved slowly, every muscle in his arms on fire, as he unfastened his helmet and goggles and pulled them from his head.

There was a sound beside him, and he turned his head—slowly!—and saw that a curious pig had wandered across. It stared at him in some fascination, clearly wondering from where he had appeared.

"Don't worry," he told the shoat. "I'll be out of your way just as soon as I can move." He realized he had to be giddy with relief—talking to a pig! He closed his eyes again for a moment. A short rest, and then he'd start on his way. He had to get back to HQ to develop the photographic plate.

Two days later, Francis Ardan was in London. It was still slightly painful to walk, but he was getting better each day. And there simply wasn't time to rest—not with the evidence he had procured about the Boche plans. Right now, he needed expert assistance, and this was the best place to obtain it. He stopped beside the Georgian house in a fashionable section of Westminster. Beside the door was a small, simple plaque:

THE GUN CLUB
London Branch
Members only

Ardan wasn't a member, but that didn't worry him. Several highly-placed contacts in the *Société Secrète des Aventuriers* had vouched for him and made an appointment with the people he needed to meet. He sounded the pull-bell beside the door, which was opened quite promptly by a liveried retainer.

"Francis Ardan," he announced. "I believe I am expected."

"You are indeed, sir," the man agreed. He opened the door, allowing the young man to enter. "Allow me to take your overcoat and hat, sir," he offered. Ardan shucked the coat and handed across his Homburg. "The second door on the right, sir," the retainer announced.

The young man thanked him and strode down the wood-paneled corridor. There were prints on the walls of all manners of military guns and howitzers, many of which were unfamiliar to him. The floor was thickly carpeted, so he made no sound as he walked, his precious package clutched firmly under his left arm.

The second door was open, and Ardan saw that within was a large room. He knocked gently on the open door, and then walked into the room.

This room was also wood-paneled, and richly furnished. Large stuffed chairs were scattered about the room, close to small tables for refreshments or books. A larger table ran the length of the far wall, and two other walls were massive book cases, the shelves stuffed to overflowing with weighty tomes. There were electric lights in strategic spots to allow for reading. None of the people in the room were so occupied.

There were two men present, who rose as he entered. There was also a sole woman, who remained seated. One of the men was stout, balding and clearly in his 50s. The second was leaner, trim and had an amused cast to his handsome features. His skin was bronzed by the tropical Sun, showing he had traveled extensively, and his eyes were blue and piercing. The woman—well, she was quite startling. Aside from the simple fact that no clubs to the young man's knowledge al-

232

lowed women inside their premises, she was one of the most startling beautiful women he had ever seen. She was young—perhaps only five or six years older than Ardan—and tall—again, almost matching him.

What was more surprising was that she somehow seemed familiar to him, though he thought he had never seen her before.

"Francis Ardan, I presume?" The older man moved forward and reached out a hand, which the young man shook.

"Just Francis—or Clark," he said.

"I am J.T. Maston," the man introduced himself. "Normally, I reside in Baltimore at our home office, but these, alas, are not normal times. This gentleman is Lord John Roxton. The young lady, of course, you already know."

Ardan was puzzled. "I am afraid I do not. There is something familiar about you, Miss, but I do not know your name."

The young woman gave him a wry smile. "Why, Clark," she murmured, "I don't know whether to be insulted that you don't recall me or flattered that I must have changed so much. We now share our last name, if that helps you to place me." Her voice was strong and pleasant, and had a decided French Canadian sound to it.

"The same name?" Ardan was startled. "Yes, of course! Aunt Pamela!" He blinked. "The last time I saw you was at Uncle Alex's wedding!"

His cousin laughed. "Yes, that was five years ago. I have changed a little. Child-bearing has a way of doing that to a woman."

"How is your daughter... what's her name?... Patricia?"

"Four, now. You should see her. She's a real little terror," she said laughing.

Pamela May Thibault had married an uncle of his, who had moved to the backwoods of Canada almost 20 years ago. Ardan had pretty much lost touch with him as a result, and had only seen her once in his life, at their wedding. No wonder he had not managed to recognize her—and why Maston had assumed he knew her.

"What are you doing here?" he inquired.

"The Thibaults are long-standing members of the Montreal branch of the Gun Club," she explained. "I happened to be in London, and when I heard you wished to consult the members here, naturally I arranged to be present."

"Naturally." One thing Ardan did recall about his Canadian aunt was her pronounced sense of curiosity and her fascination with excitement.

"I hear you have somethin' special for us, young man," Lord Roxton said, clearly eager to get down to business.

"It is something you might be able to help me with," Ardan agreed. He removed the photographic plate from the bag he carried and laid it on the nearest table. Roxton and Maston bent to look at it, and Pamela shifted in her chair to get a better view.

"Must have been risky gettin' this," Roxton murmured.

"Slightly," Ardan agreed, not wishing to detail his adventures. "It was taken at a height of about 1000 feet. It is an enlarged view of the interesting area of the resulting picture."

"I'll say," Pamela agreed. "It's a railway gun, clearly."

Ardan knew this much, but little more. "It's a new Hun weapon," he explained." The barrel is approximately 100 feet long. It is mounted on a railway flatbed to enable it to be draw by an engine."

"Must have an impressive range," Roxton offered.

"It has," Ardan agreed. "It is located in the forest of Coucy, and it has been shelling Paris—at a distance of 75 miles—since March."

"Ah!" Pamela exclaimed with delight. "The famous Paris Gun! I've long wished to see it!"

"So have the Allied High Command," Ardan informed her dryly. "And they wish to destroy it. But it is well defended and mobile to a degree."

"At those sort of ranges, it can't be too ruddy accurate," Roxton said.

"It doesn't have to be," Ardan said. "It can shell Paris without any warning, and causes a great deal of panic. No one can tell when the next bombardment will commence, or what may be the target. It is a weapon more of terror than siege, but it does its job well. Morale in Paris is low."

Pamela sighed. "And I assume your task is to destroy it? It does seem a pity."

"The inhabitants of Paris might not agree with you," Ardan said, dryly.

"Oh, I understand that," Pamela said hastily. "And I quite agree. But..." She picked up the plate. "It is *such* a magnificent gun. Made by Krupp's, obviously." She had named the largest German manufacturer of weaponry. "And designed, undoubtedly, by Von Kimmel."

"Yes," Maston agreed. "He was a member of the Gun Club before the War," he explained to the young man. "He often spoke with me about his wish to produce the biggest gun in the world. It would appear he has achieved his aim." He shook his head. "Such a perversion of all we stand for."

Ardan looked at him curiously. "But what other point is there in building guns if not to destroy life and property?"

Maston was shocked. "Sir!" he exclaimed. "The *point*, as you put it, is to *learn*. We strive to extend the frontiers of man's knowledge, to discover his capabilities."

"Besides," Pamela pointed out, "it was a gun that launched your grandfather—and Mr. Maston's father, along with Mr. Barbicane—on their wonderful trip to the Moon."

"Considering the forces involved, they were all astoundingly lucky not to have perished in the attempt," Ardan replied. "And one exception does not negate my point—the sole reason to build such guns is to kill and destroy. Men can advance their knowledge in far more peaceful ways."

"But not as much fun," Pamela complained.

"I think we'd best leave philosophical matters to the philosophers," Ralston said. "I meself am a man of action, and it's clear that's what is called for here. Do you have a plan, young man?"

"My thought is for a small band of men to penetrate the German lines," Ardan stated. "Less than five would stand the best chance, and three might be optimum. Well-placed thermite charges should cause sufficient damage to the barrel to prevent it from functioning."

"That might work," Pamela agreed. "Provided there are no spare barrels."

"Why would the Germans have any spares?" Ardan asked.

"Because of the tremendous velocity the shells will achieve on being fired," she explained. "Simply firing a shell would cause measurable wear inside the barrel. The barrel would need to be replaced on a regular basis or else the weapon would be rendered useless."

Ardan had failed to consider this, and he felt a pang of embarrassment. It was his way to attempt to consider all the possibilities, and he had overlooked this one. "Then more than the barrel must be destroyed—the rail car itself. I cannot be certain that the Huns do not have more of these weapons ready to replace the gun, but it would seem unlikely. Given the state of the war, they would surely have utilized them."

"Agreed," Maston said. "And casting and placing such a weapon would be a delicate and far from simple process. There is a likelihood that spare barrels have been cast—but it would take considerable time to install one and align it. A variation of even a fraction of an inch from the bottom to top of the barrel could be disastrous."

Roxton gave a barking laugh. "It sounds extremely chancy and dangerous to me, young fella. Count me in—I wouldn't miss it for the world."

"Me too," Pamela said, eagerly. "Next to building a gun like that, blowing one up is probably the most fun I'll have had in years."

Ardan stared at her, aghast. "You are most certainly *not* coming along on this mission. It is far too dangerous for a woman. If we are captured, we will be shot as spies—and the Germans have proven that they are quite as happy to execute women as men."

Pamela's eyes blazed. "Clark, I did not think you would be such a chauvinist! Do you think women have less courage than men? That we would shirk our duty because we are more afraid of consequences than you?"

"War is no place for a woman," Ardan said, firmly.

"It's no place for men, either!" she snapped. "But while war exists, we must all do our duty and attempt to bring it to the swiftest end. I am coming, and that's final."

Ardan looked to Roxton for help. "Surely you agree with me?" he asked.

"On general principals, certainly," the English Lord said. "However, in this particular circumstance, I have to agree with the young lady."

"What?"

"Certainly." Roxton gave him a frank look. "Miss Thibault has shown that she is the expert here in the matter of the Paris Gun. She has already made one good point that you overlooked—not your fault, of course, you can't know everythin'—and she may be able to make more on the spot. If you really want that gun blown up, then I'd say she'll be an invaluable member of the team."

"Thank you, your Lordship," Pamela said, smirking at her nephew.

"Don't thank me, young lady," Roxton replied. "Our young Mr. Ardan might well be right, too—this is a very dangerous mission, and we might all end up dead and the gun untouched. But I've fought dinosaurs and men, and I'm not goin' to sit this one out."

"And nor am I," Pamela said, firmly, glaring at Ardan and daring him to disagree.

What could he do? Much as he hated the idea of leading his cousin into danger, she and Roxton had a valid point. She clearly understood this weapon better than he did, and it was imperative that it be destroyed.

"Very well," he said, gritting his teeth. "We leave at 4 a.m.—perhaps you had best prepare for this mission by writing out your will."

"Did anyone ever tell you that you're a sore loser?" Pamela asked.

"I do not make it a habit to lose," Ardan informed her.

She gave him a sweet smile. "I'll try and make it as gentle an experience as possible, then," she promised.

Ardan could see that this was not going to be easy on his nerves...

Getting across the English Channel to France was simple enough, if a little wearing on Ardan's nerves. Pamela, it seemed, threw herself into every endeavor with a whole-heartedness that worried him. She had read up on the Coucy region where the gun was based and memorized pages of information. That was all well and good, but he hoped it would not make her over-confident when they arrived. She had managed to confine her changes of clothing to a minimum—not a simple thing for a woman in the young man's experience. And she had brought along a small arsenal.

Ardan distrusted guns. Even the best of them had the potential to jam at the moment you needed it most, and he tried to avoid using them unless absolutely necessary. Pamela, however, having been brought up in the backwoods of Quebec, had been hunting since she was a child, and had several rifles and a pistol, all of which she had obviously cleaned on a regular basis. He could hardly forbid her from bringing them along—they would probably be absolutely necessary. Besides, Roxton had his own bag of rifles and he could hardly forbid Patricia what his other companion was carrying. But it disturbed him to see a woman with a weapon.

He had trouble understanding women. Partly, he knew, it was simply that he was unfamiliar with them. His mother Jacqueline had died when he was a child, and he had been raised by his father and a group of all-male tutors. The other part was that he simply did not know how they thought. Pamela, for example, was clearly very intelligent and insightful, but he could never predict what she might be capable of saying next. He wished over and over that she had not come along on this mission.

The trip to the forest of Coucy was long but uneventful until the final stretches. Once they entered the area under German control, Ardan halted their advance for a quiet conference. They all wore identical clothing—dark pants, a long, dark great-coat and dark hats. These served to cover his and Patricia's light-color hair, which might otherwise give them away. Roxton and Pamela both had rifles slung over their shoulders and pistols in holsters at their waists. Ardan had no gun, but carried his usual supply of scientific devices he preferred to utilize secreted about his clothing.

"The Boche patrol these woods on a regular basis," he informed his companions softly. "We shall have to take great care from here on. Make as little noise as possible, for stealth is essential."

"Teach your grandmother to suck eggs," Pamela jeered. "Roxton and I are both hunters, and if we weren't adept at silence, we'd hardly catch much, would we?"

Ardan strove to keep his temper in check. "I am merely reminding you both," he said. "You do not have to take every comment as a personal challenge."

"If you didn't mean them to be, it would be a lot simpler," Pamela retorted. "I know you resent my being here, but I *am* here, so stop acting like I'm a liability and allow me to do my job."

Ardan nodded, stiffly. "I am endeavoring to do just that."

"Under protest," his aunt argued.

"Um, please," Roxton broke in. "Let's not have this discussion again, eh? We're here, the gun's there, and we'd better be on our way, eh?"

"Right," Ardan agreed. "Come along."

As the slipped through the thick woods, the young man realized that Pamela had been quite correct—she and Roxton made almost as little noise as he himself did. Both were clearly excellent hunters and adept at stealth. Why, then, did this information not make him feel any better about his aunt being there?

Was it possible that she was correct, and he *was* a male chauvinist?

They passed close to three patrols, all of which they detected soon enough to enable them to hide until the enemy had passed. It was clear from the casual manners of the soldiers that they feared no Allied attacks this deep in their occupied lands. That confidence, if shared by the rest of the Huns—might make their task a whole lot simpler.

A short while later, Roxton tapped him on the arm and pointed. Through the trees ahead he saw the glint of metal on the ground—the railway line to Paris. They were getting closer to their target and had to take even greater care as they moved.

There were more patrols, and these were more alert than the farther-flung ones. They were close to their superiors and wanted to make a good impression. In each case, though, Roxton and Pamela hid in the undergrowth while Ardan took to the branches of the trees above. In the event any of them were discovered, then the others might be able to offer assistance. It turned out to be unnecessary, however, as their approach remained undetected.

The Paris Gun itself was surrounded by a battery of smaller guns for protection against any Allied raids—as well as by the flyers of Rittmeister Von Hammer's squadron, who would fly over the site on regular patrols once it was light enough. Probably in less than an hour. It was a little incongruous in the depths of the woods to see the guns manned by sailors, but the Paris Gun was commanded by a German Admiral as it was technically a naval gun, even though they were far from the ocean. The Huns were sticklers for protocol. So the guns were all operated by men and officers of the Navy, while the patrols were regular Army.

Ardan and his companions moved slowly and stealthily through the enemy forces, skirting the guns as widely as possible. And their target came into all-too-clear sight.

Even though he had seen it from the air, Ardan was still startled by the sheer size of it. The barrel was almost 100 feet long, and had to be strongly braced lest it might bend even a fraction of an inch. It sat on a large flatbed, which stood itself upon a concrete base to take the weight, which had to be in excess of 200 tons. Shells for the gun were in smaller, separate trucks. The flatbed was placed on a turntable to allow it to be aimed, but it clearly would take a long time to reposition it.

He, Pamela and Roxton studied the gun from concealment, and then crawled away some distance before they discussed their options.

"What do you think?" he asked Roxton, softly.

"Well, there's several points where we can destroy it," the hunter replied. "The supports for the barrel, for one thing—shear them and its own weight will bring the blasted thing down. Even simply cracking the concrete supports or blowin' up the railcar it's on would do the trick. A few sticks of dynamite down the barrel..." He shrugged. "Plenty of possibilities, m'boy."

"Not one of which will work," Pamela stated firmly, echoing Ardan's own fears. "Oh, they'd all do the job fine— provided we can get close enough to the gun to actually *use* one or all of them. But there's over 200 men surrounding that gun." She glared at her nephew. "I don't care how quiet you are, or how stealthy—nobody could get through those men and plant any bombs unseen. *Nobody.*"

"I agree," Ardan stated, and he saw the flash or surprise in her eyes. He cracked the smallest of smiles. "I don't disagree with you purely as a matter of principal, you know."

"I was beginning to wonder," she murmured. "So, what do we do?"

"The two of you will destroy the gun," Ardan said. "Any of Roxton's suggestions sound fine to me. Or you could try this." He pulled a small container from his clothing and handed it to Pamela. "A thermite paste of my own devising," he explained. "Smear some of this on a few of the projectiles.

The heat from firing the gun and the friction of the projectiles in the barrel will cause it to heat up and expand the projectile."

"Trapping it in the barrel," the young woman said gleefully. "I like it." She took the container. "But we still can't get close enough to use it."

"I will create a diversion," Ardan assured her. "As soon as it commences, the two of you head for the gun."

"What are you plannin'?" Roxton asked curiously.

Ardan smiled. "There are a lot of men on the ground around the gun. But not one *above* it..."

Getting to the German airfield wasn't too difficult now that he was on his own. Francis Ardan used all of his skills to slip silently through the woods, and avoided all of the patrols. At the edge of the field, he paused to reconnoiter. There was a fair amount of activity, with mechanics checking over various aircraft. Workers were fueling a few of the craft, so it looked like an aerial foray was being readied. With a smile, he spotted Von Hammer's blood-red Fokker sitting alone. A worker was driving a fuel truck away from it, so it was clearly ready for flight, and merely awaiting the arrival of the aviator himself.

What better disguise could he employ? The young man moved from cover, and sauntered toward the craft. His long, dark coat looked sufficiently like a flying jacket that he aroused no suspicions. It was early and no one was expecting any intrusion at this remote, guarded field, and this played in his favor. As soon as there were no eyes upon him, he sprinted for the Fokker and swung into the cockpit.

He'd never been in a Fokker tri-wing before, but he knew that if Biggles were here, his friend would be saying, as ever: "If you can fly a Sopwith Camel, you can fly anything." The controls were basically very similar, though Ardan was certain the Fokker would handle very differently once he was aloft. This should prove educational...

Once he had fired up the engine, he received some attention—especially since the ground crew knew that Von Hammer had not yet arrived. A handful of people started to move, puzzled, toward him, as he taxied and then began gunning the engine to gather speed. The ground had been cleared and roughly leveled, but the plane shook and bumped. Then he had sufficient speed to get aloft and he hauled back on the stick.

Mechanics flattened as he flew low over their heads. He was starting to get the feel of the controls as he maneuvered for height. It would be a while before anyone would be able to get aloft after him, but he couldn't spare too much time to experiment. Instead, as soon as he was 200 feet up, he turned the plane and headed back toward the Paris gun.

He checked the craft's Spandau's, firing short bursts from both to be certain they were working properly, and smiled grimly. He was now ready.

The flight back was swift, and it was barely five minutes before he could see the huge barrel looming ahead of him. Men were working on it, and he realized that it was being readied to be fired. Paris would suffer another terrifying barrage if he and his companions didn't succeed.

He sent the Fokker into a downward spiral, and held his thumbs over the firing controls. Despite the fact that they were enemy soldiers down there, he was reluctant to actually take a life. After the war, he intended to train as a medical doctor, and he preferred to save life rather than kill. Accordingly, he sent his first burst slightly to the side of the gun.

Incredulous eyes glanced up, and obviously saw that their attacker seemed to be their own top ace. Accordingly, nobody moved initially. Ardan sprayed a second burst closer, and now saw realization and panic set it. Men threw themselves from the gun and ran for cover. It was a shame he had no bombs aboard the Fokker—he might have caused serious damage if he had—but he kept up a continual stream of fire as he passed over and over the gun. He saw the gun crews heading toward the anti-aircraft guns, having finally realized this was an enemy and not their defender. The sky would start getting uncomfortable for him very shortly.

Then he saw two figures running *toward* the gun—obviously Roxton and Pamela. He swooped in lower to provide them covering fire as they committed their act of sabotage.

The Huns had managed to get one of their ack-ack guns in operation, and started firing in his direction. Dodging the one gun wasn't too difficult, but then a second and third came into operation, and the sky was starting to get very unpleasant. At this altitude it wouldn't be long before he was hit. He strafed the emplacements as best he could, but they were dug in well, and impossible to hit. Glancing back at the Paris Gun, he saw that Roxton and Pamela were retreating back to the forest, their work presumably accomplished.

Now he could break off his attack and retreat. Stretching the Fokker to the limit of its endurance, he made a sharp left wheel. He could hear the fabric and wires groaning about him as he did so, but in moments he was out of the range of the enemy fire.

But only for seconds. Then a stream of bullets from *above* slammed into the right side of the plane. Ardan glanced about ands saw three more Fokkers—all metallic gray—swooping toward him. He tried to whirl out of their way, but he was still not an expert at the controls, and the plane was sluggish. More bullets tore through his wings and came dangerously close to hitting him.

Von Hammer had arrived...

His own guns were almost empty by now, so attempting to fight was impossible. The Rittmeister knew these planes far better than he did, and this would be a fight Ardan would lose. He did the only thing he could in the circumstances—pointed the nose of his plane down, and aimed to land.

Von Hammer held his fire—he was not a brutal man, and there would be no glory for him in killing an opponent who was clearly surrendering. Besides, he probably wanted his own plane back.

As Ardan taxied to a halt, German soldiers surrounded him rapidly, their rifles raised. The young man cut the Fokker's engine and clambered slowly out of the craft. A Captain, his Luger carefully aimed at Ardan's head, came forward.

"I surrender," the young man said calmly.

"A wise move. Your attempted attack has failed." The German smiled. "Paris will be shortly under siege once more." He gestured toward the big gun, where activity had commenced again. Men were loading a shell into the huge breach. There was no obvious signs of damage, and he could only trust that his companions had achieved their mission. His captors led him away.

There was a transport truck waiting on one of the roads away from the rail line, and the Captain gestured the young adventurer toward it. "You are not the first of today's captives," the German said with satisfaction. "You will join your companions."

Ardan felt a momentary tightness. Had Pamela and Roxton been caught? He was prepared to suffer what he must, but the thought of his pretty aunt as a prisoner of the Boche was almost unbearable.

Then all Hell broke loose. There was a tremendous explosion, and a wave of fire. Ardan was completely deafened, and blown off his feet. He shook his head, attempting to clear it, and saw that the Paris gun was in flames. The barrel was shattered and twisted, and the rail car warped. Germans— some with their clothes aflame—were running for cover. They were probably screaming, but the young man could hear nothing.

His companions had performed their task well. For the first time in his life, Ardan realized that sometimes having people with him to aid him might not be such a bad idea. People like Roxton and Pamela, people he could trust and rely upon... Though it was rather academic at the moment. He was a prisoner still, and unlikely to be doing any more fighting for the foreseeable future.

His hearing gradually began to return, and he could hear feverish commands being yelled in German. People were attempting to quell the fire before it spread to the ammunition cars. Ardan staggered uncertainly to his feet, and checked himself over. There was a web of blood upon his forehead where a small piece of shrapnel must have struck him a glancing blow, but otherwise he was unharmed.

"Get those prisoners out of here," someone called in German. His hearing was returning, thankfully. The Captain used his Luger to gesture the young man into the waiting truck. Two of the armed soldiers followed him to act as guards. As he stood ready to climb aboard, friendly hands reached out to help him clamber aboard. With great relief, Ardan realized that they belonged to two men he had never seen before. So Roxton and Pamela had made good their escape! That made him feel a lot better.

"Come on, you hairy ape," one of the men grumbled. "Let's get this hero aboard." He was a tall, slender man with impeccable, unbelievably neat clothing.

His companion was shorter and stockier, and indeed looked almost more anthropoid than human. "I'm not the one slacking off, you over-dressed shyster," he complained. Then he gave the young man a massive grin. "Nice work, partner. It's good to see that gun out of action."

"Much as it pains me to ever agree with you," his companion said, "in this case, I concur."

Ardan settled onto the floor of the truck with the two of them. The guards sat on small benches, keeping an alert eye upon the captives. The van started up with a jerk, and then rumbled away. The other two prisoners had started up some argument about who it was of them that had managed to get them both captured. The young man ignored them as best he could, instead watching with considerable satisfaction as the Germans strove to save what they could from the disaster. Then the van turned away, and he could see the destruction no more. Yes, indeed—having people he could trust and work with had been a great advantage here, and might well be again. It all depended upon him finding the right people, of course.

"You monkey-brained, prehistoric remnant!" the natty dresser yelled at his companion.

"Yeah? What do you know, you fashion plate?"

It was going to be a long trip...

You know when you ask an author "Where do you get your ideas?" and they can't tell you, mumbling something about "inspiration" and other vague excuses? Well, in this case, I can tell you exactly *where I got my inspiration:* Natural History *magazine. It ran an article on the mystery of the jet-black* lisianthius nigrescens, *and how the locals used it as a cemetery plant, and my imagination went into overdrive... I promptly wrote a short story with* my *explanation of what is was all about. And couldn't sell it. I sent it out dozens of times, with the same result – a rejection slip. Finally, though, I found an editor who liked the* idea *of the story – just not the way I'd written it. So she said she was interested in it, if I'd do a re-write. So I did a rewrite – and she rejected that, too. The version that follows is my third attempt, which she finally accepted. It's an illustration of that old adage of try, try and try again, I guess. But I still like my first version the best...*

The Cemetery Plant

"Mother, are you still carrying on that ridiculous feud with Cordelia Oshansky?"

Julia Gordon glanced up sharply from the carpet where she was playing with her grandson. The boy gave a whimper at the loss of her attention, but then set about trying to steal one of the toy cars from his Hispanic playmate. Julia's only son, Richard, was looking down at her with an odd, amused expression on his face.

A feud?

Julia would never call it a feud. It hurt too much for that. She could still bitterly recall the smug look of victory on Cordelia's face as her roses took first place in the Maine Garden Club finals. And Julia's took second place.

For the fourteenth year in a row.

No, it was no feud.

It was war...

Richard had inherited Julia's passion for flowers and turned it into a stunningly successful career. At the age of 32, he was in charge of his pharmaceutical company's research plant here in South America, charged with discovering potential new cures in the botanicals from the various jungle plants.

"It's not a feud," she protested.

"You brought me up to always be truthful—can't you follow your own advice?" Richard was very dear to her, but the half-smile on his face now annoyed his mother.

"I'm certain she cheats with her roses. I wish I could expose her, destroy her reputation with the club."

"I can do better than that for you." Richard grinned fully now. "Leave Francis here with Juan and his mother and come along with me."

Julia followed her son from the family part of the house to the research side. Richard's company had invested a great deal of money into this venture to pry potential cures from the native plants, and her son was working brilliantly to that aim. Here in the laboratories he and his team were taking apart many of the local plants to extract the often complex compounds within, and examining their potential medicinal uses. Richard led her into one small room, and gestured dramatically at the thin plant in a small pot on the table.

The first sight took her breath away.

It was black. The petals were long and thin, opening at the bell to reveal long, yellow-tipped stamen. The flower was only an inch and a half long.

"The only truly black flower in all of nature. It's unique, and quite a puzzle."

Julia stared into the jet depths. "How so?"

"Nobody knows how it's pollinated. Insects can't see black as a color - red looks black to them, and red is a whole lot easier a color for a plant to produce. Why would evolution go to all of the effort of growing a black flower unless there was something to be gained by it?" He shrugged. "Just about the only creatures it attracts are humans - and we certainly don't pollinate it."

"It's the most beautiful flower I have ever seen." Julia didn't want to take her eyes away from it.

He waved at the pot. "It's yours."

"You mean that?"

"Be careful with it, and don't be surprised if you hear some stories about the plants from the locals. They call it la flor de muerte, 'flower of death'. They plant it near the graves of the recently deceased. They're a rather superstitious lot."

"Thank you, Richard—I shall treasure this, and tend it carefully." She picked it up gently, and carried it back to her room.

Maria, the maid her son had assigned her, was dusting when Julia entered, bearing her treasure. She placed the Lisianthius on the end table below the window.

The maid paled and crossed herself. "Madre de Dios!" she exclaimed, her voice shocked. "Señora Gordon, take that thing away!"

Julia frowned. "It's beautiful." She could annihilate Cordelia at the next show! Everyone would then have to admit that Julia Gordon was the true genius of the Garden Club.

Seeing that smug look wiped from Cordelia's face would be worth almost anything…

"Sometimes beauty hides the deadliest sins," the maid replied. "It is evil. It is dangerous, Señora."

Julia laughed. "Come now, child—that's simply superstition."

"Return it to the cemetery, where it belongs."

"I shall do no such thing." Julia was starting to get annoyed with the maid.

"Then promise me you will move it to another room when you sleep, at least." She gripped Julia's arm. "Please, Señora… I would not ask this if it were not important!"

Julia could see fear in the girl's eyes. "I promise I will not sleep in the same room with this plant. Now, are you happy?"

"Think me a simple peasant if you will—I do not care. But listen to me, and keep your word."

As the day wore on, Julia found that she couldn't ignore the warning. She had moved the Lisianthius into the empty room next to hers to placate Maria, but she returned time and again, entranced by the black flower. She couldn't resist it, nor could she forget the intensity of Maria's fear.

The natives might know something her son didn't. He believed so firmly in his science that he sometimes dismissed others who were less educated than he. It was a touch of arrogance his late father had also possessed. It was her son's one flaw.

Curiosity and apprehension warred against her son's science, and by the time night had fallen, Julia knew she had to do some research of her own. She had to know.

On her way back to her room after dinner, she met Paco in the hallway. Paco was a good-natured youth, but with a strong weakness for the local tequila. He staggered past her, heading for his small room, an almost-empty bottle clutched in his feverish hand. He hadn't even seen her.

She could test the Lisianthius on Paco... He would be stretched out in his room in a few moments, and she could bring the plant... Maria said it was only dangerous if you slept in its presence. She would watch and stay awake. If anything looked like it would happen, all she needed to do was to pick up the plant and remove it from the room. There would be no real danger to the young man.

Her desperate need to know fought her conscience, but it was an extremely one-sided battle. Nothing could possibly go badly wrong—and, besides, Maria's fears were probably just a folk legend, with no basis in the truth.

But she had to know... She had to know everything about her wonderful new specimen...

She hurried off and collected the plant, and then retraced her steps to Paco's room. She found she was feeling absurdly guilty, but she knew that was foolish. What was the worst that might happen? Perhaps the flower produced some lethal gas that would slay a sleeping person—but she would be awake, and at the first sign of trouble, she could act. This would be a perfectly safe experiment. Perfectly safe.

Paco had indeed fallen face-down on his bed, snoring softly. The now-empty tequila bottle lay on the floor beside the bed. The servant hadn't bothered (or, more likely, been able) to get undressed, which was a good thing. She wouldn't have felt comfortable in a room with a naked youth. She set the Lithianthius down beside the bed, and then settled into the small chair close by, and prepared to wait.

She sat there, watching, the lights turned off, for less than an hour. Every five minutes, punctually, she leaned over Paco and checked that he was breathing regularly, and that his pulse was still strong. And each time there was no change.

There was nothing to worry about. In fact, she was starting to feel stupid for even thinking that there was any substance to Maria's ridiculous fears.

Then Paco's breathing pattern altered. He'd been snoring gently, but suddenly the sounds broke and then stopped. He gave a faint choking sound. Julia leaned forward, eager, excited. Was something happening? She glanced at the black plant, almost invisible in the faint light of the room. It had shown no evidence of doing anything. She sniffed, but detected no odor. She herself felt perfectly fine.

But Paco gave a gasp, and even in the darkness, she could see that his body convulsed slightly. What was happening? She leaned forward, alarmed, and reached for the boy's throat. Placing two fingers over the jugular, Julia gave a start.

There was no pulse.

Julia jerked back in her chair, feeling a slight shock and confusion. The boy had been quite healthy - merely drunk. What had happened to him? She glanced at the Lisianthius on the dresser.

Why had the youth died? She felt a growing certainty that somehow the plant had done this to him. Well, the plant— and her. Despite her resolve, her best intentions—the boy had died. And she was to blame. She felt growing guilt and shock, but, overriding that, she felt a burning curiosity. Since there was now nothing she could do for the boy—she had never learned CPR, and doubted it would help even if she had - she managed to bury her feelings for the moment, all but her curiosity. She stared at the flower, wondering what it truly was.

Then she felt a sudden chill flowing across her entire skin. A vague movement had caught her eye, from the bed. But Paco was definitely dead! What could possibly...

The body was as still as it had been, but something was happening... She stared at the dead boy, spellbound, unable to look away. It was as if a thin mist was forming over the youth. She peered closer, and saw that it seemed to be rising from the corpse. Some atmospheric condition, perhaps? The body was, after all, still warm. But - if it was something to do with the atmosphere, shouldn't mist be rising from her also?

The mist rose, but didn't thin. Instead, curiously, frighteningly, it seemed to coagulate. It should be dissipating, but it wasn't - it was growing thicker, and more distinct.

She shuddered as she realized it was taking form. The pale mists writhed, and moved, shaping into...

Paco.

Or, rather, a copy of the boy. Julia was breathing shallowly, her eyes focused on what was happening. The mist was thin and the light indistinct through the room's single window, but the features were clearly that of the dead boy. The shape was unclothed, and its masculinity was without doubt.

A ghost, Julia realized. The boy's spirit had risen from the fallen body, and was standing beside the bed.

She gave a faint whimper, her hands shaking. Did the thing know she had been responsible for his death? Was it after revenge? Or was this what happened naturally after death, and the spirit was simply departing this world? She barely breathed, watching the faint form. Perhaps, if it was here for revenge, she deserved such retribution.

But it simply stood there, the dead eyes firmly fixed. But not on her. The ghost didn't seem able to see her - or, perhaps, it simply wasn't interested. It might have more important things on what was left of its mind. Julia couldn't move, could hardly think.

Then she realized that its eyes were fixed on the Lithianthius. It was staring absorbedly at the black plant. It seemed enthralled.

And perhaps that was exactly the right word to describe it: enthralled. It was focused on the plant as if nothing else existed in the entire Universe.

The ghost finally made a movement. It raised its right hand, wispy, transparent, and reached slowly for the plant. Paco's spirit was insubstantial, she realized. The hand reached through the wood of the small dresser as if there was nothing in its path. It cupped the flower, as if striving to hold it, and failing. For the first time, some expression crossed the shadowy features of the ghost's face. Paco looked anguished, pained. The hand reached again, but could touch nothing.

Or, rather, very little. As the hand moved through the bell of the flower, Julia could see small dots of substance that appeared to cling to the misty form of the arm. Curiosity overcame her fear and guilt, and she leaned forward again, peering closer. It was pollen! Pollen from the flower was somehow being carried by the almost-nothingness of the ghost's hand...

Pollen... Light, almost insubstantial itself! The material that composed the ghost was so thin it could interact with virtually nothing - except the pollen...

Julia shivered again as she finally understood the truth. The Lithianthius had, as scientists suspected, a rare pollinator. But they had no idea just how rare... The Lithianthius had evolved a symbiosis with humans, it seemed. It used their spirits to carry its pollen. The spirits of the dead had little use for anything - except, perhaps, they could still feel the tug of beauty. Paco's ghost seemed literally entranced by the plant.

A thrill of discovery coursed through her, driving out fear and shock. She knew what none other did - that the Lithianthius bred by killing people, and then capturing their ghosts to act as unwitting pollinators...

Fascinating! Wonderful!

And... useful...

Julia had been raised in a Catholic household, and had attended church until she had drifted away in her teenage years. She knew, almost unconsciously, the beliefs in temptation. That the Devil could plant within the souls of the unwary, desires that would be very hard to ignore. Only through the grace of God could such temptations be fought, for human frailty made other battle impossible. And the Devil knew precisely what one's darkest, deepest desires were, and played upon them.

It had to be true, or else how could she explain the next thought that came into her mind? She was not a bad person, not one who held grudges, not one who envied other people. Whatever her feelings about Cordelia Oshansky, surely she didn't really hate her.

Then why was she thinking that she could use the Lisianthius to eliminate her rival—simply, silently, undetectably? She wasn't the sort of person to wish evil onto anyone.

Except, perhaps, Cordelia...

No! She tried to shake the temptation from her mind. But it was rooted now, and growing.

A small gift of a delightful plant, one that Cordelia would find it impossible to refuse... A single night, and then...

She would be unrivaled in the Garden Club. She, alone, would be the queen bee. No more Cordelia and her smuggness at every competition. No more of whatever cheating she performed to win.

No more second places—ever!

No more Cordelia—the thought was growing to become irresistible. No matter what the source of the thought, the idea was growing stronger

And she also knew that she lacked the will and the strength to fight this temptation. The God she no longer believed in couldn't save her from her own nature.

In that awful instant, Julia peered into her own soul, aided by the beauty of the Lisianthius—and she saw the same darkness within as the petals of the plant possessed.

She clutched the potted plant to herself, and stared down at the dead youth. Guilt still stabbed at her soul, but she could control it with the new strength of purpose she had. "I am sorry," she murmured to the boy. "Truly, I am sorry. I did not mean this to happen. I did not know it would. But I cannot turn back time, and I cannot give you your life back. I take what small comfort I can from knowing that the tequila would have killed you eventually. And I shall bear the guilt as long as I live." With a final nod, she fled the young man's room, afraid to look back.

But at least, in the morning, his death would be assumed to be an accident. Nobody would ever suspect that she had been involved. She was safe from retribution.

She returned the Lisianthius to the spare bedroom next to hers, and then hurried into her own room. As she prepared herself for bed, she couldn't stop herself from reflecting on what she was planning to do.

She knew that her plans for Cordelia were evil. There was simply no other word for it. Evil. And she was shocked at herself. She had always believed that she was a good person. She donated to charities, she had raised her son well, and she had sympathy for those less fortunate than herself. She wasn't an alcoholic, didn't do drugs, didn't sleep around.

But to discover the hatred within her soul that would allow her to contemplate—no, plan—murder... That shocked her. She had always disliked Cordelia, but it was a long fall from dislike to murder. And yet, here she was, aiming to kill her rival.

And, worse, she didn't feel bad about it. She felt good. This world would be better off without Cordelia Oshansky in it. Her world would be better without that bitch.

Julia took her sleeping tablets, and changed into her night gown before slipping between the comforting covers of her bed. Killing Cordelia would be something she would enjoy—in anticipation, and in the act.

Never again would she be second.

Richard Gordon moved through the silent house, aching a little. It had been along day, but a good one. It was always so pleasant when his mother came to visit, and it had been a joy watching her playing with her grandson. And then, when he had sprung his surprise on her, he had really loved seeing the enraptured expression on her face. He had known she'd love that odd flower. It had been a great idea to give it to her.

He passed the empty room next to his mother's, and saw that the door was ajar. As he moved to close it, he saw the Lisianthius plant on the table by the window He frowned. How had it come to be there? He was certain his mother wouldn't let it out of her sight.

Then he realized what must have happened. Maria, with her ridiculous native belief in the dark magical powers of the plant, must have taken in from his mother's room and moved it here. He shook his head in disgust. Superstitious claptrap! His mother would be annoyed and worried in the morning if she awoke to find her beloved plant missing.

Richard picked it up, and moved quietly to his mother's room. He rapped softly on the door, but there was no reply. Opening the door, he saw that his mother was in bed, asleep. Well, the poor darling needed her rest. Without making any noise, he slipped into the room and placed the Lisianthius on the bedside table. When Julia awoke in the morning, the first thing she would see would be this enthralling plant.

Smiling happily, Richard left the room and shut the door behind him.

I grew up on (among other things) TV Westerns. They were always on TV when I was younger. I wanted to be a cowboy. Since I lived in England a hundred years too late (and am in fact allergic to horses), this was never going to happen, but that didn't stop me becoming addicted to TV Westerns to this day. Although it was never my favorite, one show that never seemed to be off the air was The Lone Ranger. *(I preferred* The Range Rider, *with future-Tarzan Jock Mahoney.) Clayton Moore always seemed to me to be so straight and stiff, and so terribly, terribly earnest. So, naturally, years later I wondered if there might not be a very good reason why he was so stiff...*

The Loaned Ranger

The filthy black storm clouds hovered over the mesa as they had all day, threatening Heaven's vengeance on the small group of riders far below. The six Texas Rangers were moving slowly toward a box canyon, following a fresh trail. But when the thunder broke, it wasn't from the skies, but from the rocks alongside the canyon walls. Rifles and handguns barked and pounded, and a metallic rain slashed through the six men.

A couple of the unprepared victims strove to draw and raise their own guns, but they were cut down with no chance of returning a single shot. One by one, the Rangers jerked in their saddles, their bodies dancing as bullets tore into them and then they fell into pools of their own blood. Screaming, terrified horses bucked and whirled. In the withering fire, most of them fell, too, bleeding and gasping beside their riders. In moments, it was over. The flashes of fire from the rocks ceased, and then flashes began far above in the skies.

Cavendish made his way out of hiding, his gun trailing smoke as he walked slowly down to the fallen men. His gang followed him, their own arms at the ready. One of the Rangers moved, his fingers inching toward his fallen revolver. Cavendish took quick aim and blew the man's brains all over the dust. That seemed to trigger a wave of ferocity in his followers, and gunfire erupted for another thirty seconds, bullets plowing into the fallen corpses.

"Enough!" Cavendish finally called, holstering his hot pistol. "The sons of bitches are dead."

Thunder cracked above his head, as if to underline his pronouncement. He glanced upward, and rain started to hammer down from the Texan sky. Cavendish grinned. "This downpour'll cover our tracks in a matter of hours, boys. By the time the Rangers find their fallen compadres, we'll be untraceable. Back to the horses, and let's vamoose."

The rain poured about them, pooling and washing at the blood on the ground, as if to scourge the earth clean. Lightning cracked across the sky above them.

"Almost Biblical in its wrath," one of the gang noted. "A presage of the apocalypse, even."

"A presage of our splitting the loot from that bank," Cavendish growled. His men were a cowardly, superstitious lot, and he didn't want them getting any wrong ideas. Their lust for the stolen gold would keep them contented for now, though.

Above them, on the rim of the canyon, a lone figure watched and waited. He observed with hooded eyes as the killers recovered their hidden horses, mounted and rode off through the downpour. None of them looked back toward their fallen victims. Once he was certain that he had not been observed, the watcher mounted his own pony, and rode carefully down the trail. Already, the dust was turning to mud, and the way was slippery, but his pony was sure-footed, and made it down the wall of the canyon without mishap.

The Indian shook his head. Damn these Anglos, and their blood-lust! He had no idea what had caused this fight, but he now had no other option than to intervene. Ignoring the rain, he vaulted lightly from the bare back of his pony, and approached the group of fallen men.

The bodies, being washed clean in the rain, still looked grotesque. They had fallen with twisted limbs, and frozen expressions of fear and shock on their dead faces. The horses, too, were warped where they lay. Blood-laced rivulets ran from the soaked corpses. The Indian, sighing, studied the dead. Most were so bullet-ridden that they were useless. He needed one without injury to the brain, but the outlaws' blood-lust had led them to almost obliterate the features of their foes.

The last man lay slightly apart. He'd been holding back somewhat, maybe worried about the way they were riding. He was one of the few who'd managed to draw his weapon, and his revolver was still clutched in his dead grip. He had been shot several times in the chest, and one shot had creased his forehead, just above the eyes, leaving a bloody furrow. The Indian crouched to examine the head. Not too bad, all things considered, and the brain hadn't been penetrated, at least. It wasn't a good subject, but it was his best bet. The other corpses were completely unusable.

He glanced around, and saw there was a slight overhang off to one side, giving some shelter from the pounding rain. There might be sufficient room for a small fire for warmth—and other matters. He whistled for his pony, and then manhandled the body he'd chosen across its back. Then he set off for the overhang, his pony trotting obediently behind him.

It took him some time to make a fire, but finally it caught and grew, crackling and spluttering with wind-driven drops of rain. Once it was going, he took a small pot from the pack on the horse's back, and then his herb bag. He sifted through them, pulling out the ones he needed. He went over the blending in his mind several times, to be sure he had it right. He had not had cause to use this potion often, so it was important that he recall it exactly. Once he was certain it was correct, he broke and mixed the herbs with rain water in the pot, and set it on the fire to boil. Then he turned his attention to the fallen man.

He wasn't the perfect choice for this, but there was none better. His companions were all too damaged to use. This man, at least, was almost intact—at least in the necessary areas. His heart had been destroyed, but that wasn't essential, and other bullets had ripped through organs that had once been vital.

Now the only one that mattered was the brain, and that appeared intact.

The Indian began the incantation. The potion was important, but without the right frame of mind, the correct prayers to the Manitou, and the proper respect shown to the other dead, this would never work. The prayers were long and involved, but he managed them without faltering. His pony stood, the only observer, beside the fallen body.

Once the words were done, it was time for deeds. He reached for the pot, stirring the thick potion with a stick until he was certain it was of the right consistency. Then he took it from the fire using a rag, and set it down beside the cooling body. It had been almost an hour since the man had died, but it wasn't yet too long.

Using the potion, the Indian drew signs and shapes across the man's face. Then he tore open the man's shirt, and worked around the bullet holes to finish the markings. He began the invocation again, and then poured the last of the potion between the dead man's lips. His prayers reached their fevered pitch, and he threw his hands up to the Heavens, beseeching the Manitou to hear his words, and to return the spirit of the slain man—even if only temporarily.

The Indian glanced down at the fallen white man. Nothing. Perhaps it was too late, after all? No, it couldn't be. He *had* to make this spell work. He repeated his prayer, filling his words with all the desperation that he felt. Then he threw up his hands again, thanked the Manitou for his power, and looked at his patient.

The fingers of the man's right hand—the one that hand been clutching his gun before the Indian had removed it—twitched slightly. Not much movement, but *any* movement meant that the ritual had worked. The Indian grinned slightly, and then breathed a sincere prayer of thanks to the gods.

The hand twitched more, and then the eyelids opened. Cold blue, dead eyes focused on his face. The dead man's mouth moved, but only a croak came out.

"Talk later," the Indian advised. "Rest for now. The storm will soon be finished." He returned to his pouch, and made a flesh selection of herbs. The undead man would require strengthening, and the Indian started another pot brewing. The white man nodded slightly, and appeared to fall asleep. His chest didn't rise and fall, nor did his heart beat. But he was still alive—or, at least, very nearly alive.

By the time the Indian's brew was ready, the white man had opened his eyes again and watched as his companion brought him a cup of the potion. The Indian supported his head, and urged the Ranger to drink of the cup. It took the dead man a few minutes to get the hang of using his mouth to swallow, but then he drained the cup. The icy eyes then fixed on the Indian.

"What happened?" he asked. His voice was as chilled as his eyes, and a whisper of death ran through the voice.

"You died," the Indian explained. "Shot." He pointed to the holes in the white man's chest. "Pretty bad."

"Then why aren't I still dead?" the Ranger demanded.

"I brought you back," his companion explained. "Your spirit is on loan from gods. Maybe short time, maybe long. Who can say? Gods are not too predictable."

The white man struggled to sit up, and accepted help gratefully. Then he stared at the Indian. "Let me get this straight," he said, slowly. "You used some heathen ritual to reanimate my corpse?"

"Pretty much, yeah," the Indian agreed. "Potions, too. Deep mystery, few know." He tapped his chest and grinned. "I know. The gods give you back. I asked nicely."

"Okay." The Ranger closed his eyes and gathered his strength before reopening them. "And why in God's holy name did you do that? Out of the kindness of your heart?"

"No, not kindness. Leaving you dead is kindness." The Indian gestured at him. "Your body is in rough shape. Heart

261

gone, liver gone. Manhood..." He made a gesture. "But the brain is okay, and brain is important. Without brain, no life." He gestured into the still-falling rain. "Other white-eyes too damaged. Only you were workable."

"Fine." The Ranger gave a sigh that seemed to come from the depths of an ancient tomb. "But *why* in perdition did you bring even *me* back to life? Is this your idea of fun, maybe?"

"No, not fun - necessity," the Indian protested. "Think about it. Six dead Rangers, one live Indian. If White-eyes find me, who will they blame?"

"I take your point." The man sighed again. "But I'm hardly a very credible witness that you're innocent of my murder, am I?"

"Not witness," his companion said. "Vengeance. You get the real killers."

The Ranger glared at him. "You think I can take on six murderous outlaws all by myself? I'll be shot to pieces the next time."

The Indian grinned. "You're already dead once - pretty damn hard to kill again."

"You mean I can't die?"

"No, you can die," The Indian said. "It's just hard. Silver can do it, through the brain. Incantations and prayers, too. But the killers do not know my magic, so you should be okay there."

The Ranger examined his hands, cold and white. Even the warmth from the fire couldn't help there. "I'm not entirely sure I *want* to stay alive," he said. "This body doesn't feel quite right. And I kind of miss some of the pieces you couldn't restore."

"Sorry - I did best I could." The Indian shrugged. "I just need you to get killers. Then, maybe, you can die again, if Manitou says okay."

The Ranger fell back to the ground. "I am not entirely certain I have the best of this deal," he complained. "Well,

262

now I must rest. I may be alive again, but dying seems to have tired me somewhat. Wake me when the rain stops."

It took more than an hour before the Indian judged that the storm had finally spent its fury, and he shook the sleeping dead man awake. The Ranger rolled over, and caught sight of his face in one of the pond-sized puddles. He reached up slowly to touch the furrow above his eyes.

"This looks bad," he commented. "I won't be an acceptable sight in polite society. I think I need some kind of mask to cover it up, or people will stare at me."

"If you wear a mask, won't people stare?" the Indian queried.

"Yeah, but at the mask, not at *me*." He went to where one of his fallen companions lay. "Lucky stiff," he muttered. Then, using his knife, he cut himself a crude mask that would cover the scar, and used a rawhide thong to tie it into place. Then he studied his reflection again. "Better," he decided. He glanced back at his fallen comrades. "I'll be back to bury you when I've avenged you," he promised them.

Only one of the Rangers' horses had survived the massacre. It had been extremely skittish before, but had calmed down during the storm as it stood with the Indian's placid pony. Now the Ranger swung himself into the saddle. He watched, curiously, as the Indian did likewise.

"You aiming on accompanying me?" he asked, mildly.

"I brought you back," his companion explained. "Now I am responsible for you."

"Well, okay," the Ranger decided. "But we'll have no more of your heathen magics, you hear? When I kill these men, I want them to stay dead. You understand?"

"Fine by me," the Indian agreed.

Together, they rode off in the direction the Indian had seen Cavendish's gang leave. Their horses splashed through puddles that were already starting to shrink. Tracking the gang wasn't hard; not expecting pursuit yet, they hadn't bothered to start hiding their tracks. They had probably sat out the storm, also, so it was clear that they weren't far ahead.

"You with me in this fight, or do I go it alone?" the dead man asked his companion at one point.

"It's your fight," the Indian answered.

"Yeah, I kind of thought you'd say that. Well, stay back when we find them, then. Wouldn't want you getting plugged by no stray bullets."

"My thought also."

It was getting on toward night when they could hear the sound of riders ahead on the trail. The Ranger took a moment to check that both his pistols were fully loaded, and then his rifle. With a grim smile, he plunged on. The Indian followed, but at a slower pace.

Rounding a bend in the trail, the Ranger could see that the men he was after were only about a quarter of a mile ahead. Perfect. He urged his horse onward.

One of the riders turned in his saddle, and called something to his companions that the wind snatched away. The others reined in, and turned to look back. Immediately, they all drew their weapons.

Their pursuer didn't care; he had been dead already.

"Jesus H. Christ!" one of the men swore. "Ain't that one of the men we done killed already?"

"I guess he survived somehow," Cavendish snarled. Bringing up his pistol, he fired three shots in quick succession.

Two whistled harmlessly past the Ranger. Hitting a riding man from the saddle was never an easy feat, which was one reason he hadn't bothered trying any shots himself. The third, though, slammed into his shoulder. He felt no pain, just the puncture of the impact that rocked him back in the saddle. Then he bent forward to ride on.

"What the hell?" Cavendish growled. "I'm sure I winged the lawman..."

"Not enough," the Ranger growled. He was close enough in now, and reined in his steed. Then his hands whipped down to his weapons. But the gang already had theirs drawn, and a barrage of shells slammed into him, knocking him from the saddle, and into the mud.

"That should bury him this time," Cavendish decided.

The Ranger sat up.

Three of the gang swore, and fired again. They could all see the bullets batter their target. He fell back again.

"What does it take to kill him?" one gunman wondered.

"More than you've got," the Ranger replied. His guns came up as he rose to his feet, and he commenced firing.

Men and steeds screamed, and the thunder of the guns was deafening. By the time it was over, five of the gang lay bleeding and dying on the ground. Their horses, howling, bolted. Only Cavendish remained untouched. The Ranger stood there, looking up from the steaming corpses of the men he had killed.

"And now it's your turn," he said.

Cavendish emptied his revolver into the man's chest, with no apparent effect. Then he threw it at the Ranger, who simply ducked. Cavendish followed his weapon, slamming into his target and knocking him into the mud. Gripping his powerful hands about the man's throat, he squeezed hard. "Go to hell," he growled.

The Ranger didn't seem to be at all bothered by the death-grip. Cavendish, of course, didn't know yet that the Ranger had no need of air. The man reached up, pushing back on Cavendish's chin until the grip about his throat ceased, and he could speak again.

"After you," he answered. With a twist, he heaved Cavendish off, and into the mud. Then he leaped upon the man, and his own hands clenched about the outlaw's throat. "This works much better on you." Relentlessly, he squeezed. Cavendish struck out, punching and chopping. The Ranger felt the blows, but without pain. His nerves were dead, and the punches had little effect on him. His own grip, however, was different. Cavendish's face was turning purple as the man struggled for breaths that weren't ever going to come. "Die, you lucky bastard." He gave one final squeeze and felt Cavendish convulse as he died. Then he threw the broken body aside and moved to each of the fallen outlaws in turn. Carefully, even if they were dead, he shot each one through the head. Returning to Cavendish, he put two bullets through the man's face.

The Indian had ridden up as this was going on. He'd caught all of the loose horses, and trailed them behind his pony. "What are you doing?" he asked, amused.

"Removing temptation from before your path," the masked man answered. He glanced up and saw the horses. "What are you doing?"

The Indian shrugged. "Horses are worth twenty bucks apiece. Figure to sell them. Owners do not need them any longer."

"Damned right they don't." He grinned. "There's a bounty on the gang, too, about five hundred, all told. And their loot should be in their saddlebags. When we return it, there'll be a reward. Should earn us both a tidy sum."

"Why do you need money?" the Indian asked, curiously. He hopped from his horse to help load the slain outlaws across their steeds and to tie them in place.

"Well, not for food or whores now, that's quite clear," the Ranger replied. "But I do want to get me some silver bullets."

His companion scowled. "What for?"

"You did say that the only sure way to kill me again was with silver through the brain. I'd kind of like the option, should I decide I've had enough of this second life of mine. I do seem to be unable to savor things the way I used."

The Indian shrugged. "That is a problem with being dead."

"So I noticed." His task done, the Ranger swung back into the saddle of his horse. "Well, now I got to go back and bury my friends—the lucky dead." He swung his steed around. "You coming?"

"Sure." The Indian vaulted onto his pony. "I have a feeling we are stuck with each other now."

"Yeah." The Ranger gentled his horse to start it moving. "I was kind of afraid of that." He glanced down at his shirt, which had been shredded by all of the bullet hits. He could see the holes in his torso created by the bullets. "You think we could dig these slugs out sometime? I hate having so many holes in me."

The Indian shrugged. "Tough."

Sources

Return To The Center Of The Earth
Tales of the Shadowmen #10: Esprit de Corps, edited by Jean-Marc & Randy Lofficier, Black Coat Press, 2013, and *Tales of the Shadowmen #11: Force Majeure*, Black Coat Press, 2014.

The Kind-Hearted Torturer
Tales of the Shadowmen #1: The Modern Babylon, Black Coat Press, 2005.

The Incomplete Assassin
Tales of the Shadowmen #2: Gentlemen of the Night, Black Coat Press, 2006.

The Successful Failure
Tales of the Shadowmen #3: Danse Macabre, Black Coat Press, 2007.

The Dynamics Of An Asteroid
Tales of the Shadowmen #5: The Vampires of Paris, Black Coat Press, 2008.

The Biggest Guns
Tales of the Shadowmen #6: Grand Guignol, Black Coat Press, 2009; reprinted in an edited and updated version in *Doc Ardan: The Abominable Snowman*, Black Coat Press, 2016.

The Cemetery Plant
Book of Dead Things, edited by Tina L. Jens & Eric M. Cherry, Twilight Tales, 2007.

The Loaned Ranger
History Is Dead, edited by Kim Paffenroth, Permuted Press, 2007.